THE BERLIN ASSIGNMENT

ALSO BY THE AUTHOR

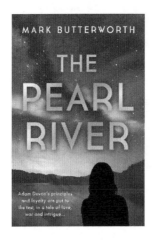

THE
BERLIN
ASSIGNMENT

Mark Butterworth

MARK BUTTERWORTH

The Book Guild Ltd

First published in Great Britain in 2024 by
The Book Guild Ltd
Unit E2 Airfield Business Park,
Harrison Road, Market Harborough,
Leicestershire. LE16 7UL
Tel: 0116 2792299
www.bookguild.co.uk
Email: info@bookguild.co.uk
Twitter: @bookguild

Typeset in 10pt Adobe Garamond Pro

Printed on FSC accredited paper
Printed and bound in Great Britain by 4edge Limited

ISBN 978 1916668 263

British Library Cataloguing in Publication Data.
A catalogue record for this book is available from the British Library.

In memory of my dad, Arthur Derek Butterworth, who introduced me to the de Havilland Dove.

ONE

Berlin, April 1952

A dirty yellow, smoke-laden mist swirled heavily over the city, as the cracked bell of a distant church chimed the forlorn announcement that it was now 6p.m. In a doorway to a long-disused baker's shop at the eastern end of Unter den Linden, Val Hetherington-Brown gazed idly at the line of bullet marks in the stone columns around the door, evidence of the vicious street fighting Berlin had seen in the closing weeks of the war.

She had been standing there for more than an hour. Waiting was part of the job. The time of her rendezvous could not be precise – soon after 5p.m. was the best estimate – so she tried to wait patiently and look as natural and nonchalant as possible. She had been met at the crossing into the Russian sector by an unknown, silent agent and left to await the arrival of her next contact, who would take her to the safe house.

The streets were clearing quickly. Few people had good reason to be out in the night; most hurried from their stale and dusty offices and workshops to catch a tram to the Berlin suburbs where they would dine on potato and cabbage soup, perhaps with half a pork sausage if they were fortunate.

A woman standing in a doorway could arouse curiosity during the day, turning to suspicion after dark.

The temperature had dropped suddenly. Val shivered, pulled down her maroon beret and wrapped her thin cotton scarf more tightly around herself. She caught a whiff of a chemical smell coming off her woollen coat – maybe mothballs, perhaps just the ugly human odour of the well-used clothes that the department had given her for this assignment from their dressing-up box. But the outfit was a necessity; she would stand out a mile in her usual Bond Street ensemble.

A thrill of nerves shot through Val's body as an East German policeman strolled slowly down the street towards her. He carried a short truncheon that he tapped absently against the wall as he looked into doors and windows. His dark green double-breasted greatcoat had a sheen of water droplets, and his face was a sallow ivory-grey in the cold air. He wore a heavy leather belt with a pistol in its holster. His peaked cap hid his eyes. When he was level with Val, she held her breath. He hesitated, then carried on. She stayed on the spot, rigid, as the policeman took a dozen steps away, tapping at the wall again.

But then he stopped, turned, and walked slowly back. He raised his free hand and pushed back his cap, revealing blue eyes and the faintest smile. Val was surprised when he spoke in English, with barely an accent. "Good evening, ma'am. I am Wolf."

Val's whole body relaxed. "I am Fox," she replied.

The policeman, if that's what he really was, nodded politely. "Come with me, please. Do not look at me, follow ten paces behind, walk steadily, and nobody will concern themselves with you."

Even in her position as the head of station in Berlin, Val did not know the identities of all of the staff and agents on the payroll. If she didn't know them, she couldn't divulge their names under interrogation. She had been advised that the contact could be anyone, male or female, from any walk of life. Support for the resistance to communism might come in many shades, many guises. Her contact tonight would take her through the near-deserted streets to a quiet corner of East Berlin. As she walked, Val took in the shabby streets. The scars of war could be seen everywhere, and there was a pervasive smell of coal smoke, river pollution and iron foundries.

***

Val Hetherington-Brown reflected on her service with the Special Operations Executive during the war in France and Holland. Her nerve had been tested many times, evading the clutches of the Gestapo. Approaching forty, tall and slim, she wore her long auburn hair in a French twist. Her vibrant green eyes shone in her pale face.

Operations were never easy. She was always nervous, but that wasn't a bad thing as it kept her focused – one mistake or loss of concentration could mean arrest, torture and death. After the war Charles Raleigh, an established MI6 agent, had taken her under his wing, mentoring her as he taught her the subtleties of political and military spying. In the way of government department hierarchies, Val was senior to Raleigh in rank, but she respected his vast experience. A two-year intelligence-gathering deployment with Raleigh in Hong Kong, monitoring the threat from the Chinese, had been followed by a spell back in the UK training new recruits in the fieldcraft that would be required if they were to stay alive out on operations.

The UK government's growing concern about the development of military power in the Soviet bloc led to her transfer to the Berlin station, where she had built her role as the powerhouse behind the extraction of vital agents and defectors who wanted to live in the West and enjoy the freedoms it offered. She just had to ensure they had something to give in return. Raleigh joined her as a senior agent at the station.

The safe house was in the eastern end of Mitte district. Here, most residents kept a low profile, not wishing to attract attention from the police or party agents. Many East German citizens had escaped to the West since the end of the war, but now the border was closing and movement between the Russian sector and the British, French and American sectors was increasingly difficult. The East German police and the Stasi secret service had been told by their Soviet masters to identify and prevent any persons of significance crossing to the West. Some people had legitimate reason – usually work – to cross from the east to the west and back every day. But they were all spied upon by the Stasi's thousands of informers and agents. Many people still succeeded in evading the guards and getting to freedom, to reunite with their families and live in a society that allowed opportunities for liberty, education and success. But many failed, and were arrested or shot on the spot if they tried to run for it. MI6 wanted to ensure that the most valued defectors, those with military or intelligence information, chose the only guaranteed way out – escorted by British secret service agents.

***

The policeman led Val on a winding route east, then north, crossing the slow-flowing River Spree, dirty, oily and dead. They headed out of the city centre and had been walking for twenty minutes when Val saw the burnt-out remains of the Nikolaikirche. The church's twin spires had been reduced by a wartime firebomb to rubble and rusting metalwork. Without saying a word, the policeman left Val at the door of a red-brick house that had once been the home of a merchant or professional. Strangely, it was in very good condition. It was a wonder that it had survived the war, and gave Val an idea of what Berlin had once looked like.

The door was ajar. As she entered, she saw a single light in the hall. Raleigh emerged from a living room to the right.

"This way," he said quietly.

Sitting on an armchair by the fire in the living room was a woman in her early sixties, small and demure. Slowly, she looked up in response to Val's greeting. Val knew the woman would be as frightened as hell, she would be regretting seeking to defect, she would be unsure if her knowledge really had any value in the West. But she couldn't go back now.

The woman held her handbag on her lap, patting the top gently. "It's in here, if you want to see it."

"Yes, certainly," said Val.

The woman opened the bag and took out a hard-backed shorthand notebook. She flipped it open at a page of handwritten notes and handed it to Val. Val saw German and Russian code names in column one and names of cities, mostly in West Germany, in column two. Some entries had London as the city, others Washington. One or two noted Paris. There was a column three, but it was blank. MI6 had been told that the woman had details of the spy network in the West, and if her notes were anywhere near complete, this would be a major coup that would enable MI6 to disrupt the entire Soviet network. British and American intelligence interceptions often picked up code names – using the woman's tables, they would be able to identify the agents.

Val's job was to assess the validity of the intelligence she was being offered and traded for guided passage through the hazardous escape route to the secure, unpatrolled crossing point a mile from any checkpoints. She was mindful of the games the Russians played: sending false information through agents, willing or unwilling, to the British, a double bluff that took time to unwind. Sometimes the efficacy of the information could never be validated.

"Tell me," she said, "how did you get this information?"

The woman's voice was very quiet. "I work at the Ministry for State Security. I made up these lists over a period of months. I have memorised the real names of agents, and I can enter these in the third column when we are safely in the British sector. My job is to communicate orders and instructions to agents. The Stasi is a formidable organisation, but no one takes any notice of a simple, hard-working secretary."

"The lists are valuable, clearly, but your knowledge is critical for us to make full use of the information. What do you want for the lists?" asked Val, although she had no doubt that the woman wanted safe passage to the West.

"I want to join my daughter and her children in the United States. She escaped in 1950. Foolishly, I stayed behind, thinking they would allow me to travel freely. Now the only safe way for any Stasi employee is to go with you. But I know it comes at a price. You will take me now?" She clasped her bag close to her chest, looking fearful.

Val smoothed out the notebook. "This agent here, code name Schwan. Real name, please."

MI6 had been interested in an agent by that name for many months.

"Angela Hauptmann – secretary at the Frankfurt American air base."

"And this one, Apfel," said Val, pointing to an agent with London as his or her location.

"That is Peter Cox, communications specialist at the Foreign Office."

"Let's try something else," said Val. "Name an agent currently working in the British secret service."

"I only know of one such person." The woman looked down at her hands and stayed silent.

"*Well?*" Val deliberately raised her voice to get the woman to talk.

"Andrew Elliott, code name Willow. Based in the Middle East. I don't know what he does there."

But Val did – he was a senior officer in the Jerusalem station. She closed the book, impressed with its contents, and longed to hear the full names of the rest of the agents. Satisfied that the woman was genuine, Val placed the book in her pocket. "Yes, we will take you. We will leave here in one hour – please be ready."

"Yes, yes, thank you so much. Thank you, madam." The woman stood and embraced Val, tears of happiness welling in her eyes.

***

In less than an hour, a black pre-war VW pulled up outside the house. Val and Raleigh had spent some time at a top-floor window, watching for any movement, anyone lingering in the street. The two quietly came downstairs and collected the woman from the living room. She was mouthing a silent prayer and shaking with fear. Val squeezed her hand and gave her a smile – she needed the woman to keep her nerve. They were standing silently in the hall when the driver knocked gently on the front door. Val opened the door to see the blue-eyed policeman, now dressed as a factory worker.

"All clear?" she asked.

"Yes. No sign of Stasi men, come now."

The front of the house had three steps down to the pavement. Raleigh was ready, his service revolver in his hand. Val carried her usual Walther PPK. "Let's go," she said.

Raleigh walked out, following the driver, who opened the passenger door and tipped the seat forward, giving access to the back seats. The early evening mist had become a cold fog, and the air was still as Val stepped out of the house. The woman followed. Then Val heard muffled footsteps to their left, and two shadows appeared from behind the church. The shadows levelled their weapons. Immediately, Raleigh read the threat and shouted to Val to get back. A volley of shots blasted through the night air, then Raleigh returned fire. The first shadow keeled over backwards. The second shadow turned to run, but just before he disappeared, Val rapid-fired four rounds into his back.

Raleigh ran to check that the men were both dead. The first man was groaning, so Raleigh fired a single shot to the head.

"Get in the car!" Val called. But as she turned back to look at the woman, she saw her lying on her back, motionless, with three red patches in the centre of her chest. Val knelt down and looked into her eyes, which were open and unfocused. She was dead.

"Hell! Raleigh, help me get her in the car."

They bundled the body into the back, and the driver started the engine. When Val and Raleigh had climbed in, the driver powered away towards the British sector, heading west to find the secure crossing. He turned into a deserted square, where they halted and switched drivers. A new man had been waiting there to take them on. Slowly, they drove down an alley that anyone would think was too narrow for a car and emerged onto a cleared bomb site. Steadily, with all lights off, the car crossed a quiet street into the British sector, near the Tiergarten, and stopped at a small warehouse. Val got out and knocked on the wicket gate set into the large wooden doors to the yard. Two men appeared. Val had a quiet word with them, and they came to the car and swiftly took the body away.

Val instructed the driver to continue to MI6's office. This was going to take some explaining.

TWO

Adam Devon sat at his desk, tucked away in one corner of the de Havilland offices, writing up his report on the morning's flight test. It had been a tough assignment, and he was hot and mentally drained. Following a triangular flight plan from their base in Hatfield, he had flown the aircraft south to the French coast at Cherbourg, north-east to overfly Dunkirk, then back along the Thames estuary and across north London. Devon's job on this mission had been to fly the de Havilland Dove at maximum speed at both high and low altitudes to recreate all aspects of the flight modes that users of the aircraft could have in future. The flight would also test the effectiveness of the new, secret navigation radar that had been fitted a month earlier.

Progress was being made on refining the radar. The technical boys who flew with Devon were all smiles when they went off to lunch, happy that the Dove was the perfect platform for their development of long-range radar systems. The project was being overseen by the RAF and everyone involved had to sign the Official Secrets Act, which served as a reminder that they were not to divulge any information to anyone outside the project.

While the radar people were pleased with the morning's flight, Devon pondered just how far an airborne radar beam could 'see'. He knew that during the Battle of Britain the range of ground stations might have been 80 miles, but only a decade later it was over 200 miles. Place a small radar in an aircraft and you have the ability to track targets over huge distances. Devon closed his notebook and was thinking about having lunch when the telephone on his desk rang.

"Adam Devon, good afternoon."

"Hello, Adam, it's Lucy. Would you mind coming up to Mr Darley's office? He would like a chat, and there's someone here to see you."

"Of course, I'm on my way," said Devon, intrigued. Why had he been summoned to the boss's office? He had only been there once before. He wasn't at all curious about his visitor; he was often interviewed by technical experts, RAF planning types, government officials and even de Havilland's investors and bankers, keen to find out how the Dove was performing. Future sales of the aircraft for military and commercial use were vital to the company's prosperity.

The managing director, Jocelyn Darley, was a tall, imposing figure in his early fifties, clean-shaven and tanned following his spring holiday in Jamaica. Dressed in a light-grey double-breasted Dormeuil suit and with a gold signet ring on his left little finger, he was the epitome of the international businessman. Well educated, he had attended Westminster School and had a first from Magdalene College, Cambridge, in history and politics. After a career with the Cunard Steamship Company selling first-class tickets for transatlantic voyages, he had been recruited by de Havilland just before the war as a project manager. He was not an engineer or a scientist; he had risen through the ranks because he was an excellent people manager and deal-maker. Darley had a modern corner office at the top of the building with a broad picture window looking out across the airfield. The office was L-shaped and furnished in the latest American white oak low-profile furniture, with modern, abstract artwork on the walls. Here, it felt as if the future had already arrived. Devon smiled at Lucy, who said he should go straight in.

"Ah, Adam, do come in. Take a seat." As well as Darley's unfeasibly large desk, the room had a matching oak coffee table, a cocktail cabinet and a black and chrome leather settee and matching chairs.

Devon recognised the guest immediately. He stood up from his chair and held out his hand. "Well, hello, Adam. Great to see you again – it's been a while."

"David! Yes, indeed, great to see you too. How are things with BOAC? What are you up to these days?" asked Devon.

"Things are going very well, thanks. After a couple of years on test flights to destinations in Africa, I'm working on the new India, Ceylon and Persian Gulf routes. All good fun. And somewhat different to our past flying roles, of course."

Jocelyn Darley cut in. "You two were together in the Far East, were you not?"

Devon turned back to his boss. "Yes, Squadron Leader Porter and I were in Malaya, Singapore and Hong Kong with 28 Squadron from 1947 to '49. Army support Spitfires. You came back to the UK a few months ahead of me, didn't you, David?"

"Yes, then after a few weeks R&R joined BOAC to develop new routes, initially to Johannesburg and Cape Town. Those services are now in operation. And you, Adam, how have you been getting on here at de Havilland?"

Devon glanced at Darley. "Very well, I believe," he said with a grin. "You'll have to ask Mr Darley if my flying is up to scratch."

"We are delighted with Adam's work, David. I think it's fair to say we have one of the best ex-RAF pilots now turned test pilot. We have high hopes for good international sales of the new Dove variant, with its advanced air navigation. But perhaps we should get to the reason for this little reunion. David, would you like to outline the proposition you have for Adam?"

"Of course. Adam, I would like to invite you to participate in this year's Battle of Britain anniversary flypast over London in September. I have been asked by the Air Ministry to put together a team of civilian and serving pilots to fly a twelve-aircraft display. We are to feature Spitfire versions from 1940 to '50, and the Ministry wants to have pilots from wartime and post-war. Nothing complicated in the display, but impeccable formation flying will be required, of course. We will rehearse the flypast from Biggin Hill on two or three dates in late August. Mr Darley has kindly agreed to let you have extra leave to carry out this task. Are you interested?"

"I certainly am. Thank you so much for the chance to take part. Will there be any other chaps I know?"

"John Corrigan now works with me at BOAC – he has agreed to participate. I'm not sure you will know the others."

"It sounds like a great project, David, thanks again for the invitation. Will I be able to put in a couple of hours flying to refresh, ahead of the rehearsals? I might be a little rusty on the Spit."

"Definitely," said Porter. "There will be a Spitfire at Biggin from late July. If you can get down there, the team will fix you up to fly a Mk XIV. Assuming Jocelyn can give you this extra time off…"

"Absolutely no problem, take as much time as necessary," said Darley. "It's always our privilege to assist the Air Ministry. Now, let's go along to the directors' dining room. Adam, you will join us? I believe our lunch will be ready, and you two can catch up on old times."

Devon was not surprised to see the dining room fitted out just as well as Darley's office. He declined the G&T offered by his boss, as he was scheduled to make a further test flight in the afternoon. He was quietly relieved by that, as he didn't enjoy daytime drinking, A waitress brought over plates of cold smoked salmon and brown bread. The main course of lamb chops was followed by peach melba. Conversation, naturally, was about the development of aircraft that would sell around the world to commercial and military customers. Porter asked several questions about the new radar navigation equipment Devon was working on. Without feeling at all uncomfortable, Devon said that he was restricted in what he could disclose, even to Porter.

"Adam has spent a considerable time with the technicians developing the radar and avionics – more than just piloting the ship," said Darley.

"Oh, really?" Porter leant forward. "Is this something you are particularly interested in, Adam?"

"Yes. I believe that the best test-flying results come from having a good understanding of the technology and working closely with the boffins."

"Yes indeed, and what new features are you working on?" said Porter.

"The ability to see ground features ahead, near and far. Very helpful in bad weather and at night."

"I see. Sounds very interesting. Perhaps you could show me around the Dove after this meeting? Maybe we could take a short flight and you could show me how she performs."

"I'd be happy to show you around the hangar. Not sure we can get a flight in today." That was about as far as Devon would go. He didn't mention the potential for radar to be developed into a way to control air-to-ground guided missiles, which the technicians were working on.

The dining staff cleared away their plates and glasses, leaving small china coffee cups and a tall, slim silver pot. Porter poured coffee for all three.

Twenty minutes later, Darley glanced at his watch. "What time are you flying this afternoon, Adam?"

"Four o'clock, sir, but we have a planning meeting at three."

"Well, don't let us keep you." Darley stood up, as did Porter. "But before you go, I can tell you that you are invited to the company's Summer Ball at the Grosvenor Park Hotel. All the directors and senior managers will be in attendance, as well as clients and other important guests. David and Mrs Porter will be there, and I would like to extend an invitation to your fiancée – Hannah, isn't it?"

"Yes, sir. That would be wonderful, thank you very much. We shall look forward to it," replied Devon, a touch more enthusiastically than was strictly necessary.

Darley moved towards the office door. Devon took his cue and shook hands with the two men. "I look forward to hearing from you about the flypast rehearsals, David."

***

Darley and Porter returned to the comfortable chairs in Darley's office. "That went very well. Thank you, Jocelyn. It's important that we take things steadily, not alert Devon that anything untoward is going on. The assignments we ask him to take on in future will be more demanding and potentially dangerous than the flypast," said Porter.

Darley nodded sagely. "I'm always keen to assist the security and intelligence services, David, and will facilitate any time off Devon requires to work with you, if that is his choice. It's for you to decide if and when you disclose your dual role at BOAC and MI6 to him."

"Naturally. I will be liaising with the MI6 people to provide the right aircraft and pilots for their operations – in confidence, of course. The objective for the time being is to get Devon comfortable with working on new and unusual tasks. The flypast appeals to his sense of adventure, as will the covert operations we might assign to him."

THREE

Henry Fitzjohn was seriously chuffed. His position as a member of the House of Commons Defence Procurement Committee had finally paid off. His selection for the committee only came about because of his RAF service. It was a burdensome job that he had not looked for and treated with disdain, but he had always felt that it might lead to something good. Fitzjohn appreciated that being the Member of Parliament for Sudbury and Woodbridge had certain advantages, of course: most notably, a very welcome expense account. And then there was the lovely Amanda Spencer, his elegant, sophisticated constituency campaign manager, an imprecise number of years Fitzjohn's senior. She had a lithe figure, Romanesque features and was very beautiful. She had guided him through the general election and helped him to be accepted by the voters and elected as one of the youngest Members of Parliament in 1951. He quickly settled into life at Westminster, with its web of intrigue, conventions and customs. Amanda was always very willing to share her expertise on parliamentary business during the daytime – and the pleasures of the bedroom at night.

But annoyingly, his roles as an MP and as a committee member were more time-consuming than he had expected. He found his weekly meetings with his constituents and listening to their petty problems so tiresome – arguments over rights of way across agricultural land, complaints about top-rate income tax, and demands from constituents for tickets for the best seats at the Queen's coronation. The opportunity to serve as an MP had appealed to Fitzjohn when he arrived back in the UK in 1950 after serving in the Far East. It had given him a way out of life on the family estate – he could leave farming and land management to his father and two older brothers. But being an MP was not his main interest in life.

Fitzjohn wanted to build up his air taxi business. His pilot, an ex-RAF Transport Command veteran, Roger Harris, who Fitzjohn had known at Millfield School, was a good sort. Harris could be trusted to carry out most of the flying: he was very experienced, never complained, and got on well with clients. Harris loved flying, and the job with Fitzjohn suited him well. Fitzjohn was satisfied that he could just about manage the business, carry out some of the flying himself, and still fulfil his duties as an MP.

After two years of running the air taxi service, he knew he wouldn't make any real money from operating his old, tired Percival Proctor aircraft. It only had three passenger seats, was cold and noisy, and was limited to local UK flights. He had another aircraft, an even older Avro Commodore, but it was barely airworthy and required renovation if it were to be put into service. There was a demand for air taxi and air charter services, with the economy in the UK and Europe finally growing – industrialists and entrepreneurs wanted to waste no time, so fast, easy travel was essential. This was how he planned to make money – his MP's salary was no more than he had earned as an RAF fighter pilot, but he felt the job carried much more responsibility. Poor though the pay was, he appreciated that no one would be coming at him from behind with a 20mm cannon and machine guns.

Fitzjohn had sketched out a plan to buy a classy aircraft, maybe more than one, offer an upmarket service and expand the routes he offered. But how could he raise sufficient funds to do this? No family money would be forthcoming, and he doubted he was good for a bank loan of any size.

But then it looked like his luck had changed for the better. In the Commons bar after a defence committee meeting that dragged on into the late evening, Fitzjohn's Conservative pal on the committee, Andrew White, ordered a couple of large Taliskers and guided him over to a quiet corner.

"Henry, I have a little proposition that you might find interesting," said White. "I've had a tip-off that Airspeed are looking to sell a couple of their surplus twin-engined Consul aircraft."

"Airspeed? Aren't they part of de Havilland now? Not sure I could stretch to two of those lovely aircraft."

"Yes, indeed. De Havilland have effectively had control for a number of years, but Airspeed is to be fully integrated in the next couple of months. The machines could be worth £6,000 each on the open market, but a special deal might be forthcoming, if you're interested?"

"The Consul is certainly a very fine machine for air taxi use, but that price is outside my budget. Sorry, Andrew, I'll have to pass on this."

"Hang on, old boy, I have it on good authority that Airspeed would let you have them…" White paused for effect, raised his eyebrows, leant forward and spoke in a quiet voice, "for £5,000 for the two. I've been given to understand they are impeccable examples, newly converted from the Airspeed Oxford and fitted out for commercial passenger service."

"Now that is an interesting proposition. But why should the Airspeed people offer me this deal? What's in it for them?"

"The practical side of the merger is going on at the moment, and two of the old Airspeed directors have been charged with the disposal of some aircraft. No one will ask who bought the machines and how they agreed a price. The price you pay would be noted in their accounts as net of a tax loss. And winning the positive influence of a member of the defence committee would be a valuable attribute that they would bring to the party around the de Havilland board table, should they need it."

"Let me give this some thought. I'll call you tomorrow," said Fitzjohn.

"Very well, Henry. But keep it to yourself, old chap. The deal has to be secret, of course. We wouldn't want the newspapers to get to hear of an MP getting a substantial discount from a defence contractor…"

"Understood, Andrew."

***

Fitzjohn finished his drink and left for the night, walking briskly to the Hotel Thames Vista in Pimlico. Amanda Spencer would be waiting for him there. He couldn't wait to tell her the news – she would be impressed that he had the chance to make some serious money. Fitzjohn trusted her implicitly to keep the details to herself.

"Perfect for use as an executive air charter, the Consul can carry six passengers in very comfortable seats with space for luggage, and it has a good cruise speed of around 160mph. It also has a range that would take in most western European cities." Fitzjohn paced the hotel room, his hands clasped in front of his chest and his eyes wide with excitement. "Bloody hell, Amanda, it's a cracking chance to get hold of a couple of really excellent aircraft and get the business going at last."

"It's a bribe, Henry, and you know it. They will want a return favour sooner than you can say scratch my back."

"Nonsense! They want to get shot of a couple of aircraft that would just be a burden on their balance sheet. I'm doing them a favour taking them off their hands."

"Oh, Henry, you do talk some tosh at times." Amanda kicked off her shoes and sat back on the bed. "And where the hell will you get the money to buy them? Don't expect me to bankroll you. I'm not that desperate."

Fitzjohn looked at her sideways and smiled. "Don't you worry, my love, I can do this deal myself." He walked slowly over to the cocktail bar and poured himself a whisky and soda. "Gin for you, my dear?"

"Go on then," she said with a warm smile.

The drinks gave Fitzjohn's cheeks an even rosier hue than normal. Nearly six feet tall, he was an imposing figure. His dark brown hair, heavy on top, swept back, was smoothed with a light touch of his exclusive Bond Street styling cream.

Without a word, Amanda turned her back to Fitzjohn. He read the sign and slowly unzipped her dress. Amanda enjoyed these nights in London to the full.

***

Fitzjohn had squirrelled away into a business account a bagful of US dollars that he had accumulated in Hong Kong prior to his departure from the RAF. He had not told anyone else about this little cache. He had resolved not to spend it, thinking of it as a long-term backup, but now he felt the time was right to put the money to good use. If he paid using the name of a subsidiary company of his air taxi business, the payment could not easily be traced back to him.

The two Consuls were delivered to Cambridge airport and immediately hangered, pending the recruitment of two new pilots to make up the team of four, including himself and Harris. Fitzjohn even managed to sell his two old aircraft for almost £2,000.

Although the interior fittings of the aircraft were new, Fitzjohn wanted to add some extras to meet the needs of the discerning businessmen and wealthy private clients he was targeting, who were willing to pay over the odds for the little luxuries in life. A small drinks cabinet was fitted in each aircraft, plus a magazine rack, and the windows dressed with maroon velvet curtains. In the airport building a passenger lounge completed the VIP service, and a leggy blonde female Cambridge student was employed part-time to welcome clients. The aircraft's silver fuselage was enhanced with the words 'Granta Air Services'. Several of Fitzjohn's air taxi clients wanted to book flights in the UK and to Paris, Brussels, Frankfurt and Dublin. Fitzjohn was confident that the new enterprise would be a huge success, and a good marketing campaign would bring new clients.

It was easy to recruit pilots; in the seven years since the war ended, so many had been let go by the RAF. Fitzjohn took on Richard Dunn, a wartime Blenheim pilot with a year's experience of working for Eire Airways on the Dublin and Cork routes from Croydon, and Joseph Richardson, a DC3 Dakota pilot with experience in the Berlin Airlift. They were soon undertaking conversion training on the Consuls, supervised by Harris. Both men had the right schooling and clipped, upper-class accents that would emphasise the exclusive standing of the company.

The first day of operations saw two flights in the UK. Harris took three passengers to Manchester Ringway and Richardson flew a wealthy couple to Southampton, where they looked at a yacht they were thinking of buying. The next morning a metals importer booked a flight for two people to Manston in Kent, to pick up another passenger, and then on to Orly in Paris. They booked return flights for three days later. Fitzjohn piloted these first sorties into Europe himself. After operating for only a month, the bookings diary was full, with UK and European flights equally balanced. Money was rolling in.

FOUR

Val knew she was in for a rough ride; being recalled to London at short notice often meant the end of an operative's career. Overt failure on an assignment had repercussions. Her actions would be examined in minute detail and her judgement called into question. Her courage would never be doubted, though, the MI6 leaders had every confidence on that score. Although she realised it was silly, the wait in the anteroom outside the chief's office was almost as nerve-racking as the challenges she had faced in the field. Kate Samways, C's secretary, came out of C's office and greeted Val with her usual warmth: a nod, a smile, almost a wink. Val thought she was a tough customer, and would be very glad of her goodwill if she ever needed to see the chief urgently. Kate asked if Val was ready for the meeting, then turned back to the red-brown mahogany door of C's office, knocked and entered.

"Miss Hetherington-Brown is here, sir."

"Right, send her in, Miss Samways."

When Val entered, she saw that C was accompanied by Angus Ballantyne, the senior officer for field operations and overseer of her

Berlin station. Val was perfectly happy to work with Ballantyne – she never regarded herself as working 'for' senior operational officers; they were all in the same line of business, and agents were regarded as equals. She had learned of Ballantyne's wartime exploits largely from other agents; it would not be proper for him to boast about his own achievements. He was a senior officer in the British intelligence services and had helped to mastermind Operation Aerial – the mass evacuation of British and allied troops and civilians from the western ports of France after Dunkirk, to escape the marauding Germans.

After the arrival of the Germans as far west as Bordeaux at the end of June 1940, Ballantyne escaped to Portugal after more than a month of forced marching and living off the land. Emaciated and exhausted, he was given time to recover before being assigned responsibility for leading the MI6 Lisbon station. His skill at building agent networks led to the gathering of vital information on shipping movements and spy recruitment.

"Take a seat, Brown."

That was the most courtesy Val ever got from the chief.

C sat back in his maroon leather chair. As he steepled his hands under his chin, his gold cufflinks caught the light. He was a well-dressed former officer, tall and straight-backed but more than a touch overweight, with a short, pointed beard left over from his Royal Navy days. Now he was commanding people's lives.

"We have been looking at your report from the operation last week, and it does not make good reading. A potentially very valuable asset was lost in regrettable circumstances. Extraction of defectors, those with helpful military or secret service information, should be accomplished successfully in every case. We do not expect the individual to be shot in the street, right in front of our own agents. Do you have anything to add to your report?"

"Agreed, sir. The loss of the defector was very regrettable. We had no intelligence that indicated she was suspected by the Stasi. I now believe she was under low-level surveillance, given her access to so much information. No doubt she attracted attention when she contacted my people in Berlin. The question of a leak in our security is being looked into, of course, but I believe the Stasi senior officers decided to have her killed as a precaution. As I mentioned in my report, fortunately we came away with the notebook listing the code names of all East German agents and many Soviets operating in the West. I accept that we do not have the real names of the agents, but the list is a good start. And of course we brought back the body."

"I find the value you place on a simple notebook hard to accept, Brown." C placed his right hand, palm down, fingers open, flat on the desk. His voice went up an octave. "Actually, I regard it as having little value. The real names connected to code names and locations is what we wanted."

"Well, sir, that's understood. But I think we are all hopeful that the notebook will be a significant source of intelligence." Val's temper was starting to show. She had great respect for C's wartime record; he had seen action in the North Atlantic and risen to the rank of vice-admiral, however he had no first-hand experience of clandestine work in the field.

But Ballantyne did. "Sir, if I may," he said. "The situation in Berlin is moving fast and we cannot always be sure we have the very latest intelligence. The pace of change is very concerning. Thousands of East Germans have crossed the border relatively easily in the last couple of years, but that's all coming to a halt as the Soviets lock down the East. It will become harder and more dangerous than ever to get out the people we want, those the Reds don't want us to have. This was an unfortunate outcome to the mission, but we should remember that the Soviets don't know the woman is dead, and will be changing and disrupting their network as we speak. With your permission, I would like to put out some badly coded messages that indicate we have the names – let's stir things up and see what emerges. Even arresting the three agents the woman gave to Val could trigger a wholesale reorganisation, and if we're lucky we may see movement in the Soviet agents already known to us, giving us a chance to identify their replacements."

C sat back. "I see your point, Ballantyne. Well, certainly we have the advantage of having disposed of the body, so no damage done there."

Val shivered. She had met the frightened lady, sympathised with her, seen her body carried away. Plenty of damage *had* been done there. But that was the nature of the work she was involved in; no one could allow themselves to be sensitised on a personal level. She listened as C continued. "I've given this careful consideration, Brown, and I'm allowing you to continue to head up the Berlin station. But you must tighten up security, make sure you have full confidence in the bona fides of the defectors and agents you deal with. The last thing we want is to lose another source of intelligence, or threaten our network."

"Yes, sir. All your advice is perfectly well understood. Perfectly well." Val raised her eyes to the ceiling, leaving C under no delusions that she felt she knew exactly how to handle her operation.

Ballantyne cowered at Val's insubordination and interjected quickly before C could react. "Come to my office first thing in the morning, Val, and I will brief you on a new task assigned to us."

"Yes, sir." Val immediately saw that Ballantyne wanted to end the meeting.

"Before you go…" C leant forward, pondering his next words. "Raleigh. Not as young as he once was. Does he still have the required skills in the field? I could arrange a very stimulating role for him in the London office to see him through to retirement."

Val was caught by surprise. She didn't see Raleigh as being anywhere near past his best. His age was indeterminate; his experience was a key factor in his effectiveness. And he was physically fit. There was little room for friendship among colleagues in the service, but there was loyalty. Val felt there was a degree of contempt in C's comments, just because he had a desk job himself. It irritated her.

"I believe he is as sharp as he has ever been." Val knew that she was ardently defending Raleigh and had to balance her views with the chief's comments, to avoid antagonising him further. "But I will give this some thought, sir."

"Thank you, Brown. That will be all." C had made his point, and in his dismissive style sent Val on her way. "Ballantyne, stay behind, please."

After Val had departed, C briefed Ballantyne on the government's concerns about the problem of spies and double agents in the diplomatic service. The discovery that Maclean and Burgess had been acting as Soviet spies had rocked the secret services. These men, highly regarded members of the British Establishment, educated at Cambridge University and holding important positions in the Foreign Office, had passed enormous amounts of secret information to the Russians. Nothing untoward had been suspected for many years, but given their membership of the communist party at university and the close network of associates they were assumed to have, the British secret services were seeking out further members of a spy ring.

No one could now be regarded as one hundred per cent trustworthy. Even long-serving officers were being revetted, their finances looked into, their social circles assessed for connections with undesirable individuals, those known to be communist activists or sympathisers. Ballantyne would be observed himself, and he resigned himself to the annoyance of being followed, his affairs dissected. But he did not worry; he was perfectly clean.

FIVE

Soon after 5p.m. on Fridays in the City of London, office workers would meet up with colleagues for a drink or two in one of the local establishments. After a hard week at their desks, they welcomed the chance to unwind, but no one stayed late. The pub landlords dimmed their lights at around 7p.m. to encourage drinkers to go home. Most Fridays Hannah Shaw enjoyed a small Port and Lemon with the girls from the bank, but she only ever had one – she had a train to catch.

The 6.15 from King's Cross to Hatfield was always busy, and Hannah was rarely able to get a seat. But the journey only took a little over half an hour, and Adam would be waiting for her in the car park. She so looked forward to spending weekends with him; they saw little of each other during the week, as she shared a flat in Clapham and he lived close to the de Havilland factory at Welham Green.

Hannah enjoyed working at the London and Hong Kong Bank much more than she thought she would. After joining the bank four years earlier, her German-Jewish background led her to be recruited by the Israeli Secret Service, and she spent nearly a year in the Hong

Kong branch of the bank, acting out her dual role of bank official and the recruitment of fighter pilots for the Israelis. The mission she was involved in failed badly when Egyptian agents attempted to assassinate her and her colleagues. They had been lucky to get out alive. The debacle resulted in Hannah being released from the service, so she now enjoyed a life free of pressure and the threat of death around every corner. The only good outcome of the mission had been meeting Adam in Hong Kong. Initially he had been a recruitment target for the Israelis to join their newly formed air force, which was equipped with Spitfires, but after considering his loyalties, Devon had declined to join, knowing he might have been required to fight British pilots. The relationship between Devon and Hannah turned to love, but she refused to follow him back to the UK after he resigned from the RAF and returned home. Their relationship only blossomed when they met again in London in 1950.

The train clanked to a halt, and a bowler-hatted gent unlocked the door and threw it open. Clouds of smoke and steam swirled around the platform as commuters walked quickly past the ticket collector. Hannah smoothed her long brown hair over her shoulder, fastened her dark-grey suit jacket and straightened her matching skirt. She wore little make-up, but had added a light pink to her lips. Her row of pearls glistened in the station lights. She spotted Adam standing by his car. The moment when she first saw him was always a thrill: she skipped out to the station car park and they embraced. He gave her a lingering kiss and held her tightly.

"Adam, so nice to see you, how are you?" Hannah said.

"Great, how are you?" Adam opened the passenger door for Hannah and placed her weekend bag on the back seat.

"I'm well, thanks. Looking forward to a lovely couple of days. What do you have planned?"

Adam put the car into gear and moved off. "Well, tomorrow I thought we could go to Cambridge for lunch and call in to your parents in the afternoon, if you like. On Sunday we can just relax in the garden – the weather forecast is good."

"That sounds marvellous. I can telephone Mother to let them know we are coming."

"And I have some news," he said. "I had a meeting yesterday with Mr Darley and a guest – none other than Squadron Leader David Porter."

"What, from Hong Kong?"

"The very man, now working for BOAC of course. He made me an offer that I couldn't turn down – to fly in the Battle of Britain anniversary flypast in September. He has put together a group of twelve Spitfire pilots from the beginning of the war up to recent times. I'm really looking forward to getting my hands on a Spit again."

Hannah felt a pang of fear. She knew that Spitfires could be difficult and dangerous aircraft to fly, and Adam was well out of practice. "Why aren't the current pilots doing the flying? It's been a long time since you flew a Spitfire," she said.

"The Ministry wants the flypast to be carried out by a cross-section of current and past service pilots. Porter himself is a Battle of Britain veteran. But I have the opportunity of doing some refresher training, and there will be rehearsals before the actual flypast. It'll be great fun!"

Hannah sat back, not wholly reassured.

"And there's more news – Mr Darley has invited us to the firm's Summer Ball at the Grosvenor Park Hotel in Park Lane. It will be a terrific night – top-class food and plenty of champagne. All the bigwigs from de Havilland will be there, as well as David and his wife and other VIPs."

"That sounds great. I shall look forward to it immensely!" said Hannah. After a few seconds she added, "I must get up to Bond Street to buy a dress to wear."

"You have plenty of lovely dresses, darling. How about that dark blue satin one you wore to the Peninsula, you looked fabulous in that one." Adam didn't understand that Hannah liked to have a new dress for a special occasion.

"I've had that dress five years, Adam!" There was no more to discuss.

***

Devon had booked lunch at the University Arms Hotel, one of the most stylish establishments in Cambridge, where the quality of the food and service could always be relied upon. They enjoyed a shared seafood platter followed by a pear cobbler with ice cream. "We could take a punt out on the river, if you like?" he said.

Hannah looked at her watch. "Perhaps another time. I'd like to get over to see Mum and Dad before the afternoon passes."

"Sure. I'll pay the bill and we can get on our way."

As the couple left the restaurant and walked through the hotel lobby, Hannah glanced across to the open doors of the bar. She faltered and involuntarily grabbed Adam's arm.

"What is it, darling?"

"Oh, it's n-nothing. Let's go."

On the steps of the hotel entrance, Devon turned to Hannah. "Really? Tell me, what's the matter?"

Hannah had gone pale. "I think I just saw Henry Fitzjohn in the bar. Bit of a shock. He was with an older woman." Hannah didn't add that for an instant Fitzjohn's eyes had met hers. She had seen a faint quizzical look in his eyes. He had clearly been trying to recall who she was. And then he had smiled momentarily at her, remembering her.

"I shouldn't wonder, he lives in this area. I heard he was back, running an air taxi outfit at Cambridge airport. The lady was probably his latest girlfriend. Come on, let's go."

Hannah smiled but said nothing. She was shaken by her memories of that awful night three years ago in Hong Kong when Fitzjohn had tried to rape her.

Hannah knew there was no love lost between Devon and Fitzjohn. Fitzjohn's dishonest behaviour on several levels in the air force and in his private life was abhorrent to Devon. At one time, as flight lieutenants with 28 Squadron in Hong Kong, they had vied for promotion to squadron leader, but neither of them was appointed and Devon left the RAF soon after. Fitzjohn left later, before he could be court-martialled. After Devon heard about his air taxi start-up he thought Fitzjohn would disappear into obscurity, and was more than a touch surprised when he read about his election as a Member of Parliament.

Back in the car, Adam asked Hannah if she was OK. He knew that she had been close to Fitzjohn; he once suspected there could be a romantic edge to their relationship, but Hannah had always denied this. He knew that she had targeted Fitzjohn to join the Israeli Air Force, as she had done with him, but it had gone nowhere. As they moved off in the car, he saw she was controlling her breathing, sitting still, trying to relax, trying to show that she was fine.

***

The Trumpington Street area is one of the most sought-after locations in Cambridge, and Hannah's family home stood just off the busy road. A large red-brick Edwardian house perfectly suited the university professor and his wife who had taken in Hannah and her brother as Kindertransport refugees back in 1939. They were two of the almost 10,000 Jewish children sent by their parents from Germany to the UK to avoid the Nazi regime. Shaw wasn't Hannah's real surname – she was a Steinberg. Soon after they arrived, the Austens had decided to change the children's surnames, to save Hannah and her brother from the teasing of spiteful children at school who took offence at a German-sounding name. They were given the surname Shaw. Professor Austen was a good friend of Hannah's father. Then when he and his wife had legally adopted the children in 1945, they kept the name of Shaw. Hannah's parents and wider family had chosen to stay in Germany. They were arrested by the Nazis and all perished in the Holocaust. Hannah carried this tragedy within her, rarely allowing herself to think about the dreadful reality.

They spent a pleasant afternoon with the Austen family, Professor Austen soon turned the discussion from county cricket to the policies of the respective political parties in regard to education funding – always a point of interest to a university professor – and listening to gramophone records. Devon selected the records from the collection that were his favourites: Holst's *The Planets* suite and Beethoven's *Pastoral Symphony*. Professor Austen even had some modern American big band records, which Hannah liked. She also played 'Waves on the Water' by Darius Delton, the American baritone: the song reminded her of the lovely warm evenings she had spent with Devon in Hong Kong.

Mrs Austen couldn't resist asking the question she always asked – had they set a date for the wedding? They had been engaged for over two years, and most people expected the wedding to follow without delay. The truth was, Adam felt no need to rush, preferring to develop his new career first. And they were planning to save enough for a deposit on a nice house in the Wimbledon area of London, which was taking time.

They took their tea out to the garden where they discussed Devon's flying job and Austen's students at the university; they avoided touching on matrimonial issues.

In the car, Hannah raised the subject of marriage again. As they arrived back at Adam's house in Welham Green, which he rented from a local solicitor, she said, "Do you think we should set a date for the wedding, Adam? I'm not pressing you, but it would be nice to have a plan of sorts." Inwardly, Hannah was indeed ready to press Adam. He had got into the habit of prevaricating whenever the subject of the wedding came up, usually citing the demands of work, the need to save for a deposit on a house – even the weather, when Hannah had once proposed a Christmas wedding.

"I haven't given it much thought but yes, you're right, we should plan ahead. Next year, perhaps, after the coronation?"

Hannah was pleasantly surprised by his response. Even if he had suggested a date a year ahead, it was good that Adam now seemed willing to commit. "That would be wonderful – say July?"

"Excellent! This is an agreement we must seal with a kiss."

SIX

Fitzjohn was delighted with the regular flight bookings made by James Mackenzie. Almost every Friday morning, Cambridge to Amsterdam Schiphol and back on the same day, with the pilot waiting at the airport while Mackenzie took a taxi to the city centre. His meetings never lasted more than a couple of hours. Mackenzie was in his mid-thirties, medium height, fair and slim, with immaculate dress sense. He usually wore a mid-grey or dark-blue Savile Row suit, Church's black Diplomat brogues and a starched white shirt. His ties spoke of class: Oriel College Boat Club, Scots Guards and MCC. His outfit was stylishly set off with a plain black trilby. He always carried a small brown leather briefcase containing no more than a few papers, business cards and a notebook.

Joseph Richardson piloted the first three or four flights, but as the summer recess effectively closed down Westminster, Fitzjohn decided to take on the next trip himself. With clear skies, the ninety-minute flight went without a hitch, and Mackenzie took his car to the city. The return flight was equally straightforward; easy money, in Fitzjohn's opinion. Over the next couple of weeks Richardson and Fitzjohn shared the flying. Mackenzie seemed to be a very satisfied customer: he got on well with the staff and was always seen through customs and immigration at Schiphol and Cambridge smoothly and quickly. The airfares were charged to his company, JRM Provisions, and always paid promptly. He told Richardson that he was an importer of high-quality food and wine from Holland, Germany and France.

***

For the next Friday morning trip the weather forecast was not looking good. Even early on the day before, the forecast showed a storm brewing in the North Sea, with strong, gusting winds, heavy rain and poor visibility. Fitzjohn asked the girl in the office to phone Mackenzie to tell him that his flight in the morning was cancelled. Mackenzie immediately asked to speak to Fitzjohn.

"Good afternoon, Mr Mackenzie, how may I be of assistance?" Fitzjohn was not used to being subservient, but he wanted to do his best to ameliorate Mackenzie's disappointment.

"It's very important that I get to Amsterdam tomorrow, Fitzjohn, at some point in the day at least. What can you do?"

"The forecast is not at all promising. We *may* be able to get to Amsterdam early morning, but the weather in England is predicted to deteriorate during the afternoon and we won't be able to get back, possibly for two or three days."

"I'm sure all will be well. I will shorten my time in Amsterdam and have my colleague come to Schiphol. I will meet you at Cambridge airport at 8a.m. sharp."

Fitzjohn hesitated. "Well, I'm not sure we can—"

"Thank you, goodbye." Mackenzie hung up.

True to the forecast, the wind swept across East Anglia during the night, with sporadic rain showers making the prospect of flying in the morning unappealing. Fitzjohn arrived at the airfield at 7a.m. and got the aircraft ready, albeit with little enthusiasm.

Mackenzie appeared with ten minutes to spare, parked his car in one of the Granta Air Services spaces and hurried through the terminal building. The passport and customs formalities were completed in less than a minute, allowing Mackenzie to go directly to the aircraft. Fitzjohn saw him coming, wearing a khaki trench coat, his usual briefcase pressed under his arm.

"What do we have, Fitzjohn? Are we ready?"

"Yes, Mr Mackenzie, but you do understand it will be a rough journey, with the possibility of being stranded in Amsterdam?"

"Yes, yes, all that is very clear. Now, shall we go?"

Fitzjohn's RAF training had included handling aircraft in all weathers, but he was used to a Spitfire, not a passenger aircraft. After take-off he levelled out at 2,000 feet – much lower than usual, but this enabled him to keep the land and sea in view. Within half an hour the weather had improved and they arrived in Amsterdam in blustery, but manageable, conditions.

From his usual seat in the coffee shop Fitzjohn saw Mackenzie exit the terminal building, meet a woman and walk to the car park with her. They sat in a Mercedes without driving off, clearly in deep conversation. Fitzjohn went to the pilots' briefing room to assess the weather forecast for the rest of the day. Conditions were pretty awful back in England, but if they got into serious trouble they could always turn back to Amsterdam. He was willing to give it a go.

Within an hour Mackenzie strode into the terminal building with a clear sense of purpose, and went straight to the row of public phone boxes. After five minutes he ended his call and met Fitzjohn at passport control. "Well, Fitzjohn, are we ready to depart? I presume the sooner the better?"

"Once we have completed the formalities, we can leave."

After take-off Fitzjohn took up a westerly heading and kept an eye on the weather ahead. It didn't take long for the cloud to thicken, giving very poor forward visibility. Gusting winds buffeted the aircraft. The good news was that the terrain ahead – East Anglia – was flat, which allowed Fitzjohn to descend and keep below the cloud base. As they approached the east coast, Mackenzie spoke to Fitzjohn.

"I'm not happy with this. Let's land at Bradwell."

"I'm not sure that's necessary. The weather is poor but stable. I think we can press on to Cambridge," said Fitzjohn.

"No, I insist we land at Bradwell. We can wait out the weather there."

Fitzjohn was put out by this: as the pilot all flight decisions were his to make. But he assumed that Mackenzie was getting nervous, and he didn't want to upset a valued customer. "Very well. I will radio Cambridge and advise them of the change in flight plan. There's no permanent passport and customs control in place at Bradwell, so Cambridge will arrange for the local man to come over. We will have to wait for him before we can leave. They will also call a taxi for us to take us to Cambridge if we get stuck there."

Bradwell sits on the Blackwater estuary and was easy for Fitzjohn to spot as he scanned the east coast. After one pass over the airfield, Fitzjohn approached to land. He did his best to stay aligned to the runway, battling against a strong crosswind and rain showers. The Consul was a solid, responsive aircraft, and on touchdown Fitzjohn was able to keep straight and slow down safely. He taxied over to the deserted tower and closed down the engines.

"Excellent flying, Fitzjohn, thank you."

Both men climbed out and walked quickly to the two-storey building that served as the terminal. Fitzjohn tried the door. It was unlocked. As no departures or arrivals were scheduled, the place was deserted.

"Please give me a couple of minutes. I need to use the facilities," Mackenzie said.

"Right-o, I will go up to the office. I have to sign in and write up my logbook."

Fitzjohn noticed that Mackenzie went straight through the hall and out to the front. He was intrigued. What was he up to? Unable to resist, he ran up the stairs to the first floor and went to the window overlooking the road. Well hidden, he saw Mackenzie walk to a Rover 75 parked in the road beside the office. Looking down, Fitzjohn could see a smartly dressed man in the driver's seat. Mackenzie, in the passenger seat directly below Fitzjohn's window, opened his briefcase on his lap, carefully unzipped a side pocket then slipped his fingers into a hidden flap and pulled out a slim box, no bigger than a cigarette packet. The other man took the box and opened it carefully, Fitzjohn was stunned to see at least a dozen diamonds rolling around on the blue velvet inside the box. The man picked one up and lifted it to his eye, replaced it quickly then closed the box. The two men shook hands, the driver handed Mackenzie a bulky envelope, then tucked the box into his jacket pocket.

Mackenzie got out of the car and returned to the terminal building. The car sped off.

"Bloody hell, so that's his game – diamond smuggling!" Fitzjohn said to himself. "Cheeky sod, using a respectable Member of Parliament as his accomplice. We're going to have a little chat about this."

SEVEN

The regular flights to Amsterdam continued, with Richardson and Fitzjohn alternating flying duties. As always, Mackenzie carried his briefcase and went off for a couple of hours in the city. Occasionally he brought back some Edam or Gouda cheese, spiced sausage or wine to show that he was running a provisions import business. Fitzjohn had decided to do nothing about the smuggling; after all, it was Mackenzie's affair. As long as he paid his charter invoices promptly, Fitzjohn was happy.

In mid-summer, Mackenzie requested a flight to a new destination – Hilversum airfield. He wanted an overnight stay to allow him to visit Utrecht, and offered to pay for the aircraft for two days and the pilot's hotel expenses. Curious about what Mackenzie was up to, Fitzjohn decided he could fit in this trip before the House returned in September.

The flight was straightforward, and Fitzjohn had pre-booked the customs and passport facility for their arrival. A taxi took them the nine miles into Utrecht. Fitzjohn was pleased that the hotel Mackenzie had booked was one of the best in the region, with a splendid dining room; Mackenzie had invited him to join him for dinner. Fitzjohn was agreeably surprised by how much he enjoyed socialising with Mackenzie. They found they had both attended good schools, Millfield for Fitzjohn and Rugby for Mackenzie. Being a little older, Mackenzie had served in the war: three years with the Brigade of Guards, ending with the rank of captain. He briefly outlined his service record: D-Day, the Normandy campaign, the liberation of Paris and Operation Market Garden in Holland. He had been slightly wounded there, and it was during his recuperation that he got to know his Dutch contacts in the provisions business. He also explained that his late father had left him a country house on the outskirts of Swaffham, then swept away Fitzjohn's obvious admiration by adding that the cost of renovations and upkeep was enormous.

Fitzjohn followed Mackenzie's lead and described his own family house and estate, farmed by his father and two brothers. Cautiously, he avoided implying that he had any real wealth; his father was uncompromising in his reluctance to help him in his business venture. Since an MP's salary was acceptable, he could live on it, but no one ever got rich on what an MP was paid. He mentioned that the air taxi business was a good source of income and he planned to grow it rapidly in the coming years.

After dinner, Fitzjohn had a single brandy then left Mackenzie in the bar.

***

Fitzjohn enjoyed a breakfast of fried eggs on toast and coffee. He wrote out the return flight plan to Cambridge and sat in the hotel lobby waiting for Mackenzie. No refuelling was needed; they had come with full tanks, plenty for a return trip. Suddenly Mackenzie arrived, in an obvious hurry. Fitzjohn stood. "Are you ready to go?"

"Yes, yes. There's a taxi waiting outside for us. Will we be able to depart promptly from the airfield?" Mackenzie was already walking to the hotel door.

"I think so. The weather is fine, and we just have the paperwork to complete at the airport. Why the hurry?"

"Never mind that, let's go. I've settled up with the hotel."

Fitzjohn bristled at the abrupt treatment, but as usual with a valued client, he shrugged it off and stepped outside to the taxi.

***

The usual passport and customs procedures were completed in just a few minutes. Fitzjohn advised Mackenzie that they would be leaving in fifteen minutes, he just needed to carry out the external pre-flight checks on the aircraft. Mackenzie didn't wait long before walking up to the open aircraft door and climbing in. Fitzjohn boarded himself, closed the door and, with his head lowered, manoeuvred himself into the pilot's seat. As he commenced the start-up, a red light flashed on the instrument panel and he heard the door open again. Turning to look over his right shoulder, he saw Mackenzie pull another man into the aircraft and slam the door closed.

"What the hell are you doing?" Fitzjohn unclipped his seat belt and started to get up.

Mackenzie came forward and pressed Fitzjohn back into his seat. "Just carry on, Henry, and everything will be fine."

"I can't take a passenger without going through passport control! Are you mad?"

Calmly Mackenzie said, "Just carry on with the flight, Henry, this man is my affair. You just do the flying."

Fitzjohn relented. He had a streak of the adventurer in him, and this development looked like a bit of excitement and intrigue. After taking off and setting the heading for England, he called over his shoulder. "It's going to take some explaining at Cambridge when they see we have a stowaway. I'll have to hand him over to the immigration people."

"No, that won't happen. We're landing at Bradwell. No radio calls, no setting up a visiting immigration man. A simple landing and immediate take-off will work just fine – there will hardly be anyone there. We will leave our friend there and continue to Cambridge. You will explain that you had a bit of engine trouble that slowed us up."

At first Fitzjohn objected strongly, but he soon gave in. He was intrigued by what was going on, and he had to admit that they were unlikely to be seen at Bradwell. He navigated so that as they passed over the Essex coast the approach to Bradwell airfield was right in front of them. He descended, made a short field landing and taxied to the buildings. With the engines still running, the man opened the door and got out. Mackenzie pulled the door shut. "Get going, Henry, and we're in the clear."

There were no awkward questions at Cambridge; they passed the customs and passport people without being challenged. It helped that Fitzjohn was well recognised by the airport officials, who would suspect a Member of Parliament of anything untoward? But Fitzjohn had his own questions. He called Mackenzie into the Granta Air Services lounge and through to his office. His patience had run out, and he was seething.

"Look here, Mr Mackenzie, I know about your little diamond smuggling game and I've turned a blind eye. But I will not be part of a people-smuggling racket. That was the last trip we will make for you. Find another charter service. If you can."

"Henry, I don't know what you're talking about! Diamonds – such a thought!" Mackenzie was overacting, but he didn't seem to care that Fitzjohn knew. "Now," he said, "I understand your reluctance to offer specialist charters, but you want to be more than just an air taxi, don't you? And of course there must be extra expenses with offering a bespoke service." Mackenzie opened the briefcase he always had with him and slid his hand into the hidden pocket. He pulled out an envelope and handed it to Fitzjohn. "There's £200 in there, and I can offer an extra £50 for routine flights where there are no… special guests. What do you say, Fitzjohn? Can we come to an arrangement?"

Fitzjohn's natural greed and desire for easy money took over. "Well, actually, I'm sure I could serve your business needs, Mr Mackenzie. But my pilots and staff must know nothing of this – and only I will fly any trips that involve special guests, as you call them."

"Excellent, Henry. I demand absolute secrecy, of course, whether I have diamonds, guests or cheese and wine with me. If you can keep to that, then I'm sure we will develop a very profitable working relationship."

EIGHT

Hannah fretted for days after spotting Fitzjohn in Cambridge. She couldn't shake off the familiar feelings of terror and sickness she had felt when he attacked her. The fear was embedded within her. She couldn't sleep, she kept checking that her doors were locked, she looked over her shoulder out in the street and took a different route to work each morning. It was three years earlier when she was given a job with the bank in Hong Kong. But that had been a front; the role with the Israeli Secret Service team charged with recruiting Spitfire pilots for the Israeli Air Force had brought her into contact with Fitzjohn. Many pilots were leaving the RAF and were looking for lucrative new jobs. But she didn't get as far as offering Fitzjohn a flying role. While she had been getting to know him, one sultry Far East night he trapped her in her bedroom, where he attempted the rape. Her secret service self-defence training stood her in good stead: she managed to fight him off and get him out of her house. She never saw him again in Hong Kong, but a fear of his return stayed with her, only fading when she returned to London.

With Hannah living in Clapham and working in the City of London there was no reason why their paths should cross. She never had cause to go to the Westminster area. She told herself to dismiss her concerns. She knew he was a Member of Parliament – she had seen it in the papers, youngest MP and all that. He wouldn't risk harming his reputation, would he? But she regularly visited her family in Cambridge and it was a reasonable bet that she would see him again there. And he would see her.

A thought came to her: she should be proactive. Hannah still had the phone number for her Israeli Secret Service handler from when she was recruited in 1949. Yoel Arbel had progressed well in his career and was now a leading agent with Mossad, as the service is known, in London. She called him and they agreed to meet in a coffee shop near St Paul's Cathedral.

Hannah got straight to the point. "Yoel, thanks for making time for me. I need a favour. I don't see any security issues here, but I would appreciate some help. You might think it silly, but something is concerning me and I would feel happier if I had some information…" She realised she was wittering on, while Arbel sat quietly, smiling, letting her talk.

"What is it you need, Hannah?" He looked at her, his eyebrows slightly raised.

"I want some information on someone. In fact, I need to know just about everything that can be found out about his movements, connections, relationships. It's Henry Fitzjohn. He was with the RAF in Hong Kong and one of our targets."

"I remember," said Arbel. "Now a famous and upstanding Member of Parliament. How does he concern you now?"

"He lives in the Cambridge area. Recently I was there with my fiancé and I saw Fitzjohn and he spotted me. Knowing he is often in London, I'm concerned that he may contact me, may want to attend to some... unfinished business with me." Hannah touched her lips, her fingers shaking. She hated being a victim of what she saw as an irrational fear, and struggled to contain it. "If I know more about his movements, I can avoid him. And it would be a great comfort to me just to know there are agents watching him."

"Hannah, I am aware of the issue with Fitzjohn in Hong Kong, his attack on you, so you have my full sympathy. But on the other hand, it was him who tipped off MI6 that you and the team were targeted by the Egyptian agents. He probably saved your life. And you will appreciate that we have to be very careful not to antagonise the British secret services – we're constantly under observation by MI5. We're not a private protection agency and cannot tail an MP without very good security reasons."

"No, of course not. I'm sorry, I shouldn't really have asked. It was wrong of me to ask for help at a personal level. I will deal with anything that comes up myself. But thanks again for your time. I appreciate it."

"That's fine." Arbel sat back. "OK, look, I will arrange a quick assessment – no intrusive investigations, just an agent or two to find out what motivates him and who he associates with. If anything interesting emerges, I will come back to you. Now, tell me about the work you're doing at the bank."

NINE

A month after the failed extraction of the Stasi secretary, Val Hetherington-Brown walked along Kurfurstendamm. She couldn't help admiring the German work ethic. Millions of tons of rubble from wartime bombing had been cleared from the wreck that was West Berlin. New buildings were going up, and even the coffee culture had returned.

She wore a mid-brown skirt and matching jacket, pale primrose blouse, low court shoes and a tan pill-box hat, deliberately playing down her natural attractiveness. Enjoying the pleasant warmth of the morning sun, she took a seat at a café table on the pavement with her newspaper and coffee, and waited.

Val had enjoyed working with the Americans during the war, and this new assignment required her to partner with a CIA agent she had not met before. Ballantyne had only given her an outline brief for the job; she understood that the Americans wanted British help to get a defector over the border. She had been given a short profile of the agent. Drake Casey had parachuted into Normandy on D-Day with the 82nd

Airborne, the 'All American' division. Casey lived up to the name: he was a typical square-jawed, muscular American paratrooper with a crew cut. When the war ended, he stayed on in the military, specialising in intelligence work seeking out and arresting Nazi war criminals. That activity would continue for decades, but it had the feel of police work, and so after five years in the job he requested a transfer to the secret service. Val and Casey had been given a description of each other, and very soon Casey stood by Val's table.

When Val looked up, Casey smiled. "Good morning. I usually buy the *Chicago Tribune* on Saturday."

"I like *The Times* myself," Val replied. Casey sat down. The greeting was easy for him to remember; he grew up in Illinois. Having got the code words out of the way, he leant across the table to shake Val's hand. He had a firm, solid hold, but not the vice-like grip that some men used to try to show their masculinity.

"A pleasure to meet you," said Val.

"And you. Have you been in Berlin long?"

"A couple of years. What about yourself?"

"I've been working in West Germany since the war, but this is my first assignment here in Berlin with the Agency. I arrived a week ago and I'm just getting a feel for the place. Hell of a mess, ain't it?"

Val was immediately concerned, and her face must have shown it.

"What's wrong?" said Casey.

"It's vital that all agents have a thorough knowledge of the city, their own sectors in particular, and the clandestine crossing points on the border with the Russian sector. You've been here a week, and you've been approved for operations already? New operatives can easily blunder into Soviet agents, and the CIA has been known to suffer from infiltration by double agents working for the communists."

"Well, you can relax with me, sister."

"We'll see. Brother."

Val decided to treat Casey with care. He had passed all the security checks, but that would count for little if her life depended on him on a job.

Casey looked more serious. "My immediate task is to get to know the priorities, look at ways we can work together. Spend some time assessing potential defectors and getting the right people out. Pretty easy stuff at first."

"Easy? Not in my experience, Drake. Stasi agents will kill in a moment if you make a mistake."

"Like that Stasi secretary? We know she wanted to come to the US, and she had some mighty interesting information. Seems she didn't get the protection she needed."

Bastard, thought Val. Wants to bitch about the one operation that went wrong. But she kept her head. "Yes, not the outcome we intended," she said flatly.

Casey placed his hands on the table, fingers interlinked, leant forward and spoke quietly. "We know you guys have intel on some of the German scientists that worked on the V1 and V2 rockets, now enjoying life on some godforsaken gulag out in the steppes. We want to work closely with you to give those who want a better life in the West a helping hand over the border. We already have many of von Braun's team, but there's a lot more out there working on the latest Soviet hardware."

Val sensed that Casey was not well informed. "None of the scientists and engineers of any significance are in the gulags, they work in some of Russia's most advanced weapons development centres. Most near Moscow."

Casey drawled out a slow response. "Well, OK, so some of them might get to like Mother Russia. But a lot want out, right? And that's where you come in. We've got some agents in East Germany that we think could produce some valuable defectors. Your job is to get them out."

Val's patience had run out. She wasn't going to have the agenda set by this Yank, or his bosses, no matter what C and Ballantyne had said. "Look, Casey, we don't work *for* you, we work *with* you. You have your priorities and we have ours. I'm happy for the Berlin station to operate as productively as possible with the CIA, but we select the operations we carry out."

"Hey, hey, relax! Sure, we want to work in the same way, but we don't want to tread on each other's toes, do we?"

Val calmed down. She knew that made sense. "No, of course not. Now, tell me about these defectors you're interested in."

"Intelligence has shown that the Soviets rounded up a team of German rocket specialists after the war and deported them to their weapons development centres in Russia. These are the ones who were trapped in East Germany, then transported east. Now these technicians, scientists and engineers have to work for a cause that they haven't chosen. The majority learned their weaponry and missile skills late in the war, playing their part in developing the V1s and V2s that could have been the turnaround weapons for Germany. It could even have led to their victory. Capturing these men and women was one of the Russians' most significant spoils of war – but now they have to motivate them to work hard for communism. They largely achieve this by intimidation, by making threats to their families, and by occasionally disappearing one of their number, usually a low-value technician, to keep the rest motivated."

"And how can we help? Be specific," asked Val.

"There's a conference coming up in Warsaw. The most senior missile specialists are coming together to share their knowledge of long-range rockets. Our agents have made contact with a guy who wants out and is willing to make a break for it. After the conference he will travel from Warsaw by train to the Russian sector in Berlin with just one Stasi minder – his mother is ill and the Reds have agreed he can visit her before she dies."

Val frowned. "That sounds very convenient. Could be a set-up. What evidence do you have that he is genuine, not a plant?"

"Gold-plated assurances from our agent at the factory that this guy has had it with the communist way. He had a fine mansion in Germany before the war and misses the good life. And we checked, his mother really is ill. Look, I know you want to be extra-careful, but this one's a cert."

"Very well. Outline exactly what you are looking for," said Val.

"We know the location of the mother's house. They will only spend one night there. In the early hours, say around 2a.m., we go in, deal with the guard, and get the scientist away and over to the British sector."

"Why not the American sector?"

"We don't want the Russians to think we have him. They know we're evolving our own systems and that Britain and the US don't always share weapons development intelligence. We will let it be known that you Brits have him."

"But in this case we're willing to act together."

"You got it. Very soon after he arrives in the British sector he will go direct to London and from there we will set him up in a nice little apartment in Washington, or maybe someplace in California, where he can tell us all he knows about rockets – and the names of any other colleagues who want out."

"When is the conference?"

"In a week's time. When he gets to Berlin he will be taken to his mother's house in Prenzlauer Berg, three or four miles into the Russian sector. I'll give you the address. And I will be with you and your team when you spring him."

"No. If this is a British operation, we do it ourselves."

Casey sat up straight. "No, no – we work together on this one. He's an important asset."

"No can do. Either we do this on our own or not at all." Val didn't want the headache of an inexperienced agent on her hands in the Soviet sector. He might not like her attitude, and might go over her head to talk to more senior officers, but she had no intention herself of referring back to Ballantyne, or indeed C.

Casey sat silently for a moment, clearly debating whether to challenge Val. "OK, have it your way. Just bring the guy back in one piece." Casey paused then added, "Please," with a touch of sarcasm. "No shooting unless absolutely necessary."

"And the guard?" said Val.

"He's expendable, of course. Maybe you would be doing him a favour knocking him over, to save him from the treatment he would get back home with the Soviets."

"Very well. I will put together a team. Do you have a picture of our man?"

"Yes, sure." Casey pulled out a folded motoring magazine from his inside jacket pocket and put it on the table. "It's in there, honey."

Val's head shot up. She said nothing but looked directly at Casey with her piercing green eyes and a solid pressing together of her lips. He got the message straight away.

"Sorry, I mean ma'am. We have assigned the guy the code name Adler."

"Adler it is." Val opened the magazine and carefully let the photograph fall out into her lap. After flicking through a few pages, she closed the magazine and gave it back to Casey. She glanced at the photo then slipped it into her handbag. "Meet me here at the same time tomorrow, and I'll brief you on the plan. If you need to contact me, call the number you have been given for the office. Stay alert, Drake. In Berlin you can expect to be watched every second."

TEN

Her mind focused on the new marketing campaign she was leading for the bank, Hannah absentmindedly answered her office telephone.

"Good morning, Hannah, how are you?" said the caller. After less than a second she recognised Yoel Arbel's voice. She knew better than to say his name, and simply responded with, "I'm fine, thank you."

Arbel suggested meeting for coffee early the next morning at the buffet in London Bridge Station. He said he had some interesting information that she might like to hear. Hannah agreed the time and place, but Arbel's call had triggered her anxiety. She tried to control her emotions, but whenever she thought of Fitzjohn she could feel panic rising inside her. She used well-rehearsed calming techniques to slow her breathing. Part of her wished she hadn't asked Arbel to help, but she had, and she felt obliged to meet him – and a strange curiosity about the information he would give her.

Hannah arrived at the appointed time of 7.30a.m. and Arbel followed a few minutes later. After buying two cups of coffee he took out a small, black, leather-bound notebook, which he opened, read in silence for less than a minute, and returned to his inside jacket pocket.

"What do you have for me, Yoel?" said Hannah. She knew they could speak openly, as there were few other customers.

"The party in question is an intriguing individual. A Member of Parliament, of course, and he's on the Defence Procurement Committee – a well-favoured young man. He is very much involved with his constituency campaign manager, one Amanda Spencer, who is influential in Westminster and no doubt hoping that Fitzjohn will go places in the Party, taking her with him. It seems that she likes her comforts and luxuries and has the financial resources to live that life. I'm sure Fitzjohn is happy to have her backing."

"Intriguing, and as you say, very interesting information. I hope this means he won't want to have anything to do with me," said Hannah, sitting back and visibly relaxing.

"But that's not the whole picture – not by any means." Arbel smiled and leant forward. "We have been looking at his air taxi business. Doing very well, plenty of work, but particularly on flights to Amsterdam. I had our people there look at his associates, and they found he is mixing with a gang of diamond smugglers. If he knows what his clients are up to – and our people in Amsterdam believe he does – he's taking one hell of a risk, so the rewards must be excellent. We don't care how he earns his living, Hannah, and we won't interfere, but I feel that he is very unlikely to disturb you."

"That all sounds incredible, but knowing the man, it's not such a surprise," said Hannah.

"Well, he's a busy man… I hope you now feel more secure?"

"Yes, definitely. Thank you so much, Yoel."

"A pleasure, Hannah – the least we can do for one of our own."

Hannah hesitated. "You mean, Jewish?"

"There's that, of course. But once you've been in the service you can never really leave – you know that. There may be a time when we need your help at Mossad. You won't mind me asking if something comes up, will you?"

"No. No, of course not."

Arbel stood up and departed, leaving Hannah to finish her coffee, pondering what he had meant.

ELEVEN

Adam Devon was in his element. He banked the Spitfire over to the left to give himself a view of the gleaming cliffs of Beachy Head, nearly 5,000 feet below, and pushed the nose of the aircraft forward. As his speed increased he pulled up, and with his left foot on the rudder and just his fingertips on the control column, made a perfect barrel roll. Everyone spoke of flying the Spitfire by the seat of your pants, and it was true: he only had to look and lean to the right or left in the compact cockpit and the aircraft responded immediately. After his second hour of practice flying, he was ready for the Battle of Britain flypast rehearsals next month. For now, it was back to work.

Test flights in the Dove had continued into the summer, with more technicians on board, new equipment installed, and even more secrecy about the project. Devon had sensed that these flights were no longer about the viability of the Dove as a commercial proposition, but its use as a platform for the advanced radar they were developing. His chats with the boffins became curt; some were reluctant to discuss the technical side, or sometimes they would not talk at all. They seemed stressed and uncooperative, but a few were happy to share information on the aims of the radar tests. Devon knew that his job was to ensure that the flights were piloted exactly as required.

After dozens of missions around the British Isles and occasionally northern Europe, instructions came through for Devon to write up flight plans for longer distances, including Geneva, Nice and Barcelona. These were at the limit of the aircraft's endurance with the weight of the scientific kit on board. Devon was asked to fly exact radar navigation headings at various levels to assess the equipment's capabilities and accuracy. He was becoming very competent in his role: all the missions were carried out on schedule and the technicians were smiling again. Then he was given a new destination: Berlin.

Devon had been briefed that after landing at Tempelhof he should taxi to the parking and reception area the Americans had assigned to British aircraft on the far side of the airport. He had been told the Americans still controlled Tempelhof, as it served as their main military base in Berlin. Since the airlift had ended three years earlier, the number of equipment and troop transports had reduced, but they were still flying in on a daily basis. He was promised that the Americans would have little interest in a British commercial flight, especially if he kept out of their way.

Devon arrived at Hatfield shortly before sunrise on the morning of the first Berlin flight and was surprised to see Jocelyn Darley already there. The MD often came down to the hangar and the pilots' briefing room, but rarely at this hour. This mission must be very important to the firm, Devon thought.

"Good morning, Adam. All set for the flight today?"

"Yes, sir. I gather the radar instrumentation has been installed, so I'm just waiting for the Met report and then we should be off. I have filed the flight plan with the Berlin Air Safety Centre, and we have permission to take the northern corridor over East Germany into Berlin Tempelhof."

"Excellent. When you arrive, you will be greeted by Artur Franken. I don't think you have met him."

"No, I don't think I have."

"He's setting up our new sales office in Germany. I would like you to give him a tour of the aircraft, if you wouldn't mind."

"But, Mr Darley, does he have security clearance? The radar boys won't like anyone getting a good look at all their equipment."

"No need to worry about that, Adam, he's perfectly secure. Been through all the vetting processes. Ah, I nearly forgot. Give him this package, would you? Some promotional material on the Dove. He'll need that." Darley picked up a handful of papers, brochures and aircraft performance information aimed at potential buyers and slid them into a large brown envelope.

"Yes, sir, will do," said Devon. He wasn't sure why, but he felt uncomfortable with this whole business. It wasn't his job to look after new people – and why should Darley want the sales rep to be based in Berlin, rather than a city in the West? Devon thought it was odd that Darley was getting involved with the paperwork; it wasn't something the MD would normally do. But Darley was known to be thorough, Devon reflected.

None of that troubled Devon any further when the Met officer brought in the forecast. He immediately set to work on double-checking his flight plans, outward and return the next day, the engineer's service paperwork, the aircraft's logbook and fuel levels. From the flight prep desk, he noticed Darley climbing the stairs from the hangar to the offices – no doubt looking forward to his full English breakfast in the directors' dining room.

***

For Devon, there was something unique about the prospect of flying into Berlin. The focus of wartime bombing by the RAF into the heart of

Nazi Germany, and then the post-war airlift, Berlin was rarely out of the news. Tempelhof was built in the 1930s and represented the Nazi image of power and superiority. The massive buildings, with their cathedral-like towering windows and enormous open areas, were designed to impress and to stir up nationalism, and they did just that. The sweeping curve of the passenger arrivals area extended to left and right, with aircraft hangars on both sides for half a mile in each direction.

After an uneventful flight and a smooth landing, Devon entered the small de Havilland office to be greeted by Darley's new man in Berlin.

"Good morning, Herr Devon, welcome to Berlin. I am Franken, but you will call me Artur, please."

Franken was very German, in Devon's view. Medium height, slim to the point of being gaunt, with thin, mousy hair. He wore steel-framed round glasses and a serviceable, if not elegant, grey double-breasted suit, a white shirt and narrow red tie. Curiously, he wore new black shoes that were clearly English, and top quality.

"Nice to meet you, Artur. And please call me Adam. I have a package for you from Mr Darley." Devon handed the envelope over, and was taken aback when Franken grabbed it eagerly and immediately moved over to a table and pulled out all the advertising material and technical papers. He flicked through the colour brochure, which fell open at a page that contained a bookmark. Franken took it out and looked it over. It was one of those corporate promotional items, a six-inch card with an embossed de Havilland logo on the front and a black silhouette of a Vampire aircraft on the back. Franken reinserted the bookmark in the same place, read a few words, then gave a small smile and nod of satisfaction. He replaced all the papers in the envelope and stood up, as straight as a statue. "Perhaps you will show me the aircraft now?"

"Yes, my pleasure. It's parked out in the first bay." Devon led Franken through the crew exit. The official at the gate simply nodded to

Devon and ignored his companion. Lax, Devon thought. He should at least check who the man was. They boarded the Dove and Devon took Franken through to the cockpit, sat in the pilot's seat and invited Franken to take the co-pilot's seat. "Have you flown yourself?" Devon asked.

"No, my background is in manufacturing," said Franken. "I worked for Volkswagen during the war and stayed on after the Americans arrived. When the plant in Wolfsburg became part of the British zone, I moved to the sales side. I met Mr Darley last year when he was touring Germany, and he asked if I would be interested in setting up the de Havilland sales operation here. I was honoured to agree."

Devon thought he saw a smug, arrogant grin. "But why have the office in Berlin?" he said.

"My wife's family are from Berlin – Charlottenburg, in the British sector. She wanted to be closer to her parents, and Mr Darley agreed to site the office here."

"Right, good," said Devon, although not with any enthusiasm. "Let me summarise some of the features of the Dove." He took the German through the key figures: cruising airspeed, maximum altitude, range, passenger and cargo capabilities, and take-off and landing distances required – particularly important if the aircraft might be used in smaller airfields. Franken looked intensely interested, nodding rigorously at every feature that Devon mentioned. Devon was amused. A typical German, in Devon's mind. Overbearing and severe in character.

Then Devon took Franken into the rear of the aircraft and described the normal seating layout for when the aircraft carried passengers. One technician sat at a small desk in front of a radar screen, writing up notes. Franken bent down and looked unashamedly over the shoulder of the man at what he was writing. The technician caught sight of him and snapped shut his notebook.

Devon spoke quickly. "Come, Artur, let's take a walk around the outside of the aircraft, shall we?"

"Very well. Please lead on."

After the tour of the aircraft, the two men returned to the terminal building. Franken ordered coffee. "I must wash my hands," he said. When he went off to the lavatory, Devon's curiosity overcame him. Quickly, he took the brochure out of the envelope Franken had left on the table and found the page with the bookmark. It was a double-page spread that detailed the possible uses of the Dove – economy and VIP seating configurations, air ambulance and evacuation and surveying work. Devon knew that this type of information was key to successful sales. No big deal. Carefully, he replaced the bookmark and slid the brochure into the envelope.

TWELVE

Val checked her gun, pocketed two spare magazines, and tightened her coat belt. She noted that her heart rate had picked up slightly. The thrill of an operation always heightened her senses. Yes, she felt a touch of fear, but in her early days with the Special Operations Executive during the war, she had seen agents with bravado and swagger who came badly unstuck. That she felt dread meant her instinct was telling her that somewhere there was a danger that she needed to manage.

Raleigh was leading this mission. He had briefed their contacts in East Berlin, and his and Val's job was to get into the defector's mother's house, deal with the guard and get the defector over the border into the British sector. At 1a.m. they drove to the eastern edge of the sector, parked the car in a quiet street, walked to the back of a bomb-damaged tenement block and waited for the agent on the other side to show himself.

They had a short wait. After an exchange of code words, the three of them walked through the building and ran quietly across an open courtyard and into another block. At the front, a small builder's van was waiting. Val and Raleigh climbed in the back, where they sat on an old, thin mattress that had been thrown in. Very considerate of them to give us something soft to sit on, Val thought, but she was less impressed when the smell of urine and stale sweat wafted up.

The driver kept to a purposeful speed, but not too fast, and with no over-revving of the engine. They passed just a couple of other cars and commercial vehicles along the road; the streets were otherwise deserted and quiet. As they neared Prenzlauer Berg, they turned left into a side street. The Russians must have bypassed the area on their advance into central Berlin, as the small terrace of three-storey houses that remained showed no signs of damage and had clearly once been owned by wealthy residents. Little wonder that the defector wanted to return to his affluent lifestyle, Val thought. The car stopped in a dark spot a hundred yards short of his mother's house. The driver let Val and Raleigh out and took them diagonally across the road and into the shell of a bombed building. From there they could see their target.

Val and Raleigh both carried Walther PPKs with silencers fitted. Just after 2a.m. they walked slowly to the front door of the house. Raleigh used his commando fighting knife to force the lock and they silently entered the dark hall. Val switched on her shaded pencil torch to give them just enough light to see by. There was a door to a large reception room to the right and, on the left, stairs to the first floor. They entered the reception room. In the faint glow of the embers in the fireplace, they could make out a figure lying asleep on the settee, and another slumped, motionless, in an armchair. Adler and his guard. As Raleigh stepped forward, a floorboard creaked and the lying figure sat bolt upright. Val knew from the photograph she had that it wasn't the defector, so it must be the guard. She aimed her gun at the man. In a swift move, he pulled a pistol from under his blanket. Val didn't hesitate. She shot two rounds into his upper left chest and he fell back, shuddered, and didn't move again.

Val and Raleigh turned to the figure in the armchair, now awake and dazed. Val shoved her pistol into her coat pocket and went to help him stand, but he pushed her away, grabbed a gun resting on a small table beside the chair and fired at Val. The shot clipped the epaulette on her right shoulder and went into the wall behind her. Before the man could fire again, Raleigh had fired twice. A clean kill.

Val shone the torch into the second man's face. "Bloody hell, neither of these men are Adler," she said, stunned.

As she spoke, they heard footsteps running down the stairs. They pressed themselves flat against the wall and gripped their guns. A figure ran in and froze, looking down at the bodies. Val took a step forward. "Adler!" The man spun round and thrust his hands in the air. Val knew she had to move quickly; someone in the neighbourhood might react to the sound of the agent's gunshot and call the police.

"It's OK, British. We're here to take you across," she said.

Adler was fully dressed. He'd been told to expect to be sprung, and stood ready. Raleigh looked into the street from the front door just as the van that had brought them pulled up. The driver was waving frantically for them to get in. The three hurried out, dived into the back of the van and pulled the door closed. Again the driver kept his nerve and drove nonchalantly towards the derelict tenements. An hour later, Val, Raleigh and the defector Adler sat with Drake Casey in an interview room at the MI6 offices in West Berlin. In a day or two he would be in London.

"There were two guards, Casey, not one. Your intelligence people need to get their act together." Adrenaline was still coursing through Val's veins. "We were lucky not to be hit."

Casey evaded the point. "Hey, you got the job done, and Mr Adler here is safe and well. Great job by you guys, if you ask me."

"Well, let's hope we don't have to work together again."

"Aw, c'mon. We could make a good team, you and me," Casey said, smiling at her.

Val wondered if Casey was insinuating something there, but let it go. "Maybe," she said. "Send your people here tomorrow evening. Our intelligence director wants to debrief Adler before we fly him to London. Then he's all yours."

"Much appreciated, Val," said Casey. "But tell me, what happened to the mother?"

"Our local people have arranged for a friendly neighbour to take her in and look after her. She'll be safe and well cared for."

"That's very thoughtful."

"We're not totally without heart, Drake."

THIRTEEN

"Do take care, Adam," said Hannah, forcing a brave smile. "Give me a call when you're back at Biggin Hill, won't you?"

She and Devon had spent Saturday together at his house in Hertfordshire. After a light lunch on Sunday, Devon had loaded his car for the trip down to Kent. Hannah would take an early train the next morning to London and her job in the City. Many of her colleagues knew about Devon's role in the flypast, and the general manager of the bank had given permission for a small group to go up onto the roof of the building to watch the aircraft pass along the River Thames on their way to Buckingham Palace.

"Yes, sure – as soon after we land as possible. Now don't worry, it will all go swimmingly." Devon gave her a gentle kiss and got into the car. After he drove off, Hannah walked back into the house. A shiver ran down her back. She knew it was nonsense, so she decided to go for a long country walk to help pass the time.

***

Devon immediately felt at home in the pilots' briefing room in the RAF station – in fact, one of the most famous fighter stations in the world. He had seen many pictures of it and heard all the wartime stories. Biggin Hill's position to the south of London meant it played a key defensive role in the Battle of Britain, and the successes of the squadrons operating out of there against the Luftwaffe was legendary.

That bright Monday morning, twelve Spitfires were lined up along the hard standing in front of the tower. The pilots had come to know each other, either as new acquaintances or as old friends and colleagues where they had served together in operational squadrons. The rehearsals had gone well, their formation flying was excellent, and they all knew the route and timings off by heart.

With half an hour to go before departure, David Porter called the group together in a briefing room. He stood by the blackboard at the front of the room. On it were coloured lines and arrows that came together in a series of parallel lines going from east to west towards central London. The Spitfires were close to the front of the flypast. The pilots were to follow a group of Hurricanes, and there would be nine Lancaster bombers behind them. A stream of other aircraft would follow, with a half-minute gap between each section.

As the Spitfires levelled out after take-off they turned in unison to the north-east and their formation point over the Thames estuary a mile south of Southend-on-Sea. They formed two sections of six aircraft: five in an arrow shape and one following the leader. Porter was at the front of the first section, with Devon to his right and James Naismith, a Canadian wartime pilot, on the outside. John Corrigan had the most challenging position, flying right behind Porter. The visibility was perfect but there was a strong northerly wind, which forced them to take a heading towards north-west London just so they could stay on track towards Buckingham Palace.

Devon could see the bend in the river, with Greenwich Park to his left and the docklands to the right. He glanced across at Porter, making sure he kept the exact distance required for the formation. But when he turned to look round at Naismith, he got a shock: the Canadian's wingtip shot across Devon's right wing. Another three feet lower, and they would have collided. Back in position, Naismith waved an apology towards Devon. But two minutes later Naismith's aircraft lurched straight at Devon, who had no choice but to dive out of the way. Instinctively he called, "Look out!" over the radio. He looked up and saw Porter take evasive action, flying up to avoid being hit.

"Mayday, may—"

Naismith's radio call ended abruptly. Devon saw him bank to the right, clear of the other Spitfires and the rest of the flypast, a thin line of blue smoke trailing behind him. Devon knew that a misfiring engine can cause erratic flying.

Naismith's voice came back over the radio. "Engine failure, oil pressure gone, turning back, will head for Hornchurch."

"Roger. All other Spitfires, form up as a five. Corrigan, go to Naismith's position," said Porter.

***

After the flypast, the pilots flew back to Biggin Hill and parked their aircraft by the control tower. Devon closed down his engine, slid open the canopy and stepped out onto the wing. Porter was already out of his aircraft and walking towards him. Devon jumped down from the wing and pulled off his flying helmet and gloves.

"Thanks, Adam, that was a nasty business. If you hadn't got out of the way, James would probably have taken us both down. That engine trouble would have caused him to struggle to fly straight and level." Porter mock-punched Devon on the shoulder. "Let's get in and find out what happened to him."

All the Spitfire pilots crowded into the debriefing room. The intelligence officer was standing there, a look of grim dismay on his face. Porter had a quiet word with him and then turned to the men, holding a hand up for silence. "Chaps, bad news, I'm afraid. Naismith didn't make it. His engine failed completely, he was too low to bail out and landed in the river. Seems the Spit went straight under. They haven't been able to recover his body yet."

After being dismissed, Devon ran to a telephone. He knew the BBC were covering the flypast live on the radio and would have reported the crash. Hannah might well hear the news and not know who had died. But he was too late, one of the main door commissionaires at the bank was listening to the BBC in his cubicle and phoned up to the marketing team who passed on the news to Hannah. When Devon managed to get through to her at the bank she was shaking with worry, and he told her what had happened. She reacted with sheer joy that Devon was still alive. Devon agreed to drive up to her flat in Clapham that evening to see her, in an effort to dispel her nerves.

FOURTEEN

He never allowed himself to admit it, but Henry Fitzjohn missed Amanda when she was away. This time she was at the wedding of a university friend in Bristol. She knew better than to invite him; that would suggest they were a couple. He was clear in his mind – he wasn't a victim of love. He was his own man, and Fitzjohn would never give up his freedom. The thought of being tied down left him cold. There were so many things he wanted to do, and being anchored to one person was not something he could imagine for himself. But he accepted that Amanda was good for him: she satisfied his needs and gave him plenty of useful advice about the madhouse – as he saw it – that was Westminster. And he knew that while he didn't mind the age difference between them now, he sensed there would come a time, not too far ahead, when his interest in other women would return.

After spending the best part of an afternoon in a committee room at the University Arms Hotel in Cambridge with fellow Conservative Party MPs from the East of England, he decided that a quiet drink in the bar was just what he needed. It would help pass the evening.

Nobody from the meeting wanted to join him. Miserable lot of bores, Fitzjohn thought.

Sitting on a high stool at the bar, Fitzjohn looked around at the room, with its elaborate chandeliers and mahogany-panelled walls. He was remembering his time in Hong Kong with the RAF, and his favourite haunt, the bar in the Peninsula Hotel. Happy days, he recalled, and smiled to himself. The Empire was long past its best, he knew, but what remained of the colonial lifestyle – luxury, position, influence and superiority – suited him well. He could have stayed in that cocooned life, with its plentiful supply of good whisky, days at the races, gambling clubs – oh yes, and girls. Plus some first-rate flying in the Spitfires. But his association with a Chinese criminal gambling club had ultimately led to his early departure and return to the UK. Such was life. He shrugged. But things had certainly picked up with the air taxi business. He had regular clients with bookings across the UK and Europe. The pilots were excellent, virtually running the business for him, and they didn't ask the earth in salaries. And there was that very lucrative arrangement with Mackenzie…

Then there was Amanda, of course. Such a gem, but would he be better off playing the field? After all, many women had made their willingness known to him. Half of them were married, many to other MPs. No, he concluded, he was nicely set up. He decided to make the most of it: money was coming in, he had a glamorous lady on his arm and a high-profile job with good prospects for advancement. Fitzjohn thought with satisfaction that his political career was going well. Politics was such a backstabbing business, he reflected: full of empty promises, self-reward, and social climbing. But he worried not, because he was good at all these things.

His second whisky and soda made him feel better, but as the evening wore on, the bar became busy and noisy. He vacated the bar stool, took his drink and sat at one of the quieter tables, then realised it was the same table he had occupied with Amanda a few months earlier. Gazing through the bar's open doors, he abruptly relived the moment he saw the girl from Hong Kong walk through the lobby. Hannah. Secret agent and all that, working for the Israelis, of all people. Got herself in with Devon. Very impressive lady, but she had given him the cold shoulder that night in Mid-Levels when he was minded to have a good time with her. Bloody shame, he thought. She would have been a delight in the bedroom.

Over the next hour his memories of Hong Kong played on his mind, and he felt the rekindling of his desire from four years earlier. He wondered why Hannah had been in Cambridge. What had brought her to the city? Fitzjohn allowed the daydream to expand in his mind. Would he spot her again in Cambridge? Maybe next time he'd have the chance to speak to her, to pick up their relationship. He would have to be all sweetness and friendliness to bring her round, of course, but he felt confident that she would be impressed with his new job. Naturally, he told himself, she would want to get to know him again. Maybe, maybe.

He concluded that her visit to Cambridge must have been something to do with Devon. Fitzjohn had heard that he was working for de Havilland, test piloting or something equally boring. Not too far away, down at Hatfield. Bloody annoying that Devon should get one over on him and enjoy the pleasures of the lovely Hannah. But there might come a time when he could put that right. A lewd grin curved the corners of his mouth and he laughed quietly at the prospect.

The clock in the bar chimed 7p.m. Fitzjohn shrugged off his thoughts and left the hotel to go home.

FIFTEEN

The race was well and truly on to develop weapons and military hardware that would give either the West or the Soviet bloc a significant advantage over the other side. The main protagonists had atomic weapon capabilities, but conventional fighting forces remained critical to offensive and defensive operations. Missile and radar expertise had advanced so rapidly during and since the war that now the balance of power might lie with those with the best scientists. Soviet advances in technology had come on in leaps and bounds since they had captured German rocket and weapons specialists in 1945, and they had developed their own innovations and construction techniques.

As a child, Ilya Leonid Demovich had always been known simply as Leonid. His first name was only ever used on official documents. He had great ambitions for himself. He believed in free enterprise, but sensibly kept that to himself in the communist regime he lived in. He felt that high achievement in his profession should be rewarded with money and a better lifestyle. He bitterly resented that the pay he received was little more than that of a factory manager, and that the serious riches were channelled towards senior members of the Party: the bureau men, branch secretaries and even district convenors. He was enveloped by angst, knowing that the German scientists and technicians who had escaped to the West were enjoying comforts that were completely out of his reach in his own life. He had been given a one-bedroom apartment in a post-war block on the outskirts of Moscow, close to his testing and development facility. His pay was enough for him to buy food and vodka, but little else in the way of luxuries.

Now he was approaching fifty, the enthusiasm and pride he had felt for Russia as a young man had evaporated, leaving disappointment, frustration and bitterness. He cared nothing for the communist ideology; peasants working in the fields or labourers in factories would always be the lowest strata in society. That was the natural way of the world, just as he, cultured and informed, belonged to the refined intelligentsia. But the state gave him little reward for all his good education and hard work.

The one consolation he had in life was that he was able to work on the leading technological advances in radar and missiles. He had developed a keen interest in machinery, electronics and engineering before the age of twelve. The local party representative encouraged his parents to send him to technical college, to develop him as a scientist who would be one of the leading lights of industry in Russia. Leonid didn't disappoint. He rose through the ranks, gaining a first-rate reputation and greater responsibility for scientific development.

Leonid never took the time to marry or build a family. But now he resented that, and hoped it wasn't too late to find a woman to spend the rest of his life with. He valued knowing that he was highly respected by the junior engineers he worked with, and openly feted by even the most experienced scientists. He never stopped to consider how his good reputation fed his ego, and consequently his view that he deserved higher rewards. He found his thoughts turning to freedom: he wanted to make the move that a few colleagues had made, although some had died in the attempt and others had been caught and were now slaving away in the hell of the salt mines.

Leonid was in no hurry. He visualised a plan that would see him talk to the people he knew were free-thinking – meaning anti-communist. He wanted to keep the line of communication as short as possible. Perhaps subconsciously, he had formed an idea of who would be able to put him in touch with the right people to get him across to West Germany – and who knows from there? The UK or the destination of his fantasies, the USA?

His technical, analytical mind allowed him to be a good, if not expert, chess player. He attended a chess club on Saturday afternoons – the nearest thing to socialising that he allowed himself. His pleasure came not from winning, although he did that often enough, but from the companionship and appreciation that came from a shared mental challenge. The members of the chess club largely came from the educated classes, but the state dictated that all should be welcome at the club. Among the members there were a few factory workers with an aptitude for chess.

Leonid sat back and closed his eyes momentarily, basking in the sound of his opponent's gentle applause, congratulating him on the bold, decisive move that had won him the game. The club member on this occasion was Boris, a long-standing friend of Leonid's. Although the usual result was a win for Leonid, there was no animosity between them. Far from it, they enjoyed each other's company. Leonid glanced at the clock on the wall. Since there was insufficient time for another game but it was early enough to remain at the club, he suggested to Boris that they take a glass of vodka together, at his expense. Sitting back in their brown leather armchairs, which were cracked and stained from decades of use, Leonid had the sudden confidence to turn the discussion to his plans. He knew it was a hell of a risk, but he also knew that Boris once had an English wife, who had been killed in the war, and hoped that Boris might have some sympathy for his ambitions.

Boris Overkov had achieved his wealth before the war, manufacturing radios, transmitters and receivers. He was able to travel widely in Europe on the premise of securing customers for the firm's products, but often included the opera, museums, galleries and chess tournaments in his tours. In 1935 he met Josephine, an English woman working as an art restorer in Vienna. They married and moved to a small apartment, finely furnished, in the fashionable Arbat district of Moscow. Boris and Josephine enjoyed socialising with the British expats in the city, mainly civil servants, journalists and import/export agents. When war came, Overkov was on a list of suspicious characters. He was distrusted by the Party, largely due to the tough bargaining position he took on providing products for the government and military. Consequently he spent most of the war in the logistics corps, in a menial managerial role, while second-rate managers ran his business into the ground. His wife volunteered to be a nurse in the siege of Moscow, was pressed into the Red Army after Stalingrad, and never returned.

Leonid hinted that it might be stimulating to meet some of the British people living in Russia who might like to play chess. To get an alternative perspective on the game, of course. Boris agreed, but in a non-committal way. Leonid held Boris's gaze and asked if he could arrange something with any of his British friends who played chess. He felt he had gone as far as he dared.

Boris was no fool, and read Leonid's comments exactly as they were intended: to open a possible link with an agent acting for the British. He had once thought about defecting to the West, but felt at his age that he would be better off enjoying his retirement, living on the reasonable wealth he had managed to retain. But he knew he had to be careful; Leonid could himself be an agent acting for the Party.

***

Three Saturdays later, Leonid sat down for a match against one of the most talented junior chess players at the club. After a promising start for the younger man, Leonid gained the advantage and had every chance to go on to win. But his attention was drawn to a game on the far side of the room. Boris sat with a man Leonid did not know, a visitor to the club. The distraction was enough for Leonid's opponent to swiftly bring the game to a winning conclusion.

At a small round table in the bar, next to the window, Boris ordered three glasses of vodka. He gestured across the room to Leonid to join him and his guest, whom he introduced as Yuri, and the three men spent the evening discussing chess moves and strategy, prospects for the wheat harvest, and Spartak Moscow's results. Leonid bought another round of drinks, and the evening drew to a close. At the door they all shook hands. They were about to go their separate ways when Yuri asked Leonid if he knew the Balalaika coffee shop. Of course he did – it was one of the most exclusive places in Moscow. Yuri asked Leonid to join him there the next morning at 11a.m. And without waiting for an answer, he quickly walked away.

Leonid spent the rest of the evening and night in a state of excitement and confusion, mixed with more than a touch of fear: the fear of not taking any action and resigning himself to a miserable existence, and the fear of the punishment, torture and death that awaited a traitor. Had Boris set him up with an agent who could lead him to the West, or was the stranger a Party informer? There could be no way of finding out without meeting him. Leonid decided that he had to take the risk.

At the Balalaika Yuri ordered coffee and cakes, sat back and without ceremony asked Leonid to describe his work. Leonid had the good sense to give only the most superficial information, but he knew instinctively that he was in the hands of an agent who had the means to get him out of Russia. He soon dropped all caution and enquired about his host's ability to introduce him to someone who might be interested in his work and knowledge. Yuri's eyes half closed and he nodded gently. He suggested that they meet at the same time and place the following week, without saying that he would be bringing along the most successful agent working for the British in Moscow.

SIXTEEN

Darley aimed to make the Summer Ball an event to remember, put on by the country's leading aircraft manufacturer and pillar of British engineering excellence. This was the first large-scale event he had hosted since he was appointed managing director of de Havilland, and he instructed his marketing team to invite 500 guests to enjoy sumptuous cuisine and the best French wines, and dance the night away in the Grosvenor Park Hotel's famous ballroom. Most importantly, it would reflect well on him: his guests would recognise his position as the UK's leading industrialist, which would lead to an entrée to the highest levels of British politics and society. No expense was spared. Rooms were booked at the hotel for all guests who required them, and gifts were placed on each dining table: a stainless steel model of the new de Havilland Vampire for the men and a silver brooch for the ladies, in the shape of a three-bladed propeller from the Mosquito.

Hannah and Devon took their time dressing in their hotel room, enjoying the luxury of the suite that had been booked for them. Hannah looked around the rooms in wonder. In her early childhood, before she came to England in 1939, her family lived a frugal life. Her father had a good job as a university professor, not well paid but sufficient. The room she was dressing in would have seemed like a fairy tale to her parents. She looked out of the window at the trees in Hyde Park, which showed the first tinges of gold and yellow, hinting that summer would soon come to an end.

Devon was happy to wear the white dinner jacket that had been made for him by a Kowloon tailor for his journey home from Hong Kong in 1949 on the Orient Line's newest ship, the *Orcades*. Wearing it again brought back pleasant memories of his luxurious first-class cabin, wonderful food and great company. He remembered the long sunny days he had spent on the ship with Barbara Blake, the Queen Alexandra's nurse he got to know when his squadron was based in Singapore. He became very fond of her on their cruise home, and smiled internally as he recalled his shock when he had learned that she was returning to England to settle down with her partner, Samantha.

Hannah wore her new dress: a full-length silver taffeta gown with a matching silk shawl. She had allowed herself the luxury of an appointment at the Grosvenor Park's hairdresser in the lobby of the hotel, and her hair was perfectly curled and set in a waving bob. Naturally, she wore her most precious item of jewellery, a single strand of exquisite natural pearls. Ready to go down, they checked each other's outfits. Devon brushed her hair gently with the palm of his hand and said how beautiful she looked. She knew she was so fortunate to have Adam's love and she glowed with joy as she felt her love for him.

In the bar before dinner David Porter found Devon and Hannah and introduced them to his wife, Penny. Only married a year earlier, they had met at BOAC where Penny was the firm's personnel director. Devon immediately felt at home with her, and Hannah also felt relaxed and warmed readily to Penny, as not all of her conversation was on the subject of flying. She mentioned that her family came from Derbyshire and then Devon recalled: he had seen their wedding announcement in *The Times*. Penny was the daughter of Lord Matlock, and their wedding had been held at their enormous country estate in the Dales.

The foursome were seated together on a large round table, loaded with glassware and silver cutlery with a centrepiece of red and white roses. Other senior de Havilland managers and their wives, plus a government official and her husband, made up the complement of twelve. Everyone was in good form, even high spirits, after the pre-dinner champagne. Hannah looked across at the table with a card inscribed with '1' in a silver holder. Devon noticed her interest and pointed out Jocelyn Darley and some of the board members. He recognised one of the guests, and realised that he had been introduced to him. It was Andrew White, the MP on the government defence committee who had shown an interest on a visit to de Havilland in ordering a number of the Dove aircraft for the RAF.

"Adam was very pleased to be invited to take part in the Battle of Britain flypast. I think he misses the excitement of RAF life," said Hannah. Porter was seated to her right, with Penny between them and Devon to her left.

Penny smiled. "Yes, but isn't he involved in aircraft development? That must be much more fun than poor David's job of flying endlessly, looking for new places to land."

The group laughed quietly.

"At least Adam is home every night. Sometimes David is away for days on end."

"That's a good point. When we're married, I will be very happy to see Adam every evening. At the moment we can only really get together at weekends, with him living in Hertfordshire and me in Clapham." Hannah glanced at Adam, who was looking down at this hands, not seeming to agree with her.

Porter broke the silence. "Tell me, Hannah, what work are you doing now? I recall you were engaged in a somewhat dangerous occupation in Hong Kong. Are you free of all that business now?"

"I've been back at the London and Hong Kong Bank since returning from the Far East. I really enjoy working at the bank, and they are lovely people. I'm in the marketing team, helping the bank attract new commercial clients."

"What work were you doing in Hong Kong that was so exciting, Hannah? I'm intrigued!" Penny said.

Oh hell, thought Hannah. Clearly Penny had not been briefed. She did not wish to dig up painful memories of the failed secret service mission that had led to the end of her relationship with Devon. But she had to give an answer, and an honest one. "I was part of a team from the Israeli Secret Service. My role was to recruit Spitfire pilots for our – I mean their – air force. Adam was one of our potential candidates, but that didn't come off, and for one reason or another the plans were abandoned. Adam and I met up again in London six months later."

"Gosh, Hannah, how exciting! How brave of you." Penny was wide-eyed and smiling broadly. Hannah tried to think how best to respond, but was relieved of the need to when the master of ceremonies announced that the dance band would be starting to play in fifteen minutes.

As they all stood and moved away from the table, Porter whispered to Hannah, "Sorry about that. I shouldn't have asked about the past."

Devon had taken Penny onto the dance floor.

"That's quite alright, David," said Hannah, "as you say, all that business is firmly in the past. But I would like to know what exotic and dangerous work you might have in mind for Adam. I'm sure he enjoyed the flypast, even though one of your team was killed," said Hannah, with more sarcasm in her voice than she intended. "But he is retired now from active service, rather like yourself."

"There are many opportunities for good pilots out there." Porter sounded defensive. "As you know, de Havilland have put a lot of trust in Adam in the radar work they are doing; it's important for national security as well as their commercial interests. I believe he is very happy in his job, don't you?"

Hannah softened. "Yes, you're right, of course. And he wouldn't want a job that was boring. It's just not his style."

Porter took Hannah to the dance floor and the two couples changed partners for the next dance. Hannah was relieved to be able to speak to Devon quietly. "Are you OK, Adam? Are you enjoying yourself?"

"Oh, I'm alright, darling. I just have so much on my mind at the moment and I'm sorry that I haven't spoken to you any further about the wedding arrangements. I know you find it annoying that we have to live apart, and I do too, but it won't be for ever. We will set a date for next year, so in the meantime we should let the subject rest."

Hannah's heart sank, largely because they still hadn't set a date. She felt that Devon was putting her in her place, dismissing her feelings. "Yes, of course, dear, as you wish," she said, knowing that she had to find a better time to discuss the wedding, and whether he really wanted to marry her.

SEVENTEEN

Leonid forced himself to walk slowly. He didn't want to arrive at the Balalaika early and seem anxious or overkeen. As he entered the café, he saw Yuri and another man sitting down at a table on the far side, the waitress standing ready beside them with her pad and pencil. Perfect timing. Leonid took off his hat and coat and left them at the cloakroom.

As he walked to the table, he felt the warmth from the dozens of wall-mounted light fittings. They lent a gold tint to the magnolia walls with their hand-painted floral murals. The cherry-red carpet was deep and dense beneath his feet, and each walnut-veneered table shone after years of wax polishing. The clientele could have been sitting in Venice or Paris. The short walk to the table gave Leonid a surge of positive feelings: this luxury was something he wanted to enjoy regularly.

"Ah, Leonid, welcome, come and sit. I have ordered coffee," said Yuri.

"Thank you, most kind."

"And may I introduce Korol? Korol is in the metals refining business."

"Pleased to meet you, Mr Korol." The two men shook hands, and Leonid gave a gentle bow.

"It is just Korol, Leonid," said Yuri quietly. "And he is a keen chess player, an admirer of the British school, like us."

Korol was a quietly sophisticated, well-educated man with a smooth voice and a gaze that could see right into Leonid. He was well dressed, of course – even in these times of hardship he must be making a good profit in his business. And if he were engaged in spying for the British then he would be very well paid for his trouble and risks. Korol said he was Ukrainian by birth and had studied at the London School of Economics and Political Science, where he developed his appreciation of alternative social structures. He took over his father's metal-refining plants after the war and built up the lucrative mining and smelting business.

"And how is the metals business at the moment, Korol?"

"There are challenges, of course, but we specialise in high-end metals like aluminium, copper and cobalt that sell well overseas. We specialise in the export market and apply the latest technology to our work. I gather you are a scientist yourself."

"Yes – I work in the arms development area. Russia leads the world in many technologies."

"And you admire the style of chess as it is played in the West," said Yuri, helping the conversation move towards the point of their meeting, but keeping the cloak of allusion over the discussions.

Without being asked, the waitress came back with a fresh pot of coffee and a plate of small pastries and carefully placed them in the centre of the table. The interruption gave Leonid a moment to think. He knew he had to be cautious. Like in a game of chess, the opening gambit was risky and required one of them to break cover and discuss a defection to the West. Leonid felt confident. "It is a great ambition of mine to play in one of the overseas chess tournaments – possibly in London, if one were able to travel freely to such a place."

"I understand your desire, Leonid. If that opportunity were to be realised, you would be very welcome, with your skills and experience," said Korol. "There are people who go on these trips and enjoy them very much – the comforts, the freedom to express themselves. The hosts of the tournament would hope that you could share your expertise in chess with them and help them improve their game. The problem is that return travel is very difficult to arrange."

"Of course – an important point to consider. But I think it would be worth it to be able to play in a British, or even an American, tournament." Leonid knew he was pushing it, but it was too late to be circumspect now.

He got the response he was hoping for.

"Well then, let us see what can be done. Most players bring with them their notes and manuals – these contain all the information they need to train the other players at the tournament. May I assume that you would be able to bring this information?"

"I would indeed. As well as my dossier, I have many ideas for game strategies in my mind."

"Excellent," replied Korol. "The very attributes that would be valued by the British. Please be aware that sometimes these chess tournaments are arranged with very little advance notice, so from here on you should be ready to travel without delay."

"Thank you. You can be assured I will be ready."

Yuri leant forward. "And of course, Leonid, we must keep our discussions confidential. We would not want competing players to hear of our plans."

***

Leonid rarely received any post, and was curious when he heard the letterbox rattle and something fall to the floor. A plain cream envelope addressed with extremely neat handwriting, using a mid-blue ink – a capitalist colour, in the minds of the state. He was ready to leave the flat for work, but took the time to open the letter. He sat down at his small kitchen table and read the letter through. And then a second time, more slowly. He was shaken to find that plans for his defection had moved so quickly. His stomach lurched, telling of his fear and thrill at the prospect. He suddenly realised that the whole charade could be a ploy to identify him as a traitor to the Soviet Union, and in a day or two he could be in a stinking jail with broken ribs, blinded in one eye and with several fingernails missing. He shook his head to push these images out of his mind, and applied himself instead to positive thoughts of a life in England, or even the US.

After reading the letter one more time – especially the part noting that the chess captain would be at his flat at 8p.m. that evening and he should pack nothing, except his chess strategy notebooks – he left for the factory. All necessities would be provided, the letter promised. Really? he thought. I should take absolutely nothing?

He spent the day at work on administrative tasks, keeping away from colleagues who might see something in his face. Arriving home at 7p.m. he opened an ancient tin of pork he had been saving for a special occasion which he would eat with the last of his potatoes. He cleaned the kitchen thoroughly and placed his technical notes on a small, neat pile on the table.

***

Korol arrived right on time, dressed in a shabby factory uniform that curiously suited him very well, and carrying a large canvas bag. He turned it upside down over the kitchen table and a pile of clothes fell out: worker's clothes, cheap, worn but clean. Everything was included: shoes, shirt, underwear, a brown woollen suit and a black, heavy, double-breasted coat. Even a pair of reading glasses to replace the expensive pair Leonid normally wore. Leonid looked at the flat cap that was included with the outfit – a symbol of the lower classes. He glanced at Korol, whose expression left Leonid in no doubt about what he should do. Leonid put the hat on, completing the labourer look that would ensure he blended in with the vast majority of the population. All of Leonid's clothes were placed in the laundry basket – Korol didn't want the house to look as if Leonid had planned not to come back. They were pretending to be electricians, moving to a new factory fit-out job. Each man had a knapsack with a few carefully chosen possessions: a spare shirt, a razor, yesterday's newspaper, some bread and cheese and a water flask. Korol handed Leonid an electrician's manual and told him to hide his notes inside it and place it in his bag.

Korol gave a quick briefing. They would go by train from Moscow to Kiev and then take the midnight train to Berlin. There Leonid would stay in a supporter's house for a number of days, to allow the initial response to his disappearance to settle down. Korol had papers for Leonid's new identity, but Korol assured him he would not be challenged on the journey if he kept quiet and made no eye contact with strangers or officials on the trains. Leonid had a compliant nature, and found very little difficulty in acting the part of a sullen, oppressed worker. As they boarded the train, Leonid was silently enthralled at the prospect of freedom and wealth, and he felt more than ever that he had a deep-seated ideological dislike of the concept of communism. He was ready to throw off the shackles of the Soviet state and become himself at last.

EIGHTEEN

David Porter entered Jocelyn Darley's office and went straight to a black leather chair. He opened his briefcase and took out a short, unsigned contract.

Darley sat back in his seat and shook his head. "Bloody close thing for you, David, at the flypast."

"Such are the risks in flying, particularly in close formation. Naismith's aircraft developed a fault that made controlling it very tricky, with power surges and drops. He might have made a forced landing somewhere, but the East End is densely populated so he opted for the river. People don't realise how hard it is to get a water landing right, and unfortunately for Naismith, he got it wrong."

"But fortunately, both you and Devon were unharmed."

"Yes, indeed."

"Now, how can I help you, David?"

"We need Adam for an assignment that may involve bringing back a valuable asset from Berlin. Our agents are confident that the party in question will come over, but he wants to talk to someone from our side who will understand the technology he is working on. And the same goes for us – we want to know that he has something of significance."

"And what is that technology?"

"Well, in strict confidence…" said Porter, keen to show he trusted Darley. "As you are so close to the project, I can outline what we're interested in, but this is not to be shared with any other party, in or out of de Havilland." Porter placed the contract on the coffee table.

"Understood." Darley quickly removed a smile that had formed at the corner of his mouth.

"We believe the Soviets are developing an advanced air-to-surface radar-guided missile system called *Blade*. It's capable of extremely accurate targeting up to twenty miles distant, on land and ships. This could outshoot any of our own systems at the moment, so it's imperative that we find out just how advanced the system is."

"And what's the name of the defector?"

Porter hesitated. Darley should not be asking these questions. "All we have is his code name. Leonid."

"Right, and you want Devon to be part of this Berlin assignment, but how can he help?"

"This could just be a smokescreen put out by the Soviets to distract us while they develop other systems in secret. We want Devon to meet Leonid, assess the delivery system, and see how the missiles can be launched by either a pilot or a flight engineer. We feel that a good test pilot, especially with air-ground attack experience, will be able to judge how viable the radar guidance is."

"Devon's not a scientist. And anyway, isn't this something for the RAF?" said Darley.

"No, not at this stage. We're worried about security, and the fewer parties involved the better. Devon will be required to cross over into the Russian sector of Berlin and perhaps travel more widely in East Germany. That's not without its dangers, of course. He doesn't need to be a weapons expert; he just needs to be able to confirm that Leonid genuinely knows enough about the system to be able to share his knowledge with a test pilot. We have to be sure the man is really involved at the leading edge of the technology."

"I see. We will, of course, be very happy to provide any assistance we can. Will you brief Devon on the assignment, or shall I?"

"I shall brief him on what's required, and from there he can agree the use of the Dove with you. There will be no need to have any other people on board. I have a contract here from HM Government for the temporary loan of the aircraft, and for Devon to come under MI6's instruction."

"Understood, David. It all does hang on Adam agreeing to be part of this. What exactly is in it for him? A lot of danger, but for what reward?"

"A certain amount, financially. We will pay quite a generous fee to him and reimburse de Havilland for his salary. I'm trusting his sense of adventure and desire to do a good job for the country. He has always liked a touch of danger, enjoys testing his nerve. I saw that many times in the Far East, and you saw it in the flypast. I'm confident that he will relish the assignment we have for him."

NINETEEN

Adam Devon was called up to Jocelyn Darley's office late one Friday afternoon when flying had finished. He doubted whether there would be anything interesting to discuss, probably just a round-up of the week's test results and a few words on the next stage of the radar development project. Devon appreciated the high status that was afforded him through the personal interest of the MD, but he wanted to get away so he could meet Hannah at the train station.

Lucy sent him into the office, where Darley sat behind his pretentious desk he so enjoyed, jacket off and with a stack of letters awaiting signature in front of him. Devon reflected that the boss had a good few hours more at the office ahead of him before his weekend started, but he seemed to be happy working into the evening. As Devon sat down in front of the desk, David Porter got up from one of the black leather chairs and extended his hand.

"Adam, great to see you again, old chap. Hope all is well with you?"

Devon was still not used to his old superior officer in the RAF being so pally. "Hello, David. All is well, thanks. Busy as usual, of course. What brings you here today? Not another air show?"

"Ha, no. Something much more challenging. I want to introduce you to a very good friend of mine – he'll be here in a few minutes. His name is Angus Ballantyne, and he's one of the government types we have to work with. In fact, he's with MI6." Porter's faint smile gave a 'don't worry' signal.

Darley cleared his throat, seeming to wish to maintain the image of being in charge. "A special flight is planned, Adam, and we at de Havilland are willing to assist any government body in their work," he said. "Berlin again, but with a different purpose this time. Ballantyne will give you the details. I don't have to remind you that you have signed the Official Secrets Act, do I?"

Devon subdued his desire to tell the MD not to be so crass, of course he didn't need reminding, but decided to take a more accommodating stance. "No, no need for that. The job sounds intriguing. Can you give me any idea what the project is about?"

Porter had dropped the nonchalance and said quietly, "As usual, you have the option to decline to participate in any of these special assignments, but I can tell you that it's important and classified as top secret. You will work with Ballantyne's colleagues in Berlin. Ah, he's here."

Darley's door was opened by his secretary, who ushered in the visitor.

"That will be all for tonight, Lucy. Have a good weekend."

Devon's thoughts turned to Hannah's arrival at Hatfield station. He was relieved to realise that if he wasn't there to pick her up, she could take a taxi and had keys to the house.

Ballantyne was not a tall man but broad-shouldered and muscular. His hair was a coppery red, and he had a moustache of the same hue. He was well dressed in a sombre grey single-breasted suit set off with a royal blue silk square in his breast pocket. He looked smart, but not showy.

"A pleasure to meet you, Devon," he said in his soft east-Scotland accent. "I've heard very favourable reports of your flying here at de Havilland and in the RAF."

"Good to know. One does one's best."

"You spent some time in the Far East, I understand."

Darley indicated they should all sit in the black chairs around the coffee table.

Devon went along with the small talk, leaving it to Ballantyne to mention the real purpose of the meeting. "Yes indeed, 28 Squadron, Mk XVIII Spitfires. With David, of course."

"Quite. You must have had some fun together. And you're now working on commercial aircraft. Sounds dull by comparison."

"Not at all, Mr Ballantyne, I'm enjoying the research and development aspects of the job and I'm guessing David enjoys the route-finding role he has at BOAC."

Porter made no reply, giving just a gentle nod.

Ballantyne's voice changed subtly to a serious tone. "My reason for coming here this evening is to tell you about an assignment that requires skilful flying and the utmost discretion."

"And this is to Berlin, I gather," said Devon.

"Yes, that's the plan. But it is not related to the radar work you have been undertaking to date."

Darley went to stand up. "Do you need privacy, gentlemen? I would be very happy to leave you all to discuss your operation."

"I'm sure there's no need for that, Darley," said Porter.

Ballantyne opened his mouth as if to say something, paused, then said, "Well then, shall we get down to the details of the assignment? The mission is to pick up three passengers and fly them back to the UK. There will just be yourself as pilot, no other crew. The date is yet to be settled, so you will continue your operations here as normal, including your regular test flights to Berlin. You will be given ample notice of the assignment when the date is known."

"Right,' said Devon. "And who will I be picking up?"

"A very valuable asset – you don't need to know the details at this time. Plus two of our own people. In fact, I believe you have met one of them – our head of Berlin station, Val Hetherington-Brown. She will be returning to the UK, plus one of her colleagues, name of Raleigh, who you probably also know from your days in Hong Kong."

"I certainly remember Val – she was part of the Government House set-up. Not sure I met Raleigh."

Ballantyne continued. "Val will be securing the party in question at a location in East Berlin. You will be taken through to the Russian sector to meet the man, and I can tell you that he is a very senior missile scientist. You will interrogate him and get a feel for his knowledge of the air-to-ground system he is working on, particularly how it is delivered in the air. But be aware, he will not tell you all the details. Even if there was time for that, he would be foolish to tell us everything now. He is trying to exchange his knowledge for safe passage to the West."

"But, Mr Ballantyne, I'm not experienced in covert operations, and there's every chance I would make a hash of it." Devon regretted his words immediately; he felt it sounded like he hadn't the nerve to take on the task. Quickly he added, "But I'm happy to be guided by your agents and perhaps get some basic training in."

"You needn't worry, Devon, you simply have to follow our agent's instructions and all will go well," said Ballantyne. "Assuming you and Hetherington-Brown are happy with the defector's bona fides, your main job will be to fly the group back from Tempelhof in the Dove."

"Understood," said Devon, "but I have a question. Why isn't this operation and the flight being undertaken by our own weapons people and the RAF?"

Porter and Ballantyne looked silently at each other for a moment. Porter spoke quietly and firmly, now sounding like a commanding officer again. "The British government cannot take responsibility for the operation. The extraction of the asset is a highly sensitive matter, and the involvement of any British or American armed forces could cause a major diplomatic incident. The Soviets might take such a situation as the trigger for a full-scale invasion of the whole of Berlin, or even West Germany. There would be little we could do to stop them, short of a war."

"So the situation is, Devon,' said Ballantyne, "if anything should go wrong, the government would deny responsibility. You would be denigrated as freelance people-smugglers, making money from illicit operations, unbeknown to your employer, de Havilland. If you or any of the team are arrested by the Soviets, no assistance will be forthcoming from the government. You would be on your own."

"Bloody hell, sounds a poor show. Why would any civilian take such a risk?" Devon wasn't being flippant.

Porter spoke next, cleverly taking an angle he knew would seal Devon's commitment. "For the simple reason that the job needs to be done and you are the one in the best position to do it. It's no different to our time in Malaya and Hong Kong – if risks were to be taken then, we were the ones to take them."

"Yes, but that was different – we were a deterrent. We only attacked enemy forces in order to protect our ground troops."

Ballantyne took up the case. "This is more important. Our understanding of developments in Russian weapons is vital, and the party you will bring to the UK will provide us with key information. We need to know exactly how the missile system works so that we and the Americans can build interception equipment. The mission is vital to our interests."

Devon felt the buzz of excitement at the prospect of a testing, dangerous mission, something he hadn't really faced since Malaya.

"Very well. I will give it some thought. I will be with my fiancée over the weekend, and I can give you my response on Monday."

Ballantyne stood up and started to pace the office, punching his fist gently into the palm of his hand. "No, no! You cannot discuss the assignment, even with your fiancée."

Devon stood up. "It's nonsense to think that Hannah is a security risk or a Russian agent. Are you mad?"

"We must maintain the utmost secrecy. Only the chief of MI6, the Berlin station senior agents and the people in this room will know the details of the mission – and of course you will be aware of the potential for Soviet agents to be at work here in the UK – and in Berlin."

Devon was indeed aware: it was headline news. He had been as shocked as anyone else when the Cambridge spy ring was exposed the year before and Burgess and Maclean had defected to the Soviet Union. The passing of secrets by such prominent members of the Establishment was hard to believe. It had spread suspicion through all areas of government and the intelligence services. Devon knew that he had to make the decision on his own; it would be unfair to burden Hannah with any details of the assignment. She might innocently give something away.

Devon sat back down and took a breath. "Very well, I will take on the assignment."

Ballantyne was the first to offer his hand to shake. He then passed Devon a heavy grey canvas bag. Devon flipped open the cover of the bag, and was not surprised to see a Browning 9mm pistol, the same as the type he was issued with in the RAF, and two magazines.

Ballantyne gave a small smile. "Take it with you on the assignment. You might need it where you're going."

TWENTY

One morning more than a week later, Devon was pleased to get a lift to the airfield from a member of the engineering team who lived locally. He threw his overnight bag and flight case into the back of the car and picked up the newspaper that was lying on the front passenger seat. He glanced at the headlines then flipped over to the sports pages and scanned the cricket scores. He was pondering what the potential business of the day might be. After he was dropped off at the aircraft parking area, he went straight over to the Dove. Climbing in, he was startled to see that all of the experimental radar equipment had been removed and replaced with two new rows of seats, making eight in the cabin. So this is it, he thought, the mysterious assignment to Berlin. He had not told Hannah about the mission; while believing absolutely in her ability to keep the secret, he didn't want to worry her. He did, however, tell her that on one of his trips to Berlin he might have to spend a few days there, and he wasn't exactly sure when that would be.

Once again, Darley was in the hangar when Devon arrived, fully suited, in polished black shoes and a starched white shirt. Devon found the man's attention to his grooming irritating; the hangar was a place for flight crew and engineers, not pomaded office workers.

"Good morning, Devon."

"Good morning, sir."

"You will see that the aircraft has been prepared for the special trip to Berlin." Darley spoke cautiously; there were other people milling around the hangar. He walked to the planning desk and picked up an envelope and a package. "Ballantyne has left these instructions for you. They cover timings and contact names. And here is some material for Artur Franken."

Devon was used to carrying packages to be handed over to Franken – they were nothing very exciting, just the usual manuals and a list of potential buyers, plus some up-to-date flight performance data with which to impress clients. Franken himself was polite and efficient on all Devon's trips to Berlin, and largely kept out of Devon's hair.

"You will be departing around midday – just you on the aircraft. The radar boys have been told that this is a sales trip and have taken all their equipment out. Do you have all that you need?"

"I think so, sir. I will get the latest weather forecast for the route shortly."

"Excellent. Well, Devon…" Darley held out his hand. "Best of luck. I hope the assignment goes all to plan." Darley walked with a sense of purpose out of the hangar and took the stairs to his office.

Devon called Hannah and told her that he would be away for a couple of days, then spent the morning on his usual preparations: reviewing the route, carefully studying his chart for waymarkers and identifying alternative landing airfields along or near to the planned route; the northern access air lane, known as the 'corridor' to Berlin, should there be a serious problem requiring an emergency landing. All this was standard procedure. He had been through the process on every trip to Berlin, and felt he knew the flight plan like the back of his hand. But it never hurt to revise and note down the distances, compass headings, high ground and obstacles en route and to visualise the emergency landing sites in the calm surroundings of the planning office – it would be a different matter if he had to make a forced landing, potentially at night.

Someone had arranged for the canteen staff to put together sandwiches, fruit and a flask of tea for Devon. He stowed these in a pocket next to the co-pilot's seat. Strange, he thought; the staff were not usually so thoughtful, but the meal was very welcome. Late morning, he stowed all his kit, closed the door, went through his pre-flight checks and radioed to the air traffic control tower that he was ready for departure. He got the clearance he required and taxied to the runway threshold. Final checks completed, he applied power and the aircraft surged forward in a short run before lifting off and climbing away. Devon felt the difference there was in performance when the aircraft was empty. The flight was uneventful, the weather clear with light winds. Devon felt as if he was on a nice little jolly.

After landing at Berlin Tempelhof, he entered the terminal building to be greeted by Franken, as he had come to expect. As usual, Franken took the package Darley had put together for him and went immediately into his office.

And now all Devon could do was wait.

TWENTY-ONE

Adam Devon never liked to be idle. The prospect of hanging around Tempelhof airport for several days was dispiriting and irksome. He had agreed to the assignment, aware that the passengers' arrival time and date were uncertain, and he had to be ready to depart at very short notice. He had the aircraft refuelled and started up the engines periodically to ensure they were running well. There would be three passengers, he was told; the 'asset,' as the MI6 people referred to their man, Val, and a colleague of hers. Devon was set up with accommodation in a hastily converted storeroom adjacent to the de Havilland office at the airport to rest, eat and sleep, and was told not to leave the airfield. His service life acclimatised him to spartan accommodation, so he found it no hardship. He had taken plenty of reading material as well as the aircraft's pilot's handling manual. He liked to memorise the whole thing; flying solo gave him no opportunity to look up flight data, stall speeds, landing approach speed in different configurations of flaps, minimum runway distance required for landing, and so on. All the vital numbers Devon knew he could easily get wrong under stressful conditions.

He was told to keep the aircraft parked close to the maintenance hangar and Val would contact him. During the daytime, people came to the enormous airport terminal building for flights, mainly to capital cities in the West. Arrivals' documentation was thoroughly examined by immigration officers before they were allowed to leave the airport, to take the U-Bahn train or the bus into the city.

The days passed quickly enough. Monday morning saw the airport much busier than the weekend. Devon felt a jolt of anxiety. Hannah would be back at work, having not heard from him for three days, as he had been told not to contact anyone in the UK. Even her patience and self-assurance could be tested to breaking point.

A little before dusk that day, he carried out his familiar routine: ran the engines, checked the aircraft security, locked the aircraft up for the night and called into the control tower for the weather forecast for the next twelve hours. There was nothing to worry about there – in any event, the Dove had excellent all-weather and night flying instrumentation. After a brief chat with the air traffic control people, Devon strolled around the maintenance hangar to stretch his legs and pass the time. As it was now almost dark, the place was closing for the evening; only the junior mechanic was there to lock up. On the far side of the airfield he could see a few lights in the American sector, but there was no one moving around.

Devon spent an hour reading a week-old copy of *The Times*, then double-checking his flight plan and route through the return air corridor. He felt a nervous excitement: this challenging mission had real responsibility, and he knew he had to get it right. His experience told him that as soon as they got going, he would relax, focusing on the task in hand. He was glad to see some action: his friends in the squadron had told him he would be bored after he had left the air force, and he had to agree that was true sometimes. This operation was more like it, giving him a sense of purpose and excitement that he had missed.

In the early evening, a car drew up outside the hangar and a tall, slim woman emerged. Devon recognised her immediately and stepped outside. "Good evening, Val, great to meet you again. How are you? What is it, three years since Hong Kong?"

"Hello, Adam. I'm very well, thanks. Yes, something like that. Good to see you too, thanks for taking on this job." Val spoke quickly; she had little time to chat. "Is the aircraft ready to fly?"

"Yes, all fuelled and checked out."

"Excellent." Val looked at her watch. "You're to come with me to interview Leonid, the missile specialist. His English is near perfect, by the way. Are you ready?"

"Sure, but where are we going exactly?"

"To the Russian sector – not far in, to a safe house. Just follow my instructions, say nothing and all will be well. There's a coat and hat for you in the car, to make you look German. It's 7p.m. now. You will have half an hour with our man, then we need to be back at the airport by 9p.m."

"That will be you, your colleague and Leonid. Three passengers."

"Ah, no. There's been a late change. We will be four – another member of the team will be joining us."

"No problem, the aircraft has plenty of space. Who is it?" Devon was just curious, and realised immediately that he shouldn't ask questions.

"A friend, a US agent," was all that Val said as she opened the door to the car. The driver didn't look in Devon's direction as he drove smoothly away.

***

The journey through the secure route from the British sector to the Alexanderplatz district only took twenty minutes, but as they drove,

Devon could vividly see the contrasting conditions between the east and west sectors. It was little wonder that so many people wanted out. He resisted the temptation to gaze around in awe at all the wartime damage still apparent, and kept his eyes forward. When they arrived at the house, he was ushered in quickly through the hall and into a small, but clean, kitchen. Leonid sat at the table with the electrician's manual containing his technical papers in front of him. Devon pulled out a notebook and pencil to record the key details, but Val told him not to make notes, to keep it verbal.

Devon was no missile expert, but Leonid's clarity in describing the potential capabilities of the *Blade* air-to-ground system astounded him. Few questions were necessary for Devon to gain a clear picture of how the radar guidance systems would work in anger, and to be able to affirm to Val that Leonid was definitely an expert in his field.

As soon as their driver returned, Val, Leonid and Devon walked calmly out of the house and into the car. Devon knew this was the most dangerous part of the mission – being stopped and arrested with a Russian defector would mean a long time in a Soviet prison for all of them. The driver was biting his lower lip, looking much more anxious than on their way in – he was clearly very frightened. They were passing through Friedrichshain district, skirting the dividing line between the Russian and British sectors, when the car suddenly did a screeching U-turn and turned back along Grunberger Strasse, heading west.

"What's wrong?" Val shouted.

"No problem, Fräulein. We must make sure we are not followed. We now go to Mitte," the driver called back.

Leonid's eyes widened and his breathing became heavy, he was gasping with fear. Devon squeezed his arm reassuringly.

"Two minutes, we change cars," the driver said in a calmer voice.

The changeover was quickly executed, and the second car moved off immediately down the quiet, unguarded street, then crossed over into the British sector. Devon saw Val breathe a sigh of relief, and Leonid covered his face with his hands.

***

When they arrived back at Tempelhof, Devon saw his other passengers emerge from the shadows at the side of the hangar. He could see the American that Val had mentioned and an older man, whom he assumed to be Raleigh.

"Wait in the hangar, stay out of view. I will need ten minutes to prepare, then come out to the aircraft and board. The door will be open." Devon returned to the office, where he collected the flight documents and his weekend bag.

As Devon was turning to leave, he was shocked to see Artur Franken come into the office. This could be difficult if Franken wants to go out to the aircraft, Devon thought. Franken greeted Devon in the way that only Germans do, a nod of the head, clicked heels, an insincere smile. Devon just wanted to deal with whatever Franken wanted and get him out of the building in double-quick time.

"Herr Franken, what can I do for you?" said Devon.

"You are preparing to leave?"

"Yes. I have been given instructions to depart tonight – immediately, in fact."

"Please wait, Adam. I must go to my car – I have a package for Mr Darley."

"No, I'm leaving right now, I can't wait."

"A few minutes only." Franken had already left the office and gone through the airport entrance to the car park at the front. Fortunately he was only away briefly.

"Please, you will take this package for Mr Darley. And please be careful, it contains a bottle of the finest German kirsch. A special gift from my wife's family for the Old Man." Franken held up a metal box, bright red with an armorial crest and the distiller's name on the lid. It was secured with tape around the edges.

Devon cringed at his words: Franzen was clearly trying to show that he was on good terms with the MD, with his pally comment and sending him a gift, like an apple for a teacher.

"That's fine. Put it on the desk, Artur. I will take it with my papers," said Devon.

"You will kindly not forget it, please!" Franzen stood to attention and stared at Devon.

"No, rest assured I will not forget your very thoughtful present."

Franken gave a little bow, clicked his heels again, wished Devon a pleasant flight and left the office, heading towards the front of the terminal.

Walking across the tarmac with the red box under his arm, Devon was relieved that not a soul was around, and his radio call on departure would announce that only one person was on board. But had Devon looked back to the office, he would have seen Franken watching his movements through a darkened office window, a satisfied smile on his face.

Devon climbed into the aircraft, turned to the right and stowed his bags, coat and Franken's parcel behind the rearmost seat, which no one would be using. He then walked down the aircraft to the pilot's seat. As he started to go through the pre-flight checks, he heard the passengers board. Val and the Russian sat in the row immediately behind him and the two others behind them. He turned his head to give instructions on closing the door, but the American had seen to it.

Devon started the engines and taxied across the parking area towards the runway. "Right, seat belts, everyone," he called. "Sit back and relax and we'll be in England in about three hours."

At last, he thought, they were under way – and he could go home.

TWENTY-TWO

After levelling out at 6,000 feet and taking up a westerly heading, Devon looked at the clock on the instrument panel. It was 9.30p.m. He couldn't help thinking of Hannah back at her flat in Clapham. He decided to ring her as soon as they landed at Hatfield, even though it would wake her.

All instruments were showing normal readings: engine temperatures, fuel reserves, electrical system charging. A great aircraft, Devon thought. It was assured to sell around the world as a comfortable passenger carrier, a tough military load bearer and a survey-and-expedition platform. He looked behind him at Val. She smiled and nodded. Devon also took in the Russian. He seemed to have relaxed and his eyes were heavy, due to the dissipation of stress and tiredness from his harrowing journey, no doubt.

The twin engines had settled into a gentle purr when Devon changed heading to ensure he stayed in the corridor. They had about fifty miles to go to the West German border when there was a shuddering jolt through the control column and an ear-splitting crack. Smoke washed through the aircraft, then a blast of cold air. Red lights flashed on Devon's instrument panel. The aircraft had lost pressurisation, but at their altitude they were able to breathe without needing oxygen masks. The aircraft lurched to the right and started to nosedive. Devon pulled on the control column but couldn't stop their descent. Instinctively, he eased back the power to the engines to try to kill the rate of descent and managed to level out.

"What the hell just happened?" called Val. Devon spun round to look at the passengers, who were all shouting at once. Past the rear seats, he could see a hole in the fuselage a foot across, and a long crack down the side of the aircraft. That explained his lack of control; the tailplane must have been damaged by the explosion. This was ominous – stress on the aircraft could tear more pieces off the tail or rip open the whole of the rear section at any time. He knew he had to make a forced landing immediately, before the aircraft broke up in mid-air. Devon's emergency procedures drill included making a mayday call. As he pressed the transmitter, he suddenly realised that it wasn't just the British and American air traffic services that would pick up the call, but also the East German authorities. He snatched back his hand, deciding that a call would attract the wrong kind of attention.

Val shook Devon's shoulder and pulled him round to face her. Devon saw the older passenger in the back row gasping and clutching his lower leg. There was blood on the seat and spattered on the floor – the explosion had blown shards of hot metal into the back of his leg. The American pulled off his tie and used it as a tourniquet, just as Val went to his aid and tried to stem the blood flow with her headscarf. Devon had to leave them to it and concentrate on landing. Looking at his flight plan, he knew there was a disused Luftwaffe airfield about four miles to their left, just a few minutes' flying time away; it might still be in a good enough state to allow them to land. He made a gentle turn, careful not to put any extra stress on the plane's structure. Devon took up a heading that he guessed was right for the airfield. As he did so, he saw moonlight reflect off a river just left of the nose of the aircraft. A glance at his map showed the River Elbe flowing in parallel to the airfield. Excellent, he thought, and called out to the passengers to tighten their seat belts, get ready for landing.

Devon strained his eyes to spot the runway, but the area was thickly wooded and he could see nothing that looked like an airfield. Devon switched on the landing lights, lowered the undercarriage and descended to less than 200 feet. Suddenly he saw to his right the smooth black shape of a runway, and yelled "yes!". But he was already over the threshold, and had to cut the power to get down immediately. As he did this, the aircraft dropped further as the damaged tail forced the nose down. Devon reapplied as much power as he dared to keep control of the plane. He realised that he had to abandon the landing or they would crash off the far end of the runway. Fortunately he could get some lift, so he climbed up to 500 feet and circled over the river and back round to the runway, this time with a good idea of where he should begin his approach.

Devon could hear the younger agent reassuring the injured man, who was gasping in agony. They could do no more for him until they landed. Devon looked ahead. All seemed fine, as the moonlight gave the runway a silvery sheen. When they touched down, Devon pulled back the engine throttles and applied the brakes hard. He could see little ahead in the headlights, and before he could take any avoiding action, the plane ploughed through a stack of empty oil drums that had been piled up halfway along the runway to indicate that the airfield was disused. The impact smashed the right-hand side of the windscreen and – as he would soon find out – broke the propeller blades on both engines and ripped the flaps off the wings. As they careered to a stop, Devon called for everyone to get out quickly. There was a real risk of a fire if the crash had perforated the aircraft's fuel tanks.

The American was first out, dragging the injured Raleigh with him. Val did the same with the Russian. Devon was last, and he grabbed two torches from behind the pilot's seat as he went. The group hurried away and hid in the trees on the edge of the airfield. Devon shone a light on Raleigh's leg and saw blood steadily running from his gruesome wounds.

"I'll go back and get the first aid kit from the aircraft. Stay here, everyone," said Devon.

"I'll come with you." Drake Casey stepped forward and crouched beside Devon, ready to run to the aircraft. Val quickly introduced Casey to Devon as her 'American friend', without going into detail on his role. Then she nodded to Raleigh and, pointing to the Russian, simply said, "Leonid". There was no need for her to make any introductions. Devon knew he was the asset they were so keen to get over to the West.

"Come on, then," he said to Casey.

The two men entered the aircraft quickly, trying to ignore the smell of aviation fuel. Devon pulled out the first aid kit, his tea flask and remaining food, and a couple of blankets from the crew stowage cupboard, and pushed them into his flight bag, which already contained his gun.

As a last thought, he stuffed the flight map in his pocket. Casey crouched in the rear, where the explosion had taken place, and picked up some blackened shards of metal and the remains of the red box, from which wires and pieces of plastic protruded.

"Devon, come here," he said. "It was a bomb. Looks like the detonator only triggered part of the explosive. Lucky – if the whole bomb had gone off, it would have blown us out of the sky."

"Bloody hell, that was a gift for Darley, our MD, Franken gave it to me to pass on – he works for de Havilland in Berlin. The bastard tried to kill us. Why the hell would he do that?"

"My guess is he's a Stasi agent, and he knew the Russian was on the plane – the real target. Someone tipped off Franken; he gave you the bomb but screwed up – it was badly made. Let's get back and fix up Raleigh's leg."

Devon collected the pieces of the box and put them in his bag.

***

Crouching among the trees, Casey told Val what they had found. Devon started to describe the damage to the plane, then stopped when he saw a look of realisation spread across Val's face. She punched a fist into the palm of her hand.

"Oh hell. Now I see. Darley has been hoodwinked by Franken – looks like the German got himself a nice job at de Havilland so he could spy on the radar developments. Question is, who gave him that information, and how? I also want to know how Franken got to know about Leonid and that he would be flown out last night. Someone at de Havilland must have told him, gave him the chance to plant the bomb with the aim of blowing up the aircraft and killing Leonid – and us, of course. We will have him arrested as soon as we can get a message through to London, and I'll have all personnel working on the Dove checked out."

"Good plan," said Casey, "but that's tomorrow's task. What're we going to do right now?"

"OK. Devon, do you know where we are?"

"Yes, we landed at this disused airfield close to the town of Burg. We're here." He pointed to the map. "Magdeburg is about ten miles south-west."

"Right, well, we'll move away from the airfield until we find somewhere to hide for the night. We can take it in turns to support Raleigh. Those first aid bandages won't last long," said Val.

They walked through forested countryside, sharp with the aroma of pine trees, their breath fogging in the clear, cold air, passing occasional small farms and timber yards. When Val decided they should rest, they had walked three miles south from the airfield away from the river they had seen from the air.

Casey did a recce of the area and found a derelict barn on the edge of a farm. The group stopped there to rest as the first light of dawn broke. Raleigh suffered largely in silence, but the team knew they had to get him to hospital urgently. Devon and Val studied the map he had salvaged from the aircraft: they needed food and drink and medical help. They agreed that Casey, fluent in German and dressed in his worker's clothes, would go into the town and locate a medical centre or doctor. They had to be quick; the sound of the crash during the night could have alerted local people, and in any event it would not be long before the aircraft was seen.

"I'll come with you," said Val. "If there's a telephone, we might be able to call London." She turned to Devon. "Come with me a moment." And she gestured to the corner of the barn. "You have a gun with you, don't you, and Raleigh has his own. Make every effort to get our Russian friend here safely across – but do not, under any circumstances, let him be taken by the Soviets."

"What are you saying?"

"If you are compromised and believe you are unlikely to outrun the Stasi agents or police, you will have to kill him." Val was deadly serious.

Devon flinched. "What? That's not for me to do. I'm a pilot, not a secret service agent!"

"Not on this assignment, Devon. You will obey my instructions. You know how important this man is to the Russians – he must not end up back in their hands."

"But…" Devon knew he couldn't argue, and she was right; this man's knowledge and work were a serious threat to the West. "Well, OK, understood." Devon checked that the safety catch was on and pocketed the gun and two spare magazines. "I can't see Raleigh being able to run very fast – or the Russian, come to that. And I don't fancy a gunfight with Stasi agents. So please get back as soon as you can. I'll bet there are search parties out looking for us already."

TWENTY-THREE

It only took Val and Casey half an hour to walk to Burg. There, the privations of post-war East Germany were immediately evident: grocery shops with empty windows, unrepaired bomb damage, tired-looking people, and only a couple of bars open. As they walked along the main street, an old lady ambled towards them.

Casey put his arm around Val's waist. "Look ill," he said firmly. "Make like you're about to faint."

Val responded on cue, and when they reached the woman, Casey asked her in German where the doctor could be found. His wife was with child, he said.

The woman's apprehensive look melted when Casey mentioned Val's condition, and she pointed to an alley on the other side of the road. Casey thanked her quickly and the couple crossed the road. Val saw a brass plate saying 'Doktor Schulze'. She opened a door into a small hall that had the reassuring aroma of disinfectant. There was no receptionist, but a small man in his fifties with a thin moustache and a stethoscope around his neck came from what was clearly the consulting room. The doctor beckoned Val and Casey in and closed the door.

"*Guten Morgen,*" said Casey.

"Good morning. I am Doktor Schulze, how can I help you?"

Val's eyes widened; the doctor spoke in flawless English. "Don't be concerned," he said. "I think I detected an accent, and you both have the look of British people. I trained at University College London Medical School."

"We are looking for a doctor to help a friend. He has a badly injured leg and cannot walk. If you have a car, we would like you to come and assist him," said Casey.

"And I need to use a telephone – do you have one here?" said Val.

"Yes, I have a telephone, but there is no international connection, if that's what you are hoping for."

"Very well, but the car?"

"That might be possible. You have the ability to pay my fee, I assume. Type of injury, please?"

"Shrapnel wounds and burns to the leg. Maybe a broken bone. Plenty of blood lost," Casey said. "There's no problem with the funds – Marks or US dollars."

"I see. I can help you, but you must wait here while I go and get my car."

"Not likely, fella. We go with you," said Casey. He pulled his right hand part way out of his jacket pocket to reveal the butt of his gun.

"Don't be ridiculous – I am a doctor."

"Just making sure we understand each other, Doc. Now, shall we go?" said Casey.

"Very well. One moment, please." Schulze took off his white coat and put on a green checked jacket and a Tyrolean hat, complete with feather. He scurried around his consulting room filling a medical bag with supplies and instruments. He was ready within two minutes, and took his keys from the drawer of his desk and pointed to a rear door. Val was astonished to see him take the time to look into a mirror, adjust his hat and straighten his tie.

A five-minute walk took them through the alleyway to a market square. Val stopped at a bakery stall and bought some cold schnitzel rolls and tiny iced cakes. As they walked on, the doctor suggested buying apple juice from another stall. The group entered a smaller square, where the doctor's car was parked. It was a Mercedes 170 – gleaming white, a four-door saloon, probably less than a year old. The doctor must be the wealthiest man in town, Val thought.

After a short drive, they had reached the barn. Casey directed the doctor to park at the rear, where his car would be hidden from view. Adam Devon went to watch from the door when he heard the car approach, pistol in hand. He relaxed when he saw Val and Casey step out of the car.

The doctor asked no questions. He quickly cleaned Raleigh's wounds of dried blood, embedded metal, cloth and dirt. Raleigh maintained a stoic demeanour, accepting the stinging of the antiseptic and the sharp pain as the doctor applied sutures. In less than twenty minutes the doctor was bandaging Raleigh's leg. He stood up.

Neat job, Val thought. He must have learned these skills during the war.

"Do not walk for three days or the bleeding will start again," said the doctor.

"Thank you. What do I owe you?" said Val.

"You can pay me for the medical treatment. But forgive me, madam, it looks to me that you need further services – perhaps a more comfortable place to rest?" said the doctor, looking around the barn.

"Yes, of course. But the most important thing we need is a telephone. How can we find one with an international connection?"

Schulze stood silently for a moment, pondering the question. "Madam, I don't know how you and your friends got here, but I can see you are in a difficult position. Anyone who assists you might well be arrested, and the punishments are severe." He looked at Leonid for several seconds. "I can see that you are not all British, or American. This makes the situation extremely dangerous. However, there is one possibility. I have a good friend – he's the deputy magistrate in town. He has an old wartime radio that you may find helpful."

"He's a legal guy – how the hell can we trust him?" said Casey.

"I believe he is a good man, likely to want to help those from a society many of us admire and wish to see prosper. Perhaps we might even seek to join you. Many people have already."

"OK, OK, enough already of the bartering. What do you say, Val?"

"We have no choice. I will go with the doctor, and you come with me, Drake. We may need your German again. The rest of you stay here. I will test the radio and, if it works, I will contact London. Don't leave the barn, keep out of sight."

"Wait a minute, Val – a word please. And you, Casey." Devon guided them both to the far side of the barn, out of earshot. "How the hell can you trust this man, or his friend? He could shop you to the authorities in a moment – and now he knows where we're hiding."

"We have no other option if we are to get word to London," said Val. "And my gut feeling is that he wants to help, he wants to do something that opposes the communists. And as you heard, he and his friend are minded to get to the West themselves."

"Leave it to us, Devon," said Casey. "If we sense that they are going to betray us, we'll cut and run."

"Just stay ready to make a quick departure, and make sure Raleigh and Leonid are also ready," said Val.

"OK, understood."

"Remember what I said – keep your gun on you and make sure you do what's necessary." Val returned to the doctor. "Lead the way, please."

"Very good, madam, let us go immediately." Doctor Schulze was already making for the barn door.

***

Just after midday, the doctor parked his car in the market square again, carefully locked it and checked all the doors. He led the way across the main square, where the stallholders were doing a steady trade. Val froze when a man in his thirties, tough and fit, looking every inch like a plain-clothes policeman, doffed his hat to the doctor and glanced at her and Casey. Without breaking his step, the doctor touched his hat in reply. The man nodded and walked on. Just a local man showing respect, Val hoped.

The doctor turned left down another narrow street consisting of a row of three- and four-storey expensive-looking apartment blocks. They were old, but had clearly been smartened up after the war. Each had a panel of doorbell buttons alongside its front door. Schulze stopped at the second building and peered at the names on the doorbells. He pressed the top one. Val's nerves jangled. This was the time of greatest risk: was he about to double-cross them, hand them over to a government official and claim a fat reward? He looked like the kind of man who had done well for himself, and would be well paid for his loyalty to the authorities. The doctor didn't make eye contact with Val. He glanced up and down the street and occasionally at the doorbell, as if staring at it would make the tenant respond.

After a full five minutes, the heavy door slowly creaked open and a middle-aged woman peered out. She seemed to recognise Schulze, and gave a faint smile, but said nothing. She looked down at Val, her eyes half closed and her lips pursed: was she curious, perhaps suspicious? The doctor said a few words to her in German and the woman, who Val now saw was wearing the emerald-green uniform of a housekeeper, stood back and opened the door fully. They walked up four flights of stairs then came to a landing with three doors to apartments. Number 12's door was ajar, and they entered. As they did, a man emerged. He walked with a stick, hampered by a shortened right leg. The doctor greeted the man politely, if not in an overfriendly way, and added a few words of explanation. The man smiled and held his hand out to Val, who responded with a quiet *"Guten Tag"*. No names were exchanged.

The man spoke to the housekeeper, who went away to make coffee. They were steered into the living room, which showed affluence and style. Annoyingly – Val felt – Casey let out a long, low whistle, showing how impressed he was with the obvious signs of wealth. The room was furnished with the best quality carpets and antiques. Everything was immaculate, clean and polished. Beautiful Meissen ceramics and Venetian glassware were on display, along with paintings of rural scenes on the walls that would not look out of place in a fine art gallery. A bookcase contained leather-bound volumes and legal journals. Val now realised the doctor was not the most wealthy man in the town; this honour fell to the deputy magistrate. German society was more class-conscious than in Britain in many ways and these two gentlemen seemed to be vestiges of the old-money landowning classes that had managed to protect some of their wealth through the war.

The deputy magistrate took Val through to an anteroom that contained a writing desk, a telescope at the window and, curiously, a collection of old mechanical toys and wooden soldier puppets with disturbingly realistic faces. A rear shelf displayed military items: naval binoculars, an *oberstleutnant's* hat, a small map of northern France dated 1917, showing red and black sequences of crosses; the front lines of the German and British trenches. Inconspicuously hanging in a wooden frame were six First World War medals, Val noted; she assumed these had been awarded to the deputy magistrate.

Among the relics was a battered child's suitcase that looked out of place in the room, but when the deputy magistrate took it down and opened the lid, Val knew immediately what was hidden in the case – a Marconi Type A Mk III portable radio, the lightweight model she had used during her SOE operations in the war. It was complete with aerial and connection cables to the mains electricity – but would the old relic work?

TWENTY-FOUR

In the early hours of Tuesday morning, in de Havilland's offices at Tempelhof, Artur Franken dialled Darley's office number in England.

Their conversation was short.

"Given you say the Dove left just after 9p.m.," said Darley, "then the flight is already several hours overdue. The security people here have alerted air traffic services in England and on the Continent. Officially, they are hoping that the aircraft landed somewhere and somehow lost radio contact. But off the record, the operations director here is assuming that, in the absence of any reports, the aircraft must have crashed in the North Sea, exactly as we planned. Good work, Artur. Your initiative in suggesting the bomb then making it yourself will be noted – and, I'm sure, rewarded."

"Thank you, sir. I'm pleased that we have eliminated a traitor to communism – and, of course, the British and American agents."

"Indeed. It's unfortunate that Devon had to die as well, but these kind of circumstances cannot be avoided in our work." After a pause, Darley continued, "I will go home now, but return to the factory in the morning. We must act as anyone would expect us to, remember: shocked, concerned, but keen to reassure everyone that the Dove is a first-rate aircraft. If we maintain business as usual, no one will suspect our involvement."

"Clearly understood, sir!" Franken stood to attention, clicked his heels and hung up. He smiled to himself. The new, united Soviet state of Greater Germany will come about all the sooner, thanks to my work, he thought proudly.

Franken had been very happy to pass to his East German handlers technical information on the development of advanced radar on board the Dove that Darley had been feeding to him. But now he was working close to the front line. He revelled in his role in the destruction of the aircraft and the elimination of a defector and the British agents. He would be seen as an important, respected player in the reinstatement of his country as the leading state in world politics, surpassing even the Russians. He would enjoy the admiration and praise of his parents, his university friends, the German people. Newspapers would interview him, laud praise upon him and recommend him for an award of a medal for his conduct. Even as the leader of the small communist cell in his hometown after the war, he knew he was destined for greater responsibility, and at last the time had come to act. Franken had been introduced to Jocelyn Darley by a cell member when they attended a business conference in Paris a year earlier, where he learned of Darley's commitment to the cause of communism. They quickly established a bond based on their ideological beliefs.

Franken now saw his role clearly. He would influence; he would act; he would be a driver of the cause. The wealthy families that had governed Germany before the war would come to understand that the rebirth of Germany's strength and position in the world could only be achieved by alignment to the communist doctrine. The foolish complaints from workers over higher food prices and wage reductions were merely minor obstacles to the rapid establishment of a socialist German state.

He expected to be given a senior position in the Party as a reward for his service and solidarity. The subjugation of the country by American and British capitalists and their military would come to an end when the East German forces, backed by the Russians, invaded West Germany. He was confident that this would happen in the very near future. Who knew? Perhaps even the French communists would rise up and destroy the bourgeois capitalists who ruled their lives, ultimately leading to a united Europe under one red flag.

Franken was so pleased with his work that he decided he was entitled to a reward – a short hiking holiday around the Brandenburg lakes. He believed in the true German pastime of exercise in the fresh air as the way to gain strength and clarity of mind. He would take his camping equipment and enjoy the freedom and peace of the countryside. It was indeed a great fortune, he concluded, that his wife was at her parents' house for a week. And being away from the office for a few days meant he would not have to face any difficult questions about the aircraft. He would be all innocence on his return, unaware of its disappearance.

Before leaving the de Havilland office, Franken left a note for callers on his desk that he would be away for two days. Satisfied with his work and leaving everything tidy, he left the airport building and drove the short distance home. He double-checked that no bomb-making materials remained in his flat, packed up his bivouac tent and outdoor gear and loaded it all into his car. He took a nap in his clothes for a few hours before calling his wife to tell her his plans, then departed just after daybreak. For the time being, he could not expect the praise and congratulations he deserved; he must be patient. On his return, he would play his part: the saddened, shocked colleague.

TWENTY-FIVE

She couldn't stand it any longer. She had to find out what was going on. Why hadn't Adam been in contact? At her desk at the bank, Hannah glanced at the calendar to confirm it was indeed Tuesday. She looked at the telephone with burning frustration: would he call this morning, or should she get in touch with his boss to find out where he was? She shivered with fear. Perhaps Adam no longer had any interest in her. Was he more concerned with his job? After all, he had put off their wedding several times. Maybe he had met someone else; he seemed to have been away more than ever recently. Instantly, she told herself that was nonsense, she must be patient, he was doing important work that he loved. But did he love *her* as much as he loved his job? She couldn't bear to think of losing him.

Hannah felt that it would be intrusive to call Mr Darley. She would look stupid if everything was alright, it would embarrass Adam, and he might be angry with her. She had met Darley before and knew him to be a busy, successful businessman; he wouldn't be happy to receive a call from a worried girlfriend of one of his employees.

But her mind turned to David Porter. She could legitimately ask him if he had heard anything. Adam and Porter were friends, and Adam had said that Porter was closely involved with de Havilland.

Hannah took the lift to the ground floor, then went through a door to the rear of the building and the telephone switchboard room. She had a good pal working there who she had known in Hong Kong, Pamela, whom she would ask a favour.

"Hello, Hannah, how are you, my dearest? Oh my, you're looking a bit peaky."

"I'm fine thanks, Pamela," said Hannah.

Pamela sat on a high chair opposite an array of plugs and cables, headphones on and a pencil in hand. She wore a tight black skirt and a ruffled shocking pink blouse, had backcombed blonde hair and a generous layer of make-up.

"Well, to be honest, I need to contact one of Adam's old friends who now works for BOAC. But I don't have a number for him and don't know where to look. I'm worried. Adam is away on a trip and should be back by now. He hasn't been in touch."

"Where does this person work in BOAC? I might be able to find him through their switchboard," said Pamela in her best upper-class English, forgetting she wasn't dealing with a bank customer.

"I… I think he has something to do with finding new places to fly to. His name is David Porter," said Hannah.

Pamela, perhaps seeing that Hannah was distressed, softened her tone. "Leave it with me, dearie. I'll go through to BOAC's switchboard to see what I can find, and let you know. Now, you go back to your desk. Don't worry, I won't be long."

She was true to her word. It was no more than twenty minutes later when Pamela called Hannah. "I have the number, dear. He works in the new destinations department, apparently, at the Imperial Airways building in Victoria. I could call the number, if you like?"

Hannah's self-confidence sank. Should she really ask to speak to Porter? Would it upset Adam to know she had called him?

"Hannah, are you there, my love?" said Pamela.

She snapped out of her trance. "Yes, yes, sorry. If you could dial the number and put me through, that would be great. Thank you so much."

Hannah heard some clicks and a buzz, then silence. A minute passed, then another. After three minutes, her nerves were shredded. She thought she might have been cut off and forgotten about. Her heart was racing. Then there was a jarring click and Pamela's voice came over the line again. "Putting you through to BOAC."

Silence again. "Hello," said Hannah, cautiously.

"Good morning, Jane Johnson speaking, Mr Porter's secretary."

"Oh, hello, Miss Johnson, my name is Hannah Shaw. I was hoping to speak to David – Mr Porter."

"In what regard, may I ask?"

"It's about my fiancé, Adam Devon. He's an old friend of Mr Porter."

Hannah heard the secretary let out a sigh. "Is this a business call, Miss Shaw?" Jane Johnson sounded wary. Hannah wondered if she was the kind of secretary who took pride in shielding her boss from any calls or visitors that she saw as frivolous or time-wasting.

"No, not really. I'm concerned: I haven't heard from Adam for three days, he's away on a flight, and I hoped that Mr Porter might be able to shed some light on where he might be."

Jane Johnson tutted. "Mr Porter is a very busy man, Miss Shaw. He plans to leave the office at noon today and has a lot to do before then. If you would like to write to him, I'm sure he will attend to your enquiry. I wish you a good morning."

"But it's impor—" Hannah slumped back in her chair. Jane Johnson had hung up.

***

Hannah decided to go out for morning coffee. She walked briskly along Lime Street, past the Lloyd's of London building and into Leadenhall Market. She wanted to keep her mind busy and try to shake off the stress of Adam's absence. After a quick coffee, she walked past the Lamb pub. Wooden beer crates were stacked outside. A florist was arranging flowers and placing bouquets in vases in the window of the shop. Crossing Gracechurch Street, Hannah stopped and looked in the window of a ladies' clothes shop. It had the latest pencil skirts and slim-fitting jackets in the window. Hannah sighed. She would love to buy some of these beautiful clothes, but she and Adam were saving hard for a deposit on a house.

All these distractions helped Hannah relax, helped her think straight and consider what to do. She walked to the corner of Cornhill and looked down towards Bank. At the far end was Mappin and Webb jewellers, where only three years earlier Adam had bought her engagement ring. The memory motivated her, and she knew she had to do something; she couldn't sit around doing nothing. And then she had an idea. She hurried back to the office and spoke to her supervisor. She needed some time off work.

TWENTY-SIX

Val sat at a beautifully burnished mahogany antique card table with inlaid green leather and marquetry. After taking down the suitcase-radio from the shelf, the deputy magistrate laid it carefully on the table, the nearest point to an electric socket. He plugged it in, unwound a wire aerial, laid it on top of a glass cabinet, and tied an earthing cable to the cast-iron radiator. Val was impressed, this man knew how to set up a radio effectively. With an almost loving touch, he brushed away imaginary dust with his fingertips, turned it on, and sat opposite Val, frowning in concentration. As the radio came to life, Val placed the headphones carefully over her ears, the sensation familiar from her SOE days.

Once an operative learns and uses Morse code, it stays in the memory for life. Val also had imprinted on her mind the wavelength for the MI6 listening station in London that was set up during the war, where messages could be sent at any time of day or night. She tuned in the set, placed her right index finger gently, but firmly, over the Morse key, and sent her message: 'VHB calling London'. She just hoped that messages were still being picked up. Nervously, she sat back, waiting for a response. Minutes passed in silence, so she transmitted again. Another long period of silence had Val's nerves tensing, but then she was pleasantly surprised when a reply came back: 'VHB switch to AW' – the coded wavelength that only senior field agents knew.

Val was able to transmit her full message. She described the explosion and crash, the position of the Dove and the condition of all passengers. Next she requested help in reaching West Germany, even though she had been warned that no help could be provided if things went wrong. She added that the aircraft had been damaged by a bomb, and ended by saying that she would make contact again in six hours. The moment after London had acknowledged her message she turned the radio off – force of habit from wartime days when the Germans had tracked transmissions to pinpoint the location of agents. But it was best practice in any event; East German police could be hunting for them.

She thanked the deputy magistrate, who nodded politely and packed up the radio. She said she would like to return for a further transmission if the doctor could drive her back, and walked through to the reception room where Drake Casey and the doctor waited. The housekeeper was preparing more coffee and sandwiches in the small kitchen. Val noticed she did this with a stern look on her face – showing her disapproval, or displeasure, perhaps, at the presence of these intruders disrupting her routine. Certainly, the woman was not as welcoming as her employer. Everyone sat down and ate and drank in silence. What could they talk about? Val and Casey could not answer any questions. When the housekeeper cleared away the coffee cups and plates, Dr Schulze stood and picked up his coat. A sign to leave. Val wanted to display her gratitude in a small way: she genuinely meant it, but also appreciated that it would help the men feel part of their cause; they were doing their bit. She held her hands together as if she was saying a brief prayer. Both men smiled.

***

When they returned to the barn, Val related the details of the deputy magistrate's radio, the message she had transmitted, and her plan for a further call. Devon and the others listened intently before Devon interjected, sounding excited.

"Val, listen, while you were away I thought up a plan to get us out of here. I've been looking at the map. There's an airfield about five miles to the south – another wartime field abandoned by the Germans. Here, look, it's in the direction of Magdeburg, name of Moser, but it's just outside the return corridor. I've seen it from a distance on previous flights, and although I can't be sure, I think the runway is serviceable. If we can get there and call in a rescue flight, I think we could all get out. It would be dangerous – we know that the Soviets are willing to attack any aircraft they see outside the corridor. All you need to do is get the RAF to put on a flight. The runway is long enough for a DC3."

Val and Devon were the only ones present who knew that the British armed forces and secret service would not be willing to get involved. Now she had to break the news to the group.

"Sorry, gentlemen. I have asked for a rescue flight, but we should not bank on one arriving. We can't expect any help from the RAF or anyone else – that was made absolutely clear to me before the operation. It's too politically sensitive. If there is official sanction from the British or American governments for this mission, the Russians are highly likely to use the incident as a reason to attack and annex West Germany. I don't think we have any option but to walk cross-country to the West German border, travelling by night and hiding up during the day."

"But, Val, I know that the government doesn't want to take ownership for the assignment but a quick in-and-out landing and take-off would only mean the aircraft would be on the ground ten minutes.

If we're all ready to board, it could be less," said Devon. "You could at least look at the map showing where Moser is."

"And you gotta be kidding about Raleigh, right?" said Casey. "He can just about stand up – it would be a huge effort to get him to the airfield, and don't even think about him walking any further. And I'm not sure Leonid here is much of a walker."

Val tried not to lose her temper, but the two men were not listening to her. "There's no argument, get that straight. We will all have to help Raleigh along. As much as I would like a rescue flight, that's just not possible. That's it." Val turned her back on them and walked across to the far corner of the barn, kicked some straw into a heap and lay down to try to sleep. "Stay quiet, everyone, and wake me in an hour."

TWENTY-SEVEN

At a quarter to twelve, Hannah was waiting at the foot of the steps that swept up to the Imperial Airways Empire Terminal in Victoria. As well as being the conduit for passengers going to Croydon and London airports, the building served as the head office for BOAC. Hannah was gambling on a hunch – that David Porter would come down those stairs at around midday and she could speak to him directly. He wouldn't dismiss her as his secretary had done, she was confident of that.

Hannah looked up at the clock at the top of the central tower of the imposing building. It was ten past, and there was no sign of him. Every minute, the doors swung open and a wave of office workers came out to go for lunch or for a walk in the park. The more smartly dressed executives hailed taxis, and some chauffeur-driven cars were parked in the street.

At a quarter past, Hannah spotted him. Carrying a bulky briefcase, he looked more stern and focused than all the other employees. He made for his car, which a garage attendant had brought up from the basement for him. Hannah had to be quick. She dashed along the street and caught Porter just as he was about to open the driver's door of the dark-blue Jaguar Mk VII. He looked startled by her sudden appearance and turned quickly. "Oh – it's Hannah, isn't it? How can I help you?"

"David, I'm very sorry, I have to speak to you. Can you spare me five minutes?"

"Ah, Hannah. Yes, we must talk."

Hannah noticed that Porter didn't seem surprised to see her.

"But I'm in a hurry, so get in the car and we can have a chat for a few minutes before I leave. I'm on my way to Hatfield to see Darley."

"Well, I can come with you most of the way – perhaps you could drop me off at Adam's house at Welham Green?"

"Good idea. Jump in." Porter said little for the first couple of miles as he negotiated through central London's heavy, slow-moving traffic. After passing through Islington and the wealthy districts around Highgate, the traffic eased and they started to make good progress.

"Hannah, I have some news for you. I have heard from de Havilland that Adam's aircraft is missing. We were expecting it to arrive in the early hours of this morning, but so far we have no news. That's why I'm on my way to Hatfield, to see if there's anything I can do."

Hannah let out a gasp and a shuddering cry. She clasped her hands over her mouth. She tried to ask for more information, but couldn't speak. Porter gave her a few moments and said, "We are doing everything we can to locate the aircraft. It's probably had engine trouble and landed somewhere remote. I gather that de Havilland are in touch with the air traffic control people, and they hope to hear something soon." Porter didn't add that the aircraft could have crashed on land or into the sea; that would be unnecessary speculation.

"Is the RAF out looking for them?" whispered Hannah.

"No, that's not possible just now. There are political issues at stake, and the powers-that-be are not willing to get the RAF or anyone else involved."

"*What?* What do you mean?" Hannah shouted. Porter flinched. "Sorry, David. But surely there must be something that can be done rather than just wait for the bloody phone to ring?"

"We have to be patient for the time being – believe me, I'm as anxious as you to find out what has happened."

Hannah collected herself; there was no point in blaming Porter or losing her temper.

They were out of London now on the A1 trunk road. Porter sped up. "Look, Hannah, I'll explain in more detail when we get to Adam's house. We're only a few minutes from the turning for Welham Green." Porter sighed. "It's complicated. Adam was doing some work for the government that is secret – something more than test-flying the Dove and the navigation radar."

"I knew he was up to something. *I just knew it.* I should have guessed it would be dangerous if you had a hand in it!" Hannah was bitter and didn't care that she was showing it. "It sounds like you've used him, knowing he likes to do risky jobs – the exciting ones, as you call them."

They had just turned into the village. Hannah pointed to the last house on the left, and Porter pulled over and parked.

Closing the door behind her, Hannah led Porter into the living room. "Well, what's Adam doing for you?" She sat down and gestured for Porter to do the same.

"This is highly confidential. What I'm going to tell you cannot be repeated to anyone, OK?" Porter didn't wait for an answer. "As you know, Adam has been test-flying the Dove on various routes, including to Berlin. This latest assignment involves bringing back some important passengers." Porter stopped. He knew he should not mention that one of the passengers was a Russian defector. But he also knew that Hannah was a determined, resilient woman – and, in his judgement, trustworthy. "Strictly between us, I can tell you that one of the passengers is an important Soviet scientist who wishes to come and work for the West. The flight was to bring him and three of our people back."

"But that shouldn't stop the RAF or anyone else searching for the aircraft, surely?" Hannah sounded firm.

"You know I'm not officially part of MI6 or any other government body. My job was to recruit the right pilots from my RAF days and the right aircraft to undertake this and other assignments. They only feed me information that I need to know. And at the moment they are saying it's impossible for anything official to be done. I'm sorry, Hannah, I know you will hate me for involving Adam, but there's little I can do now. If you wish, you can come with me to Hatfield to see Darley. He may have more information he can share with us."

"No. No, thank you, David. I will give you the telephone number for the house here and my office number so you can let me know if you hear anything." Hannah's tone had softened; she didn't wish to alienate Porter. Suddenly she wanted to be alone, and she stood up. "I'll be alright from here, David. Thanks for updating me."

***

Hannah spent a restless couple of hours waiting for news. She had nightmarish visions of Adam lying in a field somewhere in Germany – or, worse, crashed in the sea. As she made herself some tea, she was jolted by the sound of the telephone ringing.

It was David Porter. "Hannah, we have had some news. Adam and the passengers are all safe. It seems there was a problem with the aircraft, and they crash-landed near Magdeburg in East Germany. We don't know exactly where at this stage. They will contact us again this evening, when we might get to know more. I'm on my way back to London, and I will keep you in the picture."

Hannah slumped down in a chair in relief. "That's great news, David. Surely the RAF can now do something to get them back?"

"I'm afraid that's still out of the question, as the position hasn't changed there. The plan is for the group to try to walk out to the West German border, but of course it's risky – they will be hunted by the East German police and security agents. We must trust in the escape skills of the agents, who are very experienced." It was a weak effort to pacify Hannah. "Please be assured—"

Hannah interrupted Porter. "David, thanks for this, but I have to go now. Please call me when you have further news." She wasn't minded to tell Porter that she had an idea.

"Yes, I'll do that, goodbye."

***

Hannah's fingers shook as she dialled directory enquiries. She asked for Cambridge air taxi services, but the operator had no listing under that name. Then she asked her to look up an air taxi or charter service in the name of Fitzjohn. There were numbers available for various members of the Fitzjohn family and businesses, but nothing relating to aviation. Hannah became frustrated. How else could she contact Henry? The operator searched patiently in silence for a minute, then came back. She had found a listing for Granta Air Services at Cambridge airport – was that the number Hannah required? Hannah accepted her offer to be put through straight away.

A well-spoken young woman answered. Hannah asked to speak to Fitzjohn, but was advised he was not in the office at the moment, he was in the hangar. He would be very happy to ring back, probably within the hour, if that was convenient. Hannah was reluctant to divulge Adam's home number to him, but now was not the time for sensitivity.

It was only twenty minutes later when the phone rang.

"Hello, Hannah speaking."

"Well, I say, such a lovely surprise – very nice to hear from you, Hannah. Henry Fitzjohn here. How can I help an old friend?"

"I need to meet you urgently, Henry."

"Really? Well, I'm very busy just now. But I would be delighted to meet you at five o'clock this evening if you are in Cambridge?"

"I'm in Welham Green, but I can use Adam's car and be there for five," said Hannah.

"Splendid. Let's say the bar at the University Arms Hotel. I believe you are familiar with the place."

"That's fine. I will see you there."

***

Hannah was tense as she sat at a quiet table with her bitter lemon. She wasn't surprised that Fitzjohn was late; she believed he lived his life to suit himself and wouldn't care if he kept someone waiting. She knew she had to bury her fears, stay focused on what she wanted from him. Her Israeli Secret Service training had included managing stressful situations, such as being interrogated. She was determined to stay in control to get what she wanted, to treat the task as she would a field operation. She saw Fitzjohn enter the lobby and come through to the bar. He collected a drink and came over to where she was sitting.

"Hannah, lovely to see you, my dear. Looking wonderful as always. How are you?" Fitzjohn bent forward to kiss her on the cheek. She overcame her instinct to shy away; she didn't want to distance herself from him.

"Hello, Henry. I'm fine, thank you. And thank you for meeting me at short notice. I have something I need to ask you to do for me. And for Adam."

"Oh, really?" Fitzjohn's cynicism was clear in his voice. "How interesting that you should want me to do something for you, especially after the last time we met, when you wouldn't do something for me." Fitzjohn gave Hannah his best lecherous look and sat back, slowly folding his fingers together. "However, setting that aside, tell me what you need my assistance with, and we will see what can be done."

"What I'm going to tell you is very sensitive. I'm sure I don't have to tell an ex-RAF officer and MP that you must keep this secret."

"Absolutely fine. I understand. Go ahead – what is it exactly you want?"

"Adam is in difficulty on an assignment he was carrying out for MI6. A flight to Berlin, returning with a valuable cargo. It seems the aircraft developed a problem on the way back and has crash-landed in East Germany, somewhere near Magdeburg, apparently. I don't know exactly where at the moment. Adam and the four passengers are all safe but they need to be rescued, and the British government are unwilling to help – in fact, they will deny any responsibility for the flight and the passengers."

Fitzjohn interrupted, guessing the nature of the flight. "These passengers – is there anything special you'd like to tell me about them?"

"You might as well know, and I'm only telling you this because you're a Member of Parliament. In addition to British field agents, there is a Russian defector. I don't know his name or anything about him but he's very important, I gather. That was the whole purpose of the assignment: to get him over to the West. The crash was inside the return air corridor. We are waiting for a radio message advising where they are exactly, where they can be picked up, and when."

"Goodness, quite a mess. But how can I help?"

"I want you to fly your air taxi over to East Germany, pick them up and return either to the UK or West Germany. You will, of course, be well rewarded for this."

Fitzjohn remained silent. Hannah could see the reluctance in his face as he took a deep breath and shook his head. "No, sorry, not for me this one, no matter what fee you would pay. The risks are just too great. I could get myself arrested in the East, my aircraft confiscated, perhaps even shot down. Terribly bad for business, and the reputation of a British MP, you understand."

"Hang on, Henry, you don't even know what we're willing to pay. You will receive £1,000 for the successful return of Adam and all the passengers." Hannah dug her fingernails into the palm of her hand as she spoke – the money was most of what she and Devon had saved for the deposit on their house.

"Very generous. Very generous indeed. But I'm sorry, it's just not on. There's too much at stake." Fitzjohn threw back the last of his whisky and went to stand. "But it's always a pleasure to meet you, Hannah. Perhaps we can meet again some time?"

"Sit down. I have something else to say. Clearly you need a greater incentive to fly the mission. Perhaps we can discuss the little smuggling business you operate from Cambridge. Diamonds, I believe."

Fitzjohn sat down.

Hannah leant forward and spoke quietly. "It would be very unfortunate if this became public. That would end your career as quick as you like, and you could face a large fine and possibly a prison sentence. Certain friends of mine who know about your business have given assurances that your extra-curricular activities will stay confidential, assuming you take on the rescue."

"This is blackmail, Hannah, and I won't have anything to do with it!" Fitzjohn was fuming.

"Don't be a fool, Henry. It's simply a business deal. You get the

£1,000 and you can go on unhindered with your air taxi and import business in peace." Hannah was getting anxious. Time was of the essence. She wanted a decision.

"These friends of yours… are they connected to a particular state in the Middle East, by any chance?" said Fitzjohn.

"I'm not willing to discuss who they are, but you can be assured they mean business and are very well connected in Westminster." That was a bluff. Hannah had no idea what links Mossad had with British MPs, but it caught Fitzjohn's attention. He sat back, a frown on his forehead, and he closed his eyes for a few moments. Then a smile slowly formed.

"Well, look, my dear, I think we can come to a mutually satisfactory arrangement. Here are my conditions. Yes, I will happily take the fee as offered, thank you. And I expect absolute secrecy over the business activities of Granta Air Services. You will appreciate that your own situation requires a degree of confidentiality – your background, let's say, and that's something I can assure you of."

"That's good, Henry…"

"But I have one more requirement if we are to strike a deal. You will recall from Hong Kong that I was very fond of you, but you… scorned me. Well, now you can put that right. I'm sure this lovely hotel has rooms free this evening that we can make good use of." Fitzjohn took Hannah's hands in his and pulled her towards him. "Give me a few hours of your time, and I will fly your rescue mission. I assume you care sufficiently for Devon to be willing to carry out this little favour?"

Hannah gasped, her heart pounded and she shook as she relived the terror of the evening in Hong Kong when Fitzjohn had tried to rape her. "No, no, I can't do it!" Her dismay and anger showed fervently in her face.

"Don't dismiss my offer too readily, young lady. It's a simple favour which I'm sure will give you great pleasure to undertake."

"You're a monster, Henry – how can you ask me to do this? I won't do it."

"Very well, then I wish you a pleasant evening. I will take my chance with your Israeli friends. Just let them try anything and they will see how well the British intelligence services protect our MPs."

This time Fitzjohn got up immediately and headed for the door to the hotel lobby. Hannah sat there in shock. The realisation that she had no other option to rescue Adam petrified her. But there was nothing else for it. She ran out of the hotel and stopped Fitzjohn in the street.

"Henry, listen." She hesitated, then went on, "Alright, it's a deal, I will sleep with you, but not tonight. We need to get going with the flight – there's no time to lose. As soon as I hear where Adam and the others are, I will ring you. But I promise you, I will honour my commitment whenever you want after you return." Hannah gripped Fitzjohn's arm and her eyes pleaded with him.

"Well, that's more like it. But am I to trust you? That's the question," said Fitzjohn slowly. "You know what, I do trust you; you're foolishly in love with Devon and will do anything to get him back. I'll go over to the airfield now. I will consult with one of my chaps who flew in the Berlin Airlift – he will be able to help with the flight plan and landing. Ring me this evening at eight o'clock. I will need to know exactly where to pick up the passengers."

Hannah agreed. With a shudder at the thought of what she had promised, she walked quickly to the hotel car park and drove back to Welham Green.

***

Hannah arrived at the house a little before 6p.m. and immediately telephoned Porter's London number. Miss Johnson must have been forewarned of a possible call from her, as she put her straight through.

Hannah told Porter that Fitzjohn was willing to carry out the rescue flight. In response to his questioning, she mentioned the cash payment she would be making, but she left out details of the other incentives to undertake the task. Hannah needed to know the name and location of the airfield where the rescue was to take place, so she could brief Fitzjohn.

Porter expressed surprise at Fitzjohn's willingness to do the job, even for £1,000, but he agreed with Hannah that she had no choice – it all depended on Val and the others being able to get to a suitable airfield at the right time for a pick-up. Porter said he would call his contact at MI6 to make them aware of the flight. A lot needed to be coordinated if the rescue had any chance of success.

TWENTY-EIGHT

Angus Ballantyne marched quickly from the lift, across the hall and headed for C's office. Kate Samways, C's secretary, raised her hand to stop him entering.

"Is he here, Kate?" Ballantyne said. "I need to see him immediately."

Kate knew when something was important or urgent, and waved him through.

"You have news for me, Ballantyne?" said C, who had been briefed on the aircraft's disappearance by phone at his home that morning.

"Yes, sir. The good news is that we've had contact from Hetherington-Brown. She has managed to get hold of a radio transmitter and sent a Morse message through to MI6 in London."

C sat up straight and interrupted Ballantyne. "Really? So they haven't ditched in the sea. That's something. We can stand down the air-sea rescue operation."

"Yes, sir. But the not-so-good news is that the aircraft crash-landed in East Germany. Seems there was a bomb on board that went off but failed to detonate correctly. They all survived but Raleigh is badly injured."

"What? Bloody hell," gasped C, "so the East Germans must have got wind of the operation and planted the bomb? There must be a mole in the operation somewhere, and they will know we have Leonid. They will be out hunting the group if they know they have survived. And Leonid – what of him in the crash?"

"No specific comment from Hetherington-Brown, but we can assume he is safe and well," said Ballantyne.

"Right. Do you know their whereabouts?"

"They are laid up on a farm somewhere near Magdeburg, maybe fifty miles from the West German border. We need to get them out by sending in a commando extraction party. I'd like your permission, sir, to set this up with the RAF."

"You know it's impossible for us to intervene. If the rescue were intercepted in hostile territory, the matter would turn into a major incident. That, Ballantyne, will create an enormous backlash. You are aware that the MoD are very concerned about Russian military manoeuvres along the whole of the Soviet bloc, and this could give them just the excuse they need to invade West Germany. No, if this blows up we will deny involvement by our government and say the affair is a private matter of people-smuggling – that was the whole point of using de Havilland and the Dove as a cover. I'm afraid the British armed forces can't help in any way. They will have to get back over the border under their own steam. When the aircraft is found, our government will simply say the pilot and passengers must have escaped to the West."

"Sir, with respect, with Raleigh wounded they will not be able to travel far—"

"To hell with Raleigh, Ballantyne; he must take his chances. You know my view on the wisdom of taking him on this mission in the first place!" C took a few seconds to calm his voice. "No, the mission's aim is to get the Russian across to the West – his weapons knowledge is vital to us. Hetherington-Brown knows this. I hope her judgement is not impaired by any misplaced association with Raleigh. And another thing: Leonid must not fall into the hands of the Germans, as they will pass him back to the Soviets. They're unlikely to execute him, he's too valuable. He will be back at work in no time, and after a thorough and doubtless painful debrief, he will be able to tell his masters all about his handlers and the flight out of Berlin. No, he must be eliminated. Make sure Brown is clear on that point, Ballantyne."

"Yes, sir, that's understood. But sir, surely we can attempt a rescue with our own agents?"

"MI6, you mean? Out of the question, man! What are you thinking of? No further exposure of British agents or military personnel will be entertained. I repeat, the group must look to their resources. Brown has extensive SOE experience, does she not? Travelling by night, living off the land, that sort of thing. Then let her use her skills to get them all, and especially the Russian, into West Germany. All they have to do is get across the border."

"Sir, that's something like fifty miles away. It'll be a hell of a job to travel there undetected. Even if they make it close to the border, the area is alive with guards."

"That's as may be, but it's the only option they have. How will you contact Brown again?"

"She will be calling in again later this evening, sir. Contact will be very short, of course, to prevent detection. I will let you know what she has to say."

When Ballantyne walked back through C's secretary's office, Kate stopped him and called him over, whispering that he should urgently contact his office. Ballantyne dashed down four flights of stairs to his own department, where he picked up a handwritten note asking him to phone David Porter.

***

Within minutes Ballantyne had returned the call. Porter told him about his meeting and subsequent discussion with Hannah, and the plan for Fitzjohn to fly the rescue mission. Understandably, Ballantyne was sceptical. He doubted that a commercial pilot would be able to find the airfield, land safely, pick up the group, and escape without detection. He told Porter this, and received assurances that the pilot was one of the best around for this type of work. Porter was clear on one point: it was essential that the passengers were ready to board the aircraft immediately – it must not wait on the ground. Ballantyne must ensure that the radio people were fully briefed on the message they had to pass to Val when she called in; there might be little chance of further messages after that.

Porter insisted that he had to have official sanction for the flight. His involvement meant he risked his job with BOAC, and even Fitzjohn could be in serious trouble unless he could cite some form of government contract or military order. The consequences of a failed operation would clearly be catastrophic for all involved, but even a successful mission could lead to prosecution for illegal flight operations and unlawful entry into the country of a foreign national.

Ballantyne had to concede that Porter was right. Even if Fitzjohn hadn't yet woken up to the risks he was taking, it was right that the mission should be endorsed by MI6. He also knew that getting C to put something in writing would either be impossible or would take days to achieve. He chose the only route open to him. He sent a telegram to Porter: *TOP SECRET STOP LEONID AND COMPANY RESCUE FLIGHT APPROVED STOP*. Ballantyne's neck was now on the block. If the mission failed or there was any leak of the telegram before the team had been rescued, he could expect serious trouble from the chief.

The next thing Ballantyne addressed was the message that the radio operators at the London listening station were to give to Val. It had to be precise and clear. It was vital that the operators got the exact location of the airfield from her so that Fitzjohn could be briefed. Ballantyne phoned the head of communications and gave her very specific instructions – they had to have the location of the rescue airfield and agree a time for the pick-up.

TWENTY-NINE

Right on time, the doctor returned. Val and Casey walked out to the car and, without stopping, opened the doors and got in, Val in the front.

"Everything in good shape, Doctor?" she said.

"Yes, I think so. The deputy magistrate is waiting to welcome you to his home again. But be careful – the other residents in the building cannot be trusted. There are informers everywhere, so we must be as quiet as possible. And this must be your last visit. If you are seen again in town, it will undoubtedly be reported to the police."

"Understood. I hope I shall have no need for the radio after tonight."

The housekeeper opened the street door promptly and led the way upstairs, as before. A coffee pot and fine china cups were already laid out. The deputy magistrate always showed hospitality to guests, no matter what the circumstances. The radio was waiting on the card table, connected, aerial in place, switched on and warmed up. Val immediately got to work. London responded quickly. Val was very surprised but thankful to hear that a rescue flight would pick them up the following evening at 6p.m., providing they could get to an airfield. The pick-up would be an hour before sunset, allowing the aircraft to land in daylight and depart under the cover of early twilight. Val was hugely relieved that Devon had named Moser airfield and given its location, so she passed this on to London. She asked what the contingency plans were if they missed the aircraft or the aircraft failed to arrive – all standard procedure for a covert operation. But in this case there was no contingency plan to get them out; they would have to fend for themselves and try to escape across the border.

When she switched off the radio, Val heard the gentle click of the apartment door closing. She wondered who had come in, or gone out. When she returned to the main reception room, the two old gentlemen were seated, glasses of brandy in their hands. Drake Casey stood admiring the pictures on the wall and the framed photographs. Silently, Casey pointed to a photograph of what looked like a very young Dr Schulze with the deputy magistrate in German army uniforms in a typical French village. Val looked at the photo. They shared a long friendship, she thought, and they were loyal: to the Fatherland and to each other.

Dr Schulze slowly drank the last of his brandy and stood up.

"I'm ready to go," said Val. "*Danke, danke schön,* Herr Magistrat."

The deputy magistrate held out his hand, and Val shook it warmly.

"What news?" said Casey.

"I'll brief you when we get back. There's no need to burden our friends here unnecessarily. But we will need more food and drink. Doctor, can we stop somewhere where we can buy food?"

"That will not be possible. Shops close early in East Germany. But I have some bread and cheese and beer in my car for you."

"That's very considerate, Doc," said Casey.

"My pleasure. As I said, we like to support alternative ideals to the regime we live under, in any small way we can. Now please, let us return to my car. I will take you back to the barn."

The group walked quickly to where the car was parked. A few other people were out in the evening, some strolling in the fresh air, others going to work or on their way home. There were also a few lucky people having a drink at one of the *stubes* in the town.

The doctor drove steadily, so as not to attract attention. Val looked over her shoulder and saw Drake Casey sitting sideways in the rear seat, glancing forward and back. After a couple of minutes, he caught sight of a pre-war VW staying too close behind them. Half a mile further on, Casey said, "We're being followed, Val – black VW."

"Can you shake him off, Doc? How about a right and right again up ahead?" Val said.

The doctor took the first right, then reduced his speed and turned left and left again, back to a crossroads on the road they had left. He went straight across then quickly turned right into a narrow, curving road, lined by thick conifer trees. Once around the corner, he stopped and killed the lights.

"Good work, fella, we've lost them," said Casey.

"I will stay for two minutes, then we can continue. This road is an alternative route to the place you are staying. But please keep a lookout."

"Sure will, no worries about that." Casey clicked on the safety catch to his gun.

***

Once they were back at the barn and the doctor had left, Val called everyone together. "I got through to London. They have arranged a rescue mission for us at Moser airfield tomorrow at 6p.m. I have no details of the aircraft, but it's not the RAF. Probably a freelancer out to earn money. Whoever it is, it's our only chance of getting out by air."

"Excellent, Val," said Devon. "Let's hope the airfield is as good as I think it is."

Val realised that Devon had taken on a lot of responsibility in suggesting a disused wartime airfield, but it was the best option they had. "Moser is about five miles away. We have to get ourselves over there by tomorrow morning and lie up for the day. But there's a problem. Someone tried to follow us here. We shook them off, but it means there are people out looking for us and we must assume they will soon find the barn. We have to move, and quick." Val looked at her watch. "It's now nearly ten-thirty. We will leave immediately, walk for an hour, then rest and sleep. We can use the remaining hours of darkness to get as close as we can to the airfield."

"I will help to get Mr Raleigh through." It was Leonid, stepping forward and speaking up for the first time. "I will carry him on my back."

"Thank you, Leonid – we will all help him along. Now, pack everything up. We need to get out of here."

THIRTY

The MI6 radio listening station operative didn't waste a moment before calling Ballantyne and giving him the airfield name and location and agreed time for the pick-up. Ignoring his sense of disloyalty to his boss, Ballantyne passed the details on to David Porter. He knew he was setting in train a mission fraught with danger for those involved and potentially career-ending for himself. He empathised strongly with the agents in the field and couldn't deny that he longed to be on the mission. It had been several years since he was operational, and he missed the physical test of action and the slow-burn mental thrill that overcoming danger brings.

Ballantyne had great respect for the Service. Anyone appointed as its chief would have to have extremely good organisational skills and a sharp focus on achieving the British government's overseas aims. But Ballantyne needed to act on his own views and beliefs. He had a clear sense of foreboding: he knew that Soviet military capabilities were increasing at a rate that could result in their leaders believing the time had come for them to take steps to dominate Europe and end any future threat from Western powers to invade Russia itself. Never again would they suffer the horror of an army at their door. Ballantyne was no political strategist, but most senior military and secret service officers were convinced that the Americans would do no more than threaten a nuclear response; they would never put together a fighting force to oppose the Russians on the scale they had committed into Europe in both world wars. Their fight against communism would be financial and strategic – once the USSR felt that they were unlikely to be attacked, a military balance would be struck and a solid, if uneasy, peace would prevail. The Americans would abandon Russia's European allies to a new life under the hammer and sickle, and good luck to them. Ballantyne saw the extraction of one or more significant weapons scientists as an easy way of painlessly neutralising the Soviet armed threat and keeping the West a free place to live.

Porter was delighted to receive the message. He knew there was no time to lose – he immediately called Hannah with the news that she should contact Fitzjohn and have him set up the rescue mission. As Porter gave Hannah the details of the airfield and timings, he was confident that all the ducks were in a row. A simple flight, landing and return with the passengers – it would be easy, he assured Hannah.

Porter then returned to his office at BOAC. Although he could hardly focus on the task, he spent time planning his next research flight to the northern cities of Canada. He knew it was important for him to maintain a business-as-usual façade over the next couple of days.

THIRTY-ONE

Val didn't have to encourage the team to get ready to leave the barn. Even Raleigh was standing at the door, looking confident and positive. The rest had done him some good. The night was again clear, cold and moonlit. They formed up for the walk: Casey at the front, Leonid and Devon assisting Raleigh, and Val at the back. They had only gone 200 yards when Val felt an impulse to look back. She was shocked to see beams of torchlight flickering in the trees around the barn. They had got away just in time, but Val was puzzled. Who might be hunting for them? She was sure that the doctor and the deputy magistrate could be trusted. Might it be the smartly dressed man in the market? Her hand instinctively went to the grip of her gun, and she resolved to keep pressing on.

Once out of the pine forest, they were able to walk across grassland, keeping to the edge of the wooded areas and occasionally walking along narrow country roads. They had no compass, but good map-reading and Casey's military operational experience ensured that they took the right course. There was no traffic. After about a mile, they saw a small village straight ahead. Val sent Casey forward to take in the options. After fifteen minutes, he came back to suggest that they followed the towpath along the Elbe–Havel Canal, which headed south. There was only one problem: they had to cross a main road to get to the towpath.

The group moved forward at a slower pace, having to half carry Raleigh. Tiredness made them pause frequently. The road they had to cross had been built higher than the surrounding land, with deep drainage ditches on either side. They would have to cross a bridge then slide down an embankment to get to the towpath. Val indicated to the group to keep low as she stepped up onto the road. Quickly, she shrank back again; any observer could easily see a figure in the moonlight up on the road. The group crouched in the ditch in a foot of dirty water and waited. Raleigh's facial contortions showed the pain he was in. Peering through the tufts of grass that lined the ditch, Val could see headlights in the distance, and within a couple of minutes a truck approached. Everyone pressed themselves down into the ditch, but as the truck passed, they could see that it was no threat; the moonlight illuminated rows of milk churns stacked on the rear platform. Val whispered that they should wait a little longer – and she was right. Soon more headlights appeared. There were two cars together, Mercedes limousines, and this time they stopped a hundred yards away, between the group and the bridge, blocking their route to the canal. The lights were switched off and a man emerged from the passenger seat of the first car with a large torch, wearing the three-quarter-length black leather jacket favoured by Stasi agents. He walked slowly across the road to the bridge, sweeping the torch from left to right. He looked down along the canal and towpath before returning to speak to the driver through the open car window. The man stayed standing outside the car, pulled open his jacket and rested his hand on the butt of a Stasi-issue machine gun hanging from his belt.

Val murmured a clear, "Stand by. Don't move. We stay here until they go." But she knew they were trapped. Any attempt to cross the road, and they would immediately be seen by the East German agents. The time to move would be dictated by their actions.

After half an hour, the milk truck returned, slowed down, and was stopped by the man with the gun. They exchanged a few words, then the truck moved on. A small VW came up behind the two police vehicles and got the same treatment, then was waved through. Casey crawled along the ditch and spoke to Val, asking if they should go back the way they had come and try to find another way round. Val wasn't keen. It was only just after midnight; they would wait it out.

The man in the black leather coat began to pace up and down, looking bored and cold – towards the group then back past the two cars. Each time he returned his steps were longer and quicker: he was trying to keep warm. In a few minutes he would reach where the group were hiding – if he glanced down, he would see them. Three times he approached them before swinging round and returning to the cars.

In the darkness Val heard an engine start. Then the lights came on on the rear car, which pulled out in front of the first car, slowly heading along the road towards the group. They all sank lower in the ditch. As the car passed them, Val looked up to see the driver and another leather-clad agent in the front – and the deputy magistrate and his housekeeper in the back seats. Val couldn't help letting out a quiet growl at the two who must have informed on them. Still the agent walked backwards and forwards, peering from the bridge along the canal towpath and shining his light along the path each time he passed. Occasionally he spoke to the driver. Once he relieved himself against a tree by the far end of the bridge, without straying more than a couple of yards from the roadway. An hour passed like this. Devon and Leonid were quiet, while Raleigh's breathing became audible and faster, spurred by the pain he was suffering.

Val realised that they now had little choice: they must make a move or be discovered. She turned to Casey. "If you can get along the ditch to the car, we can shoot the driver and the agent simultaneously and get out of here."

"Sure thing," said Casey enthusiastically. "And then I'll move the car into the trees, so if the other car comes back they will think their friends have gone."

"OK, get along the ditch and wait. When you're in position I will shoot the guy as he comes close to us. The moment I do that, you see to the driver." Val crawled along to Devon, Leonid and Raleigh. "Get ready to move. Casey and I will take out these two and move the car. Then we'll make our way along the canal as fast as we can."

No one said anything in response. Val shuffled a few yards away, checked her gun and got ready to kill the Stasi agent.

THIRTY-TWO

Hannah went to bed at 11p.m. and immediately fell into a deep sleep. The stresses of the past few days had taken their toll: she was exhausted, her body shut down, pushing away the thoughts that had troubled her mind. But at just after 6a.m. she woke suddenly, refreshed and alert. She had an idea that she needed to act on without delay. She used the bathroom quickly, dressed, and went downstairs to the telephone.

Yoel Arbel was used to calls at any time; he often took or made calls during the night, given the time difference in Israel.

"Yoel, it's Hannah Shaw. Sorry to disturb you so early."

"Hannah, no problem. What can I do for you?"

"Another favour, I'm afraid. It's a long story that I can't tell you, but I need a gun and some ammunition. Perhaps a Webley or a PPK, if you have one. And I need them urgently – this morning, in fact. I'm at my fiancé Adam's house in Welham Green in Hertfordshire at the moment, but I can come down to London to meet you."

Arbel gave no more response than a slow inhalation of breath.

There was silence. After a while he said, "You will have to tell me why, Hannah. We don't just give out guns without a very good reason."

Hannah knew that her request for a gun was stretching favours to the extreme, and Arbel wouldn't help unless he could justify his actions to his superiors. "It's Adam. He's involved with an assignment to Berlin to bring back an important passenger and two or three MI6 agents. His aircraft has crash-landed in East Germany and the British government will do nothing to get them out – they will deny any knowledge of the operation. So I've arranged – well, blackmailed – Henry Fitzjohn into undertaking a rescue flight."

"*What?* Fitzjohn? I thought you wanted to avoid him like the plague."

"Under normal circumstances, yes. But he's my only hope in the time available. I'm paying him £1,000. I told him I knew about his diamond racket, but not how I got to know, of course."

"I see. Nice touch."

"The flight will leave around midday today, and I'm going to be on it. I may need to protect myself when we get to the pick-up point. Hence my request."

"Yes. And the important passenger, who is he?" said Arbel.

"I don't know exactly, but he's defecting to the West, so he must be someone valuable, someone the British government want badly enough to try to get him safely over the border. But it's so sensitive that they can't admit to being involved."

"Enough said. I think I can help you. But you will realise that the service has been assisting you of late, and there is a return favour I must ask of you. I will drive up to Welham Green this morning and explain when I get there. I will leave shortly."

"I don't mind coming to meet you," said Hannah.

"No, no. It would be better if I came to you. It's 6.30 now, I will be there in about an hour. Give me the address, please."

***

Yoel Arbel arrived just ahead of time at Adam's house. Hannah saw his car pull up and went to open the front door to let him in. She had made coffee, and poured two cups. "Thanks for coming up here at such short notice."

"That's fine." He placed a black leather holdall on the table. "I have the gun for you, but it's not what you might have been expecting." He unzipped the bag and took out a small machine pistol.

Hannah was unfamiliar with the gun. She had never been trained to use it in her time in the Israeli Secret Service. "What is it, an American job, or Czech maybe?"

"No, it's a new Israeli design that we are still testing. It's called an Uzi." Arbel pulled back the short metal folding stock and took a magazine out of the bag. "The usual stock is wood and fixed. We're trying this folding arrangement to see if it helps with concealing the gun, makes it easier to carry. As you can see, it has a short barrel and the magazine is inserted here, into the pistol grip."

"Unusual," said Hannah.

"Yes – makes for a much more compact design. It's small enough to carry over your shoulder. There are two more magazines in the bag. Each holds twenty-five rounds of 9mm bullets, making seventy-five in total – far more than you should need. The gun's designed to get you out of trouble, not for you to take on a well-armed opponent. Its purpose, of course, is close-range fighting, but it's effective up to around 200 yards. What we want from you is feedback. Is it easy to carry, fold up, keep clean? – that sort of thing. Hopefully you won't have to use it in anger, but if you do, we want information on how it performs in the field, any operating difficulties that you encounter. It has been tested at the factory and firing range, of course, but now ahead of rollout to our forces we are seeking user experience in different environments. Are you happy with that?"

"Yes, sure." Hannah slid the thin black strap over her shoulder. She tucked the gun comfortably under her arm and pressed her hand against the folded stock. "Fits nicely and not at all heavy. Is that what you're looking for – a report on how I find it?"

"Yes. I mentioned that the service might ask you to do a return favour, and this is all you have to do," said Arbel.

"OK, that's no problem. Run me through how it breaks down for cleaning and clearing any jams."

Arbel then spent twenty minutes training Hannah how to handle, use and maintain the gun.

"Thanks, Yoel, I really appreciate your help. I'll return the Uzi to you as soon as I return, and I'll let you know how I got on with it. As you say, let's hope I don't need to actually fire it."

***

After Arbel had left, Hannah dialled the number for Granta Air Services and was pleased to find that the receptionist was at her desk, even at 8.30 in the morning. She was told that Fitzjohn was in the airport Met office, getting the weather forecast for the day, and would be available in half an hour if she would like him to call back. The receptionist added that Mr Fitzjohn would be leaving at 1p.m. and would be away for two days.

Hannah declined, saying she would call again later in the week. She tidied up her handbag, taking out letters, bills and make-up, keeping some cash, her hairbrush and mirror – and, importantly, her passport. She found a small torch, some boiled sweets, a box of matches, gloves and a cotton scarf and slid these into her bag along with the two spare magazines for the Uzi. Not the most comprehensive kit for field operations, but it would have to do. She noticed her hand tremble slightly, felt her heart rate increase, and knew that the sense of purpose engulfing her would drive her on.

She changed quickly into warm layers: trousers, her strong walking shoes, a zip-up bomber jacket with the gun hidden under her arm, her handbag. Hannah picked up the house and car keys and took one last look round.

"Right, let's go," she said to herself.

THIRTY-THREE

As he parked his car outside the Granta Air Services offices, Fitzjohn felt building within him more uncertainty and apprehension at the flight ahead of him. He would be searching for an airfield in unfamiliar territory just before nightfall. Why had he agreed to the mission? He knew that the fallout from exposing Mackenzie's diamond import business would be bad enough, but it would inevitably lead to uncovering the people-smuggling racket – a very different kettle of fish. He was relieved that Hannah had not mentioned this. If it ever came out that he was involved, he would be guaranteed a long prison term. He resolved to end the racketeering business after this rescue job – it just wasn't worth the risk.

Fitzjohn wanted all the help he could get. He was very glad he had called Joseph Richardson the night before to ask him to come over to the airfield early in the morning. Richardson's experience in the Berlin Airlift would be invaluable in planning the flight. Fitzjohn would have to outline the rescue plan – he had no choice but to trust the man, although he would keep as much to himself as possible.

Fitzjohn unrolled the air charts for West and East Germany, spread them across the flight planning desk and weighed them down with a mug of strong tea, his notepad, a slide rule and a thick red pencil. He wanted Richardson to double-check his flight time calculations, fuel consumption, headings and altitude. Fitzjohn described the mission, jabbing his finger on the chart showing the target airfield, Moser.

"This is where I'm off to – take me through the options, Jos," he said.

But Richardson stood back. "Why are you taking on this charter, Henry? It's not the sort of work we're set up for. If you get caught, there will be a heap of trouble."

"Look, I can't say any more, I'm afraid; it's confidential. But it will pay extremely well, and with the fee for this job and the rest of the income this month we could well be in a position to put a deposit on another aircraft. But I know it's a tricky job, Jos, so give me the form."

"OK. As you know, flights into Berlin from West Germany still have to use one of the two entry air corridors. There's one exit corridor back, directly west from Berlin – here." Richardson ran his finger along the chart. "The route you will have to take on your way in is the northern corridor – let me draw it on your chart. In the airlift, British aircraft landed at Gatow in Berlin, so that's the airfield I'm familiar with. It's not in general use now, so for your trip you will use Tempelhof, which is still the American air force base, plus it's used for commercial purposes by other airlines and cargo carriers.

Fitzjohn nodded and said, "Understood, old boy."

"It's about 600 miles in, plus 150 back out to, say, Hanover, which means you will have to refuel at some point before you can get back to the UK. That could be in Berlin, which would give you enough fuel for a direct return to the UK, or you could wait until you get to Hanover. You must file a flight plan ahead of departure, noting your take-off time from Cambridge and your landing time in Berlin. You should allow about three and a half hours from Cambridge to Berlin," said Richardson.

"But look, as I said, the field I'm heading for is Moser – here, just outside the return corridor. It's about halfway between Berlin and the West German border." Fitzjohn waved a pencil across the chart. "Can't I cut across the last hundred or so miles and go straight there?"

"Absolutely not! You may well be flying against the flow of air traffic. You have no choice. You will have to land in Berlin then head back along the return corridor, diverting at the last minute to Moser. The East Germans will be monitoring your flight, and if they see on their radar that you have strayed outside the corridor they might send up a couple of MiGs. At best they will escort you out of East Germany, but you know there's a risk that they could shoot you down. They did that to a French aircraft that strayed outside the corridor."

"Yes, I'm aware of that. Right, I'll refuel at Tempelhof and then I must take off again quickly, back into the corridor. When I divert to Moser I shall maintain radio silence, even if the air traffic people contact me. Then I'll pick up the guests and make all speed for the border. They wouldn't dare to shoot down a British aircraft in the corridor."

"You'd hope not, of course. Henry, this is a hell of a chance you're taking, flying this route solo. Do you want me to go with you, to share the flying or act as navigator?"

"That's really generous of you, Jos, but no, there's no need to embroil you in this business. I expect a call from my contact shortly to confirm the details, and then we can get the aircraft ready and go over the flight plan once more. Given the flight time to Berlin, and allowing for a landing, I'd like to leave here by 1p.m. Thanks hugely for your help, old chap."

"You're welcome. Best of luck. Watch out for Soviet fighters."

THIRTY-FOUR

Val shivered, not just because of the cool night air, but because of the tension she felt at the prospect of executing the Stasi agent in cold blood. She had seen plenty of fighting in France during the war, and had felt the inner surge of controlled violence and aggression against an enemy that was out to kill you. But silently lining up a victim was a different piece of work, and it did not sit well with her.

Val could see Casey in position along the ditch, looking back towards her, waiting for her to make the decision about when to shoot. As soon as she opened fire, he would stand and fire at the driver through the car window. The man in leather was returning to his car, walking away from Val. He said nothing to the driver as he passed. This gave Val time to look around, assess their next move once the agents had been dealt with. She had naturally good night vision, and the light from the moon allowed her to see perfectly well the bridge to her right and the canal stretching ahead.

When the man turned back, Val knew this was it. She had to make sure it was a clean kill. She could see him clearly through the clumps of grass. With her thumb, she clicked off the safety catch. A quick glance down at Casey told her that he was ready to go. Val decided to let the man get within twenty-five yards of her, but as he approached, the car's headlights came on and the driver gave a blast on the horn. The Stasi agent spun round, ran back to the car, and wrenched open the passenger door. The car set off at speed as the man slammed the door shut. Everyone in the group cowered in the ditch as the car shot past them. Val waved to Casey, who ran back, splashing through the ditch. Without waiting any further, Val called to everyone to get up onto the road, walk quickly along to the bridge and clamber down to the towpath. Even in the cold, beads of sweat formed on her face.

After they had walked as fast as they could for more than two miles along the canal towpath, Devon, who was leading, stopped and waved to indicate to everyone to get down. He had spotted a pair of lock gates and a lock-keeper's hut. He came back to speak to Val, told her he would try the hut door and, if he could, break in. He crept forward and peered through the window. All he could see was a desk and a chair and some keys hanging on a hook on the wall. He tried the door handle and found it was unlocked, and there was no one inside. Val gave orders for the group – apart from Casey – to shelter in the hut, have a quick drink and a bite to eat and warm up. Drake Casey had the uncomfortable job of staying outside in the cold keeping an eye out for any activity. She looked at her watch. The green illuminated hands showed it was just past 4a.m.

Devon crouched down beside Raleigh and pulled out a clean bandage from his jacket, along with a wound dressing and a single-use morphine injection that the doctor had given him. "Have we got time to change the dressing, Val?" he said.

"No," she said, but she sounded hesitant. She didn't want to stay any longer in the hut, but Raleigh's strained breathing and closed eyes told her that he was in serious pain. "Oh, alright, go ahead and make it quick. And get the morphine in."

Ten minutes later, Casey tapped gently on the door, then entered.

"Is it clear, Drake?" Val asked.

"Yes, ma'am. There's no one to be seen, but we can be sure those Stasi agents will still be out there looking."

"Agreed. Everyone, we leave in five minutes – get ready." She took a close look at Leonid, pleased to see that he looked alert and apparently happy. She needed him to be resilient, to stay strong. After all, he was the purpose of the assignment, and she wanted very much to deliver him safely to the British weapons people.

***

Devon's map was folded to show the location of the airfield and the surrounding area. Since its purpose was for flight navigation, it contained little geographical detail; it showed towns, rivers and main roads, but no minor roads or villages. Devon estimated that the airfield was around a mile and a half further west from where they were beside the canal, and they should now cut across country. The faint light on the horizon told them that dawn was not far away. They needed to be hidden in the vicinity of the airfield within an hour.

"This is the route I suggest." Devon crouched with Val and Casey and ran his finger across the map. "We start following that hedge to our right across the fields and then into the woods we can see in the distance. We should find the airfield on the far side, so we can check our position exactly and then lay up in the trees out of sight. I'd like to have a look at the runway to check it's in good shape. If the surface is not usable, we're in trouble."

THIRTY-FIVE

Hannah left her car in the main passenger car park, collected her bags and walked into the passenger terminal of Cambridge airport. There were only a handful of flights scheduled that day and the place was quiet, with only a short queue at the ticket sales desk and a dozen or so passengers having coffee in the lounge. The departure board showed a flight to Guernsey and another to Manchester Ringway. Both were on schedule, and the clock showed 11.40a.m. She went up to the viewing window and saw the two Granta Air Services Consuls across the tarmac on the right-hand side of the airfield, one with its engines running, the other static. She had a sudden bolt of fear as she thought the aircraft about to leave could be Fitzjohn's.

She strode back to the enquiries desk, where she was informed that the Granta flight leaving shortly was a private charter on its way to Exeter. The next departure after that was another charter flight leaving at 1p.m. The assistant didn't know the destination. Hannah went over to the immigration desk and handed the assistant her passport, explaining that she was taking a flight to Berlin. Without hesitation, the assistant stamped her passport and handed it back to her.

After a quick coffee and a sandwich, Hannah walked through the airport building and found the reception office for Granta. The tall, blonde receptionist looked up as Hannah entered, and put on a fake smile. "Welcome to Granta Air Services, madam. How may I help you?"

"I'd like to speak to Mr Fitzjohn, please," said Hannah.

"Sorry, madam, I'm afraid he's not available today. He will be leaving soon on a charter."

"Go and find him and tell him that Hannah Shaw is here to see him. Do it now, please." Hannah's frustration and nerves got the better of her, and she couldn't help raising her voice.

"There's no need to be like that," she said, clearly piqued. "I'm very sorry, madam, but I'm not allowed to disturb Mr Fitzjohn."

Hannah noticed a door behind the reception desk that could only lead out to the aircraft parking area. She stepped around the desk and went to open the door, but the receptionist jumped up to block her way. She had more gumption than Hannah expected.

"You can't go through there."

Hannah's frustration was about to boil over. She knew that time was short and Fitzjohn would soon be departing. "Just get out of my—"

The door opened and Joseph Richardson walked into the office. "Everything alright, Annabelle?" he asked.

"Yes, Mr Richardson," the girl whimpered, "but this lady wants to see Mr Fitzjohn and I have told her he's busy. She tried to go out to the aeroplanes."

"Could I be of assistance, madam?"

Hannah recognised Richardson as someone with authority who could help. "Thank you, yes. I'm here to see Mr Fitzjohn, Henry. It's about his flight this afternoon to Berlin."

"Right, so you know about the charter." Richardson's demeanour changed immediately to one of concern when Hannah mentioned the destination.

"Yes, I'm Hannah Shaw, a friend of Henry's, and I need to speak to him urgently. I assume he's outside getting the aircraft ready. Could you take me to him, please?"

"Yes, of course. Come with me," said Richardson.

Hannah walked past the glaring Annabelle, out into the bright sunlight and across the tarmac to the Consul. Fitzjohn was in the pilot's seat.

Richardson knocked on the side of the fuselage and called out, "Henry, someone to see you." He turned to Hannah. "Shall I leave you here, Miss Shaw?"

Fitzjohn had got out of his seat and was heading for the door.

"Yes, thank you."

Fitzjohn jumped out of the aircraft, a look of surprise on his face. "What brings you here, Hannah? You could have phoned. I tried your number this morning, but no answer. No problem with the flight, I hope?"

"No, Henry. Everything is as we discussed, but I'm coming with you," said Hannah.

"What the hell are you talking about? What good could you possibly do?"

"Help with the search, for one thing, first to find the airfield and then Adam and the group."

"Don't be stupid, Hannah! I can do all those things. You'll just get in the way. Now get back to the office. I'm leaving in fifteen minutes." Fitzjohn turned to climb into the aircraft but Hannah grabbed his arm. He spun round in indignation. Hannah stepped up to Fitzjohn, her face inches away from his. "And I'm going with you – get that clear in your head." She swept open her jacket, allowing Fitzjohn a glimpse of the Uzi under her arm. "Are we agreed?"

"Bloody hell, girl, you mean business. But you'll have to go through immigration."

"That's done. My passport is stamped and in order."

"Alright, get in then. Sit next to me up front, right-hand seat. I'll be back in a moment. If we're going tooled up, I'll bring my own piece of kit."

THIRTY-SIX

The moon had set, leaving the last part of the night, before the sun illuminated the ground, in a solid blackness. Devon led the way, staying close to the hedge bordering the field, but progress was slow, with their visibility limited and the need to assist Raleigh. On the other side of the hedge was a narrow road that had grass and weeds growing down the middle, showing very little traffic use, but Devon kept a watchful eye out and listened for any farm workers who might be going to work.

At the end of the hedge line they came to the woodland Devon had seen on the map, and they entered the silent, still pine trees.

"Val, let's go deeper into the trees. The airfield should be a few hundred yards further on," said Devon. Val agreed, and the group moved cautiously forward.

Headway was slow, with fallen branches and tree roots making walking treacherous. "Shit!" Casey called as he suddenly fell headlong into a deep depression that was overgrown with bracken. The hole in the ground was bowl-shaped, thirty feet across and fifteen feet deep at the centre.

"Are you OK, Casey?" Devon slid down the first few feet of the depression and helped him back up. "It's a bomb crater," Devon went on. "There will be more, I guess, from the war. When the airfield was operational it would have been attacked by allied bombers, leaving craters all around the area."

Val spoke quickly and quietly. "Right, let's continue but keep a good watch everyone. I don't want any broken legs."

It took them another fifteen minutes to get to the other side of the wood. By the time they had reached it, the light in the sky outlined the horizon and the flat fields beyond the woods. And there it was – Moser airfield.

They had stopped at the edge of the trees, where they found another overgrown crater. Val told everyone to crawl carefully into it – it made an excellent hiding place. She then turned to Devon. "Bloody good map-reading, Adam."

Devon nodded. "Wait here, everyone. I'll go out and have a look at the state of the runway. Don't get worried – it will take me a while to walk the full length of the runway and back, it's about 900 yards long."

Half an hour later, it was completely light and Devon had not returned. Val had everyone stay low while she had a look around. She crawled forward to see along the full length of the runway. It ran exactly east to west; they had arrived on the north side. A hundred yards to the right she saw a figure approaching and pulled out her pistol, just in case. She soon saw that it was Devon, peering into the woods, trying to relocate the group.

"Here, Devon," whispered Val, and he crept back into cover.

"It's fine – a few broken areas of tarmac but no big obstacles. Looks like the airfield has been used at some point since the war – there's a hangar and storage buildings at the far end – but there's no sign of use now. I'm sure the rescue aircraft will get in and land OK. What could be a problem is the trees at the end of the runway – they've been allowed to grow very tall."

Val and Devon rejoined the others. "OK, everyone, now we wait."

***

The group had to pass a whole day hidden in the crater in the woods, patiently awaiting the late afternoon when the rescue flight would arrive and they could escape the mess they were in. They all took out the remains of the food Val had given them the night before. Some only had a couple of mouthfuls. They would just have to go hungry. Devon took his empty tea flask and filled it with water from a brook by the side of the runway. They were all desperate for a drink, and Devon refilled the flask twice before Val told him not to go out of the trees again; they were pushing their luck.

Val sat down with Raleigh. "How are you, old chap?"

"I'm bearing up, ma'am. Let's hope the aircraft gets in. I would struggle to walk to the border. In any event, make sure you get the Russian over. Make it all worthwhile." Raleigh coughed and winced at the pain in his leg.

"Lie down here and try to get some sleep." Val helped him slide down the side of the crater into the long grass.

Devon sat alongside Leonid. A chat would help to pass the time, and he was keen to find out more about the man. "Tell me, what made you want to come to the West? You must have had a good life in Russia."

Leonid looked at Devon and smiled. "I'm thinking you don't understand how the communist party treat their so-called comrades. Harsh working conditions, poor food and housing, few luxuries. My family were once wealthy – bourgeoisie, you could say – and escaped the ravages of the revolution. For sure, as a child I had a good life compared to many others. But my loyalty has not been appreciated, and certainly not rewarded."

"Do you believe you will be able to advance your work better in the West? You must still want to enhance your knowledge and reputation for scientific excellence."

"That is true, Mr Devon, and of course I plan to continue the work I have been leading on radar-controlled armaments, but I want to work on behalf of the free world. I'm a believer in the concept of deterrent – and a balance of power between nations. It would be disastrous for Europe's safety if Russian military capabilities outstripped those of the US and Britain. The systems I have been working on – if they were ever fully developed, they would give Russia the ability to hit targets at great distances with extreme accuracy. But let me say also, we all need some comforts in life. I'm looking forward to a nice house, good food and the chance to play chess in one of your famous London gentlemen's clubs! What about you, Mr Devon, why are you doing this dangerous work?"

"It wasn't my intention to get into covert operations. I'm just a test pilot. But I suppose I was attracted to the idea of a bit of excitement. After five years of front-line service in a Spitfire squadron, I miss the adrenaline rush you get on operations," said Devon.

"Do you have a wife or family?" asked Leonid.

"I'm engaged. We are looking at maybe getting married after the Queen's coronation next year, but we haven't set a date. It's not something I often think about."

"Why not, if you wish to be married? Is it that your lady is reluctant?"

"Good question. No, I guess it's me. I was engaged once before but my fiancée broke it off when she met someone else – she didn't want to wait until I had finished my RAF service. I know Hannah is very keen to get married, but I just can't seem to come to terms with being married, settled, living in a nice semi-detached house in the suburbs.

But I suppose that will come in time, and I hope Hannah is happy with the way we are just now."

"I hope so too, Mr Devon. But, if I may say, I doubt it. And I thank you for all your efforts to get me to the West. I'm sorry to have brought you to this trouble."

"Not your fault, Leonid. We didn't know that one of our de Havilland people was a Stasi agent. When we get back to England, we can get that individual arrested."

"Yes, indeed, it's important to—"

"Quiet!" Val waved a hand towards Leonid then pointed towards the airfield. On the south side, two cars moved slowly along the perimeter track. They were the Mercedes staff cars they had seen during the night by the bridge. The cars came to the airfield buildings and stopped. The heavy in black leather got out, gripped his machine gun, walked over and opened the door to the largest building, a hangar, and looked around inside. He then went to all the other buildings and huts and checked them out. Seeming satisfied that they were empty, he turned to face the cars and waved a hand. One of the rear doors of the second car opened and the deputy magistrate and the housekeeper emerged.

"Jeez," said Casey. "Val, will you look at that?"

The housekeeper had a gun in her hand, and was directing her boss to a small office building. It looked like she was going to shoot her employer.

"Well, that explains a lot. That goddam housekeeper is an agent and betrayed the magistrate. It must have been her we saw following the doctor's car."

The deputy magistrate entered the building, the housekeeper standing at the door, her pistol in a two-handed grip.

"She's going to kill him," said Val.

A minute later Devon said, "No, wait, look."

The deputy magistrate emerged from the building with a handful of valves and wires, and all three hurried back to the cars.

"He's disabled the radio – taken some components out so it can't be used."

"Why not smash it up?" said Val.

"That's what the Stasi agent would have done but this way, with the magistrate's knowledge of radios, they could come back, fix it up and use it."

After the cars had turned and departed, Devon spoke to Val. "They obviously think we could be picked up at an airfield around here. Did you tell the doctor or the magistrate about the rescue mission?"

"No. All messages were in Morse, and I'm sure I was out of earshot with the Morse key. They're just being thorough, checking out the airfield. Are there any others shown on the map in this area?"

Devon lifted the map. "Yes, a couple, but they're more than ten miles away, on the far side of Magdeburg. If they wake up and realise this airfield is the only realistic way out of here, other than walking, they'll be back."

THIRTY-SEVEN

Fitzjohn said little for half an hour after take-off, by which time they were out across the North Sea. Everything on the aircraft was working perfectly and the weather forecast continued to be accurate, with clear air, light winds and little cloud. Perfect flying conditions. Fitzjohn made a couple of radio calls to air traffic control, then set the heading for Hamburg and the entry point for the northern corridor into Berlin.

"Now, Hannah, as we will be together for the next couple of hours, why don't you tell me something about yourself? I never understood how a lovely thing like you got involved with the Israeli Secret Service and all that pilot recruitment business in Hong Kong."

"You don't need to know anything about that. Anyway, it's all water under the bridge now. Please just concentrate on your flying."

"But didn't you want to recruit me? We all knew that the Israelis were desperate for Spitfire pilots in 1949 – wasn't that what you were after? Wasn't that what all the amorous approaches were all about?"

Hannah was irritated. "There were no amorous intentions on my part. I was talking about a business arrangement – a well-rewarded role for you in Israel. That's all."

"Oh, come on. OK, I was a bit heavy-handed, but don't deny you were trying to get me in bed. And when that didn't work, you succeeded with Devon where you failed with me."

Hannah laughed in astonishment. "That's bloody ridiculous! Yes, Adam and I fell for each other, but his unwillingness to join the Israeli Air Force was all about his principles. And anyway, as you know, there was a change of plan and he decided to come back to England."

"And you followed him. Goodness, Hannah, you could do a lot better. He hasn't even set a date, has he?"

"That's enough, Henry."

Fitzjohn leant across and patted Hannah's knee. "Don't write me off, my dear, you know what high regard I hold you in. When you come to your senses, you and I could have a wonderful life together."

"Are you mad? And keep your mind on flying."

"Let's just wait and see, shall we? And I still don't know how you got involved with those Israeli types in the first place. How did that all come about?"

Hannah didn't mind telling him how she and her brother were sent to Cambridge as part of the Kindertransport movement as the anti-Semitism of the Nazi party became a threat to all Jews. She never saw her parents or the rest of her family again; they were all sent to concentration camps and murdered by the Nazis. She explained to Fitzjohn that she was approached after university to join the Israeli Secret Service and she didn't hesitate – she wanted to play her part in building the new State of Israel.

"I didn't feel I was doing a whole lot of good in Hong Kong, so I resigned and returned to the London and Hong Kong Bank in my original job in London."

"But I gather you have stayed in touch with your old colleagues, haven't you? How else would you get hold of that interesting piece under your arm?"

"I'm not in touch on a regular basis, but they are always there for one of their retired agents."

"Retired? That's a laugh. In my estimation, these people never let you retire. They own you and will have you jumping to their tune at any time."

"The relationship is two-way, Henry, as you know. If they can do something for me, I'm very happy to reciprocate if I can. Yes, Mossad agents in Holland discovered your diamond-smuggling racket and passed that on to me. They don't care what you do to make money, but if you should think of causing harm to an agent, or ex-agent, then they are very likely to take action. This flight is a personal arrangement between you and me. All they wanted was for me to take the Uzi – the gun – and provide a report on its practical use in the field, whether or not I have to use it. So far I'm happy with it. It's light and small enough to hide away."

"There you are – see what I mean? You're back on the firm without realising it," said Fitzjohn.

"That's as may be, Henry. Now, enough about my background, I have a question for you. Who was the lady I saw you with at the University Arms Hotel?"

"Very good. I'm impressed, Agent Shaw – excellent observation. Are you sure you have resigned from the spying game?"

Hannah stared at him. "Just answer the question."

"That was a business meeting. Miss Amanda Spencer, my constituency campaign manager, and I often meet at the University Arms. Also at the hotel I use when in London for parliamentary business. Always a pleasant occasion, I must say."

"I think I understand you. She's rather older than you, wouldn't you say?"

"I hadn't noticed. Now you mention it, you could be right, but she has great charm and is a godsend in Westminster." Fitzjohn took the chart from the pocket by his seat and noted with a red pencil the time at the second waymarker, the city of Hamburg.

"Everything going well?" Hannah asked.

"Yes, we're on course, and on time. I expect to be landing at Tempelhof on schedule and will refuel. We will then be able to make an accurate estimate of the flying time to Moser, where we're due to land at 6p.m. I gather that Tempelhof is mainly tenanted by the US Air Force, but we will be able to tuck ourselves away at the parking area assigned to British commercial flights."

Fitzjohn quietened down as he concentrated on flying an accurate heading through the inbound northern corridor at the required altitude of 6,000 feet. The weather continued to be benign, and he had no trouble in identifying the towns, cities and rivers shown on the chart. With around ten miles to go, Fitzjohn began to make out the grey spread of the city of Berlin, and called Tempelhof air traffic control for permission to land.

THIRTY-EIGHT

The group soon fell silent, each person reflecting on their situation. Val and Casey took turns to keep watch, alternating every hour. In the early afternoon, Casey crawled out of the crater and across the bracken to the edge of the wood where Val lay, her arms folded across a thin fallen tree trunk, looking out to the runway.

"All quiet, Val?" Casey asked.

"Yes, at the moment, but I can't shake off the feeling that those guys will be back. Think about it – the housekeeper understood that we were contacting London, probably seeking an aircraft to pick us up. Walking out to the border would be unlikely, given we had a wounded colleague. It would be easy for the Stasi to identify this and one or two other airfields, stake them out, and wait for us to show up."

"Yep, let's hope the aircraft is on time and he can get in – and away – quickly. In fact, we should be sure that everyone is ready in case it arrives early."

"OK," said Val. "It's about three o'clock now. I'll check on Raleigh shortly and take him for a slow walk around to keep his leg mobile."

"Good idea." Casey hesitated. "He's a risk to us, you know, Val. Our priority is to make sure we get Leonid out of here. We can't let an injured player mess up the team."

"I'm quite aware of that, Drake, but he's a strong character and I'm sure he will be alright."

"You've worked with him for a long time."

"About six years, first in the Far East and then in Berlin. He was with military intelligence during the war and then he had a couple of years in the MI6 London office setting up the network of agents across Europe. But he's a field agent at heart, and got back to operations in 1947. We've been working together since."

"And you like him, I can see."

"Like? Come on, Drake, he's a valued colleague. I admire his professionalism; there's no room for anything more in our line of business. In the SOE we had girls who couldn't stop talking about their boyfriends. Some were never seen again after dropping into France or Belgium. It would be crazy for anyone doing what we do to get too close to someone, in or out of the service."

"If you say so, Val." Casey looked at Val and she looked back, holding his stare for several seconds before smiling gently and crawling her way back to the crater.

***

Val helped Raleigh to his feet and walked him deeper in the woods, ensuring they couldn't be seen by anyone on the airfield. "How is it, Raleigh?" she asked.

Raleigh's breathing was rapid and thin, and he spoke in a whisper. "Not too bad, ma'am. The morphine has worn off, but it's nothing that can't be tolerated. What's the plan when the aircraft arrives?"

"I've discussed that with Devon. The wind is coming from the west, pretty well straight down the runway. He says that as soon as we hear an aircraft overhead or approaching, we get out to the runway threshold at the eastern end and use the torches he recovered from the Dove as makeshift landing lights. He's confident this will show the pilot the direction for landing – it's important he approaches and lands into the wind. The pilot will know he has to taxi back to get ready for the take-off."

"Rather risky, ma'am, breaking cover," said Raleigh.

"I know, but Devon's view is that without our guidance the pilot could well spend time circling, trying to check out the wind direction, and that would be worse. The quicker he gets down, and back to the end of the runway where we're waiting, the better."

"Understood. Do you want me to assist Devon?"

"No, I'll get Casey to help. Now, you have your gun to hand?"

"Yes, right here." Raleigh patted the pocket of his jacket.

"And spare ammunition."

"Of course. I will be ready if we have uninvited guests trying to gatecrash the party."

Val smiled. "I do trust you. But you also know that we can't let Leonid fall into Stasi hands, come what may."

"Understood, ma'am. I know exactly what to do."

THIRTY-NINE

The group was silent, their sense of anticipation palpable. They had less than an hour until the arrival of their transport home – and, for Leonid, the blessed gift of freedom and the prospect of a fulfilled life. The birds in the trees had roosted and fallen silent, so the westerly breeze stirring the leaves was the only sound they could hear, even though they were all unconsciously straining their ears for the distant hum of an aircraft. Lack of food, water and proper rest was increasing the stress on them all.

It was Casey's turn on lookout. Suddenly, he shot back from the edge of the wood into the crater where they were all hidden, and beckoned to Val.

"Those Kraut cars have come back, but this time there's three of them. They've stopped on the track approaching the buildings. There's five or six Stasi agents walking around, all armed to the teeth. Plus the housekeeper, who seems to be directing them. If they're still here when the aircraft arrives, we're sure gonna have ourselves a firefight."

"Get back over where you can watch them, Casey, and check to see if they move off. So long as they are in sight, we can deal with them."

"Like how? They're sitting tight at the far end of the runway. If we move, they'll see us immediately," said Casey.

"OK, here's how. We will make a move now to our left, parallel to the runway, but staying in the trees. It's only a couple of hundred yards to the beginning of the runway. We will hide there until the aircraft arrives. From there we can get round the far end. You and Devon will be ready at the runway threshold with the torches. Got that?"

"Sure, good plan. Let me go check on what they're doing. Will you brief the others?"

"Yes. Now off you go." Val crawled back into the crater and spoke quietly to Devon, Leonid and Raleigh. They all immediately got to their feet. They were tired of lying around in the undergrowth and were relieved that at last something was happening. Val outlined the plan, and when Casey returned they all moved off, silently and slowly, staying hidden in the trees.

Val found a new resting point and had everyone lie in the last line of bushes before the runway. Stretching away to their right they could see the whole airfield, with the hangar, radio room and other buildings only two hundred yards from them. The Stasi men were pacing the ground, occasionally looking into the sky. The man in black leather from the river stopped and had a few words with the housekeeper. She looked at her watch then pointed the gun she was holding first to the right, down the runway, then across the airfield to the far side. Two men took up positions a short distance away from the buildings, and two more ran across to the other side of the runway, opposite where the group had been hiding. They were setting up an ambush on both sides of the runway.

"How the hell did they know to come here?" said Devon.

"I doubt they knew. They just did some good anti-insurgent work. Some of these guys are probably ex-Gestapo, now committed communists," said Casey.

Val turned to Devon. "Could be a problem with the torches, if the aircraft arrives before the Stasi depart."

"It will be OK if we get as far down the runway as possible and hide in the bracken, staying out of view and directing the lights towards the approach line of the runway for the pilot to see as he comes in," said Devon.

"Right, be ready to do that. In the meantime, we wait here."

***

Fitzjohn taxied the aircraft to the Tempelhof refuelling station then, after filling up, parked outside the de Havilland office. Hannah walked over to the door, but it was locked and no one was around. There did not seem to be any commercial flights departing that evening, and the airport buildings were quiet. On the far side of the curved terminal building Hannah could see several US planes parked and servicemen milling around.

"We need to be away in about twenty minutes," said Fitzjohn. "I'll go over to the traffic control tower and file our flight plan. Don't wander off, please."

Hannah felt a surge of nervous tension as she contemplated the next leg of the trip: landing on a disused airfield outside the safe zone of the return corridor. "No problem. I'm ready to go whenever you say."

***

"It's a quarter to six. Let's hope the aircraft is late – these Stasi guys don't look like they're about to leave in the immediate future," said Devon.

"No," said Val. "But if they're still here when we hear the plane, then we're going to have to deal with them. Casey and I will handle the two by the buildings, plus the housekeeper and her agent. It looks like there's one more man in the third car. Raleigh, can you get into position at this end of the runway? Hide in the bushes to cover those two up on the other side. Take them out if you have to. You move over there too, Leonid."

"Will do, ma'am." Raleigh seemed to have forgotten about the pain in his leg as he crawled fifty yards through the bracken and into the woods in the direction of the East Germans and settled in. Leonid crouched in the undergrowth behind him.

Ten minutes later the sound of an aircraft could be heard in the distance, and Devon saw a twin-engine machine heading their way from the east. He turned to Val, who had also seen it. Quietly, she called over to Casey and Devon. "Get into position with those torches. Stay well hidden."

Val saw the Stasi agents react as the aircraft approached. The housekeeper waved her gun to the two teams of two men, who waved back in acknowledgement. The ambush was set.

***

"See anything?" Hannah asked anxiously. She hoped that Fitzjohn's RAF flying experience had honed his natural sense of place and he would simply fly direct to the airfield. In fact, she was not far from the truth and Fitzjohn spotted the town of Magdeburg, and knew they were only two or three miles from their destination. "Look out to the right 45 degrees – we should see the airfield in a couple of minutes," he said. Just a moment later he saw it, and made a gentle turn that would take them directly overhead.

"Are you sure it's the right one?" said Hannah.

"I am now – look." Fitzjohn pointed to the torches signalling just ahead of the nose of the Consul. "They're indicating the runway threshold – standard practice – which means we will land into the wind. Well done, chaps, very helpful. We'll go around in a left-hand circuit pattern and make our approach. Tighten your seat belt, please!"

Fitzjohn took a wide arc around the airfield and lined up to land. At first, the torch signals were visible, then he lost sight of them. He ignored this and continued his approach to land, muttering his sequence of checks to himself: "Flaps down, undercarriage down, fuel pumps on, airspeed good." He made a perfectly smooth landing right at the start of the runway and allowed the aircraft to slow a touch before gently applying the brakes. He couldn't be sure how good the tarmac surface was, so treated it cautiously.

His pleasure at a perfect landing was violently dispelled when he heard gunfire to his left and the clang of bullets hitting the fuselage. "Bloody hell, we're being shot at! Hang on!" Fitzjohn applied a short burst of power to both engines and sped further down the runway before turning the aircraft onto the grass verge on the right and stopping the engines. "Quick – get out and head for those trees."

Hannah slid out of her seat, opened the aircraft door and jumped out, Fitzjohn right behind. They ran into the trees then turned to look back. There was a line of bullet holes across the rear section of the fuselage and the rudder.

"Oh great, look at that damage," said Fitzjohn.

They could see two men on the far side of the runway firing into the trees with machine guns. Gun smoke rose up – at least one person was returning fire. They saw more East Germans shooting on the side of the airfield where they were crouching, but they were shooting away from Hannah and Fitzjohn, towards the runway threshold.

"Adam and the others must be somewhere down there," Hannah called. "Get your gun out, Henry. We can get through these trees and hit them from behind." She already held the Uzi, pointing it towards the airfield buildings.

"Tally ho, old girl – let's bag ourselves a couple of communist bastards." Fitzjohn was revelling in the prospect of being the hero of the day, the one to clear the way for the rescue and triumphant return to the UK with the Russian defector.

They were within sixty yards of the agents, who had stopped firing to watch the shooting on the other side of the runway. Fitzjohn waved to Hannah, mouthed an exaggerated "Three, two, one!" then they both opened fire. Fitzjohn saw his bullets strike the wall of the building behind one of the agents, who turned in shock and ran around the building into cover. Hannah fired a burst of four rounds at the second man, who was armed with a pistol, but her grip on the gun was weak and the recoil kicked it up and to the right, so the bullets flew harmlessly into the trees. The Stasi agent went down on one knee and fired back. Hannah pressed herself hard against the tree, pulled the stock more firmly into her shoulder, wrapped her fingers tightly around the magazine grip and fired again. This time her aim was true and the man spun to his left, grabbing his arm, where two of the four bullets fired had hit him. Frighteningly for Hannah, grimacing and screaming, the man fired back at her. Hannah slid around behind the tree trunk for more protection.

Fitzjohn took several steps forward, out of the cover of the trees, to get a clean shot at the agent, but he had forgotten to count the shots he had fired and the gentle 'click' of his pistol showed that he was out of ammunition. He tugged at his jacket pocket to reach another magazine, but the agent had seen his chance. He stood up and took careful aim. Fitzjohn froze. Before the agent could shoot, Hannah fired another sustained burst. The storm of bullets hit him full in the head and neck, and the agent cartwheeled into a bloodied heap and stayed still.

"My god, that was close. Good work, Hannah!"

She ignored him and was quickly replacing the empty magazine with a new one. Coolly, she made a mental note to mention in her report how easy it was to overfire the Uzi and risk running out of ammunition.

Fitzjohn called again to Hannah, and pointed to a line of trees less than thirty yards from the buildings. When he shouted, "Now!", the pair dashed forward and took up positions behind the trees. The remaining agent turned away from firing at Devon and his group and levelled his gun at them.

***

Concerned that Raleigh and Leonid were in danger of being overrun, Val called out, "Get back, you two!" She shouted as loud as she could; there was no point trying to stay hidden after the aircraft had arrived and the shooting started. "Casey and I will cover you – get back to this end of the runway." She saw two figures move in the trees: Raleigh and Leonid. Then she saw the two Stasi men emerge from their ambush, now only fifty yards away. She opened fire with her PPK, even though she was on the edge of the bracken and clearly exposed. They had the advantage in weaponry, and returned fire. A volley of rounds from a machine gun dug into the ground just a few feet in front of her. Raleigh saw the danger Val was in, turned back to face the enemy, and fired twice at the first man. He fell and lay writhing on the ground. Raleigh was raising his revolver to aim it at the second man, but he was too late. The Stasi agent fired three rounds at him. The bullets slammed into Raleigh's chest, killing him instantly. Leonid ran forward and, crouching low, grabbed Raleigh's gun and ran back into the trees, dodging shots from the agent.

"Keep back, Leonid! Don't try anything!" Val shouted.

But Leonid calmly stood up, held the pistol in both hands and, with one eye shut, aimed and fired two shots. They struck the agent in the leg and he staggered sideways, at the same time pulling his machine gun level. Leonid crouched down, keeping his head low but watching out for the agent. The Stasi man charged forward. He was within twenty yards of Leonid when Devon stood up and fired a single shot into his chest. He collapsed to the ground. Leonid jumped up and ran to pick up the man's machine gun. He even had the nerve to wave and smile at Devon, calling out a thank you.

More fire came from the other agents by the buildings. Casey shot a few rounds towards them then dashed to Val, who lay on the ground, frozen in shock, tears welling in her eyes. "Oh, Raleigh, you fool," she said. "I could have dealt with those bastards and—"

There was another burst of machine-gun fire, and they both instinctively dropped their heads. But Devon saw what was happening, and called across to Val and Casey. "Look – the agent by the building, he's shooting away from us, along the runway. Must be aiming at the pilot." Devon ran forward and hit the ground next to Casey. "I'll run over to Leonid and get his machine gun – you two keep these agents busy."

Before Val or Casey could stop him, Devon ran across the runway to the far side, where Raleigh lay dead and Leonid was hiding. Devon heard bullets clatter across the tarmac, but reached the trees unscathed and dived down beside Leonid. Devon took the machine gun but left his pistol with Leonid, telling him to lie down in the bracken away from the line of fire, then worked his way back to behind Val and Casey. From her position at the runway threshold, Val saw the remaining Stasi agents and the housekeeper manoeuvre into position behind the buildings, responding to the fire that was coming from the direction of the aircraft.

"There were two people in the aircraft, and they're both firing at the Germans. Who on earth are they?" Val shouted.

Devon could hardly believe his eyes. "Bloody hell, Val, it's Hannah and Henry Fitzjohn! What the hell's going on? I was expecting RAF or MI6 people!"

"Fitzjohn must be the pilot. No idea how Hannah has got in on the act. Keep covering fire, Devon. Drake, come with me."

Devon had not seen the Granta Air Services logo on the fuselage from his position in the undergrowth with the torch, but now he realised that the aircraft was not the military Airspeed Oxford, but the civilian Consul version. He recalled that Fitzjohn's air charter service had a couple of Consuls, but he couldn't imagine how Hannah had got involved.

Val and Casey ran over to the first building, keeping low. They had the Stasi agents trapped. Casey had an agent in his sights, and fired two shots to take him out. The remaining agent, the man in black leather, was more cautious. He and the housekeeper worked their way to the far side of the buildings. Fitzjohn and Hannah could see them clearly, and opened fire. The agent in black leather made a dash back towards the cars, but only made it about ten yards before Fitzjohn shot him in the head.

The housekeeper, clearly seeing that it was futile to carry on, threw her gun down, raised her hands in the air and stepped forward into the thinning gun smoke. No one fired at her. Instead, everyone walked out to the edge of the runway. Leonid marched across the runway to join them.

Val hurried over to Raleigh, bent down by him, straightened his jacket, smoothed his hair and touched his cheek. She took his identification papers from his inside pocket and removed his watch and signet ring; she didn't want any communists benefitting from his belongings, and knew he had family in England. Kneeling by Raleigh, she smiled fondly at him. "Goodbye, my dear," she whispered, then stood up and strode back to the group.

Devon ran up to Fitzjohn and Hannah. "What's going on? Hannah, why are you here?" He held her upper arms and looked searchingly into her eyes.

Hannah was almost hyperventilating as the adrenaline began to wear off. Breathlessly she said, "Oh, darling. I had to do something to help get you out of Germany, and Henry was our only hope. He agreed to rescue you." Hannah folded away the Uzi stock and pushed the gun under her arm.

Val nodded. "Well done, you two. Thanks. Now let's get go—"

A gunshot rang out.

The housekeeper had drawn a small pistol hidden in her jacket pocket and shot Leonid. Val didn't hesitate; she fired two rounds into her chest, straight through the heart. The housekeeper fell backwards. Val's anger burst through her emotional control: she took a step forward and fired at her again, then screamed and fired again into the dead body. Casey took her arm and pulled her away. "Val, leave it! No, Val, it's done."

"If it wasn't for this bitch, Raleigh would still be alive." Val came close to shooting again but after an internal tussle, her self-control won. She forced her personal feelings from her mind and turned her back on the housekeeper. Casey put his arm around her and walked her away. Spontaneously, she rested her head on his shoulder and sobbed briefly. He patted her back, and she turned to him and gave him a smile in thanks for his touch of kindness.

Devon was helping Leonid to take off his jacket. He pressed a handkerchief into the cut on his forearm to stem the flow of blood.

"It's OK, Val, just a flesh wound to the arm," Devon said.

"Casey, go and check the third car – the agent might still be in it. Find out what happened to the magistrate. I need a minute." Val walked away from the group, pocketed her gun and covered her face with her hands. Her shoulders shook as she released the emotions she couldn't control.

"Yes, of course," said Casey.

Val was right – a fresh-faced young agent had been left in the car to guard the deputy magistrate. He was in the front passenger seat, talking frantically into the microphone of the car radio. As Casey approached, he fired a round into the air as a warning, and the agent put his hands up. Val arrived just as Casey ordered the man out and took away his gun. She opened the rear door and the deputy magistrate emerged, smiling broadly.

The voice on the radio was asking for the message to be repeated. *Wie bitte, Heinz, wie bitte?*

"The bastard's been calling in help." Val grabbed the young man by the throat and pressed the barrel of her gun into his temple. "Casey, get him to tell us who he was talking to. If he bluffs, I will kill him."

Casey started to question the young man, who looked frightened out of his wits by Val. But the deputy magistrate called out that he had been speaking to the Stasi controller, who was in touch with the air force.

"Right. I'm going to set the kid free, Drake, tell him to run for it." The youth sprinted away into the woods.

"Herr Magistrat, tell me what happened," said Val.

"My housekeeper, so loyal and hard-working she has been for me for three years – I had no idea she was a communist and an informer. After your radio transmissions, she betrayed us to the Stasi men, who followed you when you left in the doctor's car."

"Well, she's dead now, and so are her friends," said Casey.

"Perhaps I am not sorry to hear this. After you left my apartment she returned with Stasi agents and they arrested me. Fortunately, the doctor had already gone, and now that these men are dead no one knows he helped you, except the boy you let go. He is from the town, and I will ensure he says nothing. I believe the doctor is safe, but he and I will make all efforts now to escape to West Germany. I've learned that no one can be trusted here."

"We will do all we can to help you both, since you have done so much for us," said Val.

"Thank you, that would be very much appreciated. But now, I shall walk into Moser village and get a taxi home."

Casey touched Val's arm. "We'd better get going, pronto."

"I'm coming. Herr Magistrat, thank you." Val shook his hand and ran with Casey back to the others.

FORTY

Fitzjohn was the first back to the aircraft. He examined the bullet holes closely. "I don't like these ones," he said to Devon. "Two bullets have gone through the lower tailplane – here, see, the elevator is bent and is jamming the hinge. I wouldn't be able to climb or descend if it locked up completely."

Devon crouched down to get a better view of the damage. "You're right – we can't fly with the tail as it is. We need to cut away or bend the bodywork so the rudder and elevator can move properly. Have you got any tools on board?"

"No, just my flight manuals and maps," said Fitzjohn.

"I've got an idea. Hannah, pass me your gun, please."

Uncertain what Devon had in mind, Hannah passed him the Uzi. He unfolded the metal stock and used the rear bar to bend the damaged tailplane bodywork away from the hinge. He took hold of the tailplane and lifted it up and down to check it travelled cleanly. "That should do it – have a look, Fitzjohn."

"I'm happy with that. Now, shall we go? The sun will set shortly and we'll have about thirty minutes of twilight. Get in, everyone. Devon, you take the co-pilot's seat."

Everyone got on board and strapped in. Fitzjohn started the engines and turned to taxi back past the airfield buildings to the runway threshold. Devon told Fitzjohn about the risk of the high trees at the far end of the runway, so he applied a short runway technique, holding the aircraft on its brakes while running up the engines to full power. The aircraft was shaking under the strain until Fitzjohn let off the brakes, when the Consul shot forward and quickly built up speed. Would it be enough? thought Devon. They had six people aboard, and almost-full fuel tanks – the weight the aircraft had to carry was near its maximum.

As they thundered and bounced down the uneven runway, the trees became ominously close. "Rotate, Fitzjohn, rotate!" Devon called as the dark pine forest loomed ahead. But Fitzjohn held the aircraft on the runway for another few seconds before pulling the control column hard back and setting the steepest climb away that he could without stalling. They made it with ten feet to spare.

"I think you will find I am perfectly able to handle the aircraft, Devon," said Fitzjohn in his most superior voice. "I'll keep to a low altitude and make a direct line to cross the border at the nearest point."

But after they had been flying for a few minutes, the aircraft shook, and everyone on board flinched as the scream of a jet engine cracked the air above them. Devon caught sight of the red exhaust glow of two jets turning away. "Fitzjohn, turn right – get into the corridor, quick!"

They were being hunted by Soviet MiG fighters.

***

In a darkened room at the RAF station at Wunstorf in West Germany, an operator pressed his alarm button. Two officers dashed from their desks into the radio monitoring room. The operator lifted a notepad and read out the information he had picked up. The RAF listened in constantly to the East German air force radio frequencies, and when two MiGs were scrambled to intercept an aircraft taking off from an airfield in East Germany, the operator knew it was the one he had been told to listen out for.

A message had come through from MI6 alerting the RAF to a flight that could be expected from an airfield in the Magdeburg area: an Airspeed Consul with five or six persons on board. It was imperative that the aircraft be protected and if necessary safely escorted across the border. The radar screens at Wunstorf picked up the Consul and the two MiGs, and the team could see them all outside the return corridor. The British aircraft was in trouble; the Soviets had fired on a civilian aircraft a few months earlier that they claimed was outside the controlled airspace. The officer in charge at Wunstorf didn't hesitate. He ordered two RAF Vampire jets to be scrambled to intercept the civilian aircraft and provide an escort back to safe airspace.

The slow-moving green dots on the radar screen had turned north, the British pilot clearly trying to get to the safety of the corridor. The faster-moving MiGs circled and were rapidly approaching the rear of the Consul. There were no other aircraft in the corridor, so the RAF pilots were vectored towards the Consul. The Vampires would be there in less than six minutes.

***

Fitzjohn headed north to reach the corridor as quickly as possible. But when Devon looked over his right shoulder, he could see the two MiGs banking to close in from behind. They screamed over the Consul, waggled their wings and turned sharply to the left. All the passengers cried out, shocked by the way the aircraft shook in the fighters' slipstream.

"They're instructing us to follow them to the south, Fitzjohn," said Devon.

"No way. Hang on, everyone." Fitzjohn pushed the throttle levers fully forward to get the maximum speed possible from the engines, and dived to 1,000 feet.

"Steady, Fitzjohn – don't forget you have a damaged aircraft," said Devon.

The MiGs came round again and followed the Consul down. This time the leading MiG came up on the Consul's right and opened fire with machine guns. Devon saw the tracer bullets draw red lines through the air ahead of them. Fitzjohn's fighter pilot instincts kicked in, and he put in a steep climbing turn out of the line of fire.

"That's a warning shot," said Fitzjohn. "He could easily have blown us out of the sky."

"I'm guessing they have orders not to shoot us down. We have a very valuable passenger on board who mustn't be killed," said Devon.

"But that will only work as far as the border – if they see that we're about to get over to the West they will shoot to kill, we can be sure of that. And they don't give a damn about the corridor – look, they're following us in."

After another half a minute the MiGs came past again, this time both firing their guns from behind in warning. As they turned away for another approach, Fitzjohn called out, "Look ahead, Devon! Two RAF planes – Vampires! Bloody good show, chaps! And we're in the corridor, so those bastard Russians had better back off or they will get it from the Vamps."

The two RAF aircraft engaged the MiGs with warning shots of their own. The Vampire was more than capable of outgunning a MiG, but it was a game – neither side wanted to shoot down opposition air force planes; that could spark a major incident. The Soviets got the message and in close formation the two aircraft banked hard to the south and climbed away, back into East German airspace. Fitzjohn was free to continue the flight westwards with Vampire fighters flanking him. He immediately got Devon to tune into the radio frequency for Wunstorf. Fitzjohn requested a direct approach and landing, and added that they had a wounded passenger on board and had lost a man. Fitzjohn had wanted to fly direct back to the UK, land unseen at Cambridge and take his reward. Landing in West Germany meant he was likely to get a good deal of exposure he didn't want, but the mission – to deliver the defector, Leonid, to the British secret service – would be a success. He was determined to get the most respect and credit for his guile and bravery when he got back to the UK.

***

Kate Samways waved Ballantyne through her office. He found C standing anxiously behind his desk.

"Well, Ballantyne, what news do you have?"

"Sir, I just had a call from RAF Wunstorf. The civilian aircraft sent to rescue the defector and the rest of the party has been escorted through to West German airspace. Apparently they narrowly escaped the attentions of a couple of Soviet MiGs, but they were shepherded over the border by a pair of Vampires and will be landing shortly. There is a report of one of the group being wounded in a shoot-out at the airfield, and I'm sorry to have to inform you, sir, but there was one fatality."

"Don't tell me it was Leonid, Ballantyne!"

"No, sir. I understand it was Raleigh."

"Well, that's a relief. Sorry to hear the news, of course, but that's the risk our agents take. And I think it proves my point about Raleigh's abilities. He was past it, in my opinion, and I'm not sure of

Hetherington-Brown's judgement in taking him on the mission. The whole affair must be looked into: it has been a shambles from start to finish. Get Brown in here as soon as they return to the UK."

Ballantyne bit his lip. C was talking rubbish. He had no experience of running agents, the risks in the field, or covert operations. He was a senior naval officer squeezed into an office job before a comfortable retirement. He was used to his orders being obeyed without question or challenge, but Ballantyne couldn't resist commenting. "I'm not sure that's fair, sir. Val has delivered a significant defector into our hands – the assignment is a success in that regard. And we know there must be a double agent or a mole involved somewhere along the line, who planted the bomb or arranged for it to be planted."

"Hmm, we must certainly get to the bottom of that and make sure our operations are secure going forward. Now tell me, who is this mysterious rescue pilot, and how did he know where the group were?"

"I will be submitting a full report in the morning, sir, that will cover all relevant points. Now if I may, I need to get back to my office urgently to talk to the intelligence officer at Wunstorf."

C exploded. "Don't you brush me off, Ballantyne! If you know the answers to my questions you will tell me now!" He banged a fist on his desk.

Ballantyne wasn't going to be intimidated. He took a few steps across the office, inhaled slowly and tried to sound relaxed to indicate that he, at least, was not losing his cool. But he felt it would be like kicking a hornet's nest if he named Fitzjohn before he had returned to the UK and could speak for himself. Ballantyne was acutely conscious that he had sent the telegram that officially sanctioned the rescue flight, and he didn't want to tell the chief that right now. "The pilot, I believe, is an ex-RAF officer now working in the civil aviation sector. He was assisted by Adam Devon's fiancée. Devon works for de Havilland, and he flew the original assignment to bring Leonid and the others back from Berlin, under our instruction. You will also be aware that the Americans are involved and their agent, Drake Casey, is working closely with Brown." Ballantyne's extended response, and mentioning the Americans, was designed to stop C from thinking about who the pilot really was.

It worked.

"Bloody Americans. Let's ensure we keep Leonid away from them. He's *our* asset and that's the way it must stay – understood?"

"Of course, sir. I will get on to Wunstorf immediately and ensure they do not hand him over."

"Do that, please, and make sure I have that report by 11a.m. tomorrow."

"Of course, sir. Good evening."

***

As soon as Fitzjohn brought the aircraft to a stop in front of the airfield reception building at Wunstorf, a military ambulance pulled up beside it. Val opened the aircraft door and helped Leonid step out. He held his wounded arm close to his body. The doctor went to take him away, but Val insisted he waited until everyone was off the plane.

"I'll go with Leonid to the base hospital," Val said. "Everyone else, go with Casey to the intelligence office and wait for me. I shouldn't be long. There is to be no discussion about the assignment or who was involved, is that clear? You are still under my control – and that includes you, Devon and Hannah. Fitzjohn, the same applies to you – no talking, no phone calls home or to the office. Got that?"

Everyone nodded or gave quiet affirmation.

Once in the intelligence office, a military policeman insisted that they hand over all their weapons and ammunition. As Hannah went to put the Uzi on the desk, Casey took hold of it. "Where'd you get this, Hannah? It's a rare piece – Israeli, if I'm not mistaken."

"Yes, how did you know?"

"From my time hunting for Nazis after the war. I made a lot of friends in the Israeli Secret Service, in Europe and the UK. I'm still in touch with a lot of them. But I wouldn't expect an English lady to be in possession of a new gun like this."

"Well, that's something for another time. Let's not discuss anything now."

"But surely you can—"

"Leave it, Casey." Devon stepped forward, took the gun and placed it on the desk with the others. "Cut out the discussions until Val returns."

"OK, OK." Casey held his hands up in mock surrender and glanced at the intelligence officer, who was obviously intrigued by their conversation. The officer said to the group that all their weapons would be returned on their arrival in the UK. The strained atmosphere in the room evaporated when a young WAAF brought in a tray loaded with mugs of tea and a tin of biscuits.

Twenty minutes later Val came into the office with Leonid, his arm bandaged and in a sling. He was all smiles as he realised he had made it. He was in safe hands, and would soon be in England – and maybe not long after, he would be taken to the United States. His ambitions – in his personal life and his work – would be fulfilled.

FORTY-ONE

The commanding officer at Wunstorf received orders from the office of the Chief of the Air Staff in London. He was required to ensure that the group remained isolated from other personnel at the air station, and were flown to the UK as soon as possible. The CO organised a flight in an RAF Douglas DC3 Dakota transport that was due to take service personnel back to the UK the next day. Fitzjohn was promised that when his Consul had been repaired it would be ferried back to Cambridge. The service personnel were removed from the passenger list and only two pilots, a navigator and a doctor would travel with the group instead. The destination was to be Biggin Hill, where cars would meet the aircraft and take everyone to a safe house in Surrey, where they would be debriefed.

Val was given the use of the commanding officer's adjutant's office so she could make a confidential call to Andrew Murray, her senior operational agent in the Berlin station. She gave instructions for a team – consisting of Murray and three agents – to get over to the de Havilland office at Tempelhof, arrest Artur Franken, seize any papers or materials that related to the Dove and its radar development, and look for bomb-making equipment. They should also try to find out who Franken's accomplices were, either in the UK or his Stasi handlers.

Casey was also given an office and a telephone, but an intelligence officer had to stay with him throughout the call to ensure he didn't plan for the CIA to interview Leonid. Casey then rejoined the others.

An accommodation block was cleared of personnel and a mess room provided for the group so they could spend the evening together. RAF Regiment armed guards stood outside; Leonid was still a potential target who needed to be protected. Devon and Hannah sat a little away from the rest of the group, holding hands and leaning in, almost cheek to cheek, talking quietly.

"Hannah, how on earth did you get Fitzjohn to do the rescue?"

"David Porter told me that no help would be forthcoming from the RAF or anyone else, so I thought of getting Henry to fly his air taxi to pick you up. David gave me the name of Moser airfield to pass on to Henry. He has a chap working with him who flew in the Berlin Airlift, and he helped with the flight planning. And I decided to come as well."

"But what's in it for Fitzjohn? He was taking a big risk. And so were you, of course," said Devon.

Hannah knew she had to tell the truth – or part of it, in any event. "Well… Adam, please don't be angry with me, but I agreed to pay Henry £1,000 for the job. I know it's nearly all the money we've saved for the house. I'm sorry."

Devon sat back and let go of Hannah's hands. At first he was speechless, then with frustration in his voice he said, "But that's put us right back where we started! It'll take years to save up a deposit again."

"But it was worth it. How else were you going to get back safely?" Hannah felt a sob rising in her chest. She took a deep breath. "You might have been arrested by the Stasi agents or killed. I had no choice!"

"Well, that's true. But even £1,000 is hardly worth it to Fitzjohn, given the risks. Think of the fallout if he – a British MP – had been caught by the Soviets extracting a defector. Seems crazy to me that he would even consider it. He must be desperate for the money."

"Maybe he is, darling." Hannah took Devon's hands again and pulled him to her. "But I think he relished the excitement of the trip." She wanted to steer Devon away from pressing her on any other motivations Fitzjohn might have had to fly the mission.

"And how the hell did you get hold of that gun? Are you still secretly a member of the Israeli Secret Service? Have you been hiding this from me?"

"No, no, it's not like that at all. I got in touch with my old London contact to ask for something to protect myself on this trip. I just wanted a pistol, really, but he asked me to take the Uzi. I'm glad I did. All I have to do is report to him about how it performed operationally. I bet they never thought it would be a useful tool to do aircraft repairs!" Hannah gave a light, unconvincing laugh.

"No, I guess not. You'll be lucky to get it back, mind you. Your Israeli friends won't be too pleased with you if you can't return it."

"No, but that's the least of my concerns. I know you're angry with me, but what would you have done? We can always save up again for the house, and I feel we should be thankful to Henry. He got you out, after all."

Devon looked mutinous. "Yes, but why did he? You seem to have some kind of hold over him – maybe it's something to do with your relationship back in Hong Kong. I've never quite understood what went on between you two. Maybe he owed you a favour…"

Hannah jumped up from her seat, fisting her hands. "Hell, Adam, I've told you before, nothing went on between us! When are you going to believe me?" She was desperate to tell Devon the real reason that Fitzjohn had agreed to the flight, but she knew she could never do that.

His involvement in diamond smuggling, the fact that she had agreed to sleep with him – Devon must never be allowed to know this.

"Alright, please calm down. It doesn't matter now; we can settle everything when we get back to the UK. I don't even know if I have a job to go back to. The Dove is wrecked and there are no other radar test aircraft at de Havilland."

Hannah sat down again and Devon touched her arm. "I'm sorry. I'm being such an idiot. I haven't really thanked you and Fitzjohn for getting us out of that mess. You did brilliantly well, dealing with those Stasi agents."

His words shook Hannah, and she realised that the adrenaline that had been flowing through her system had dissipated. She felt the effects of shock begin to rise in her, and she started to tremble as she realised that she had killed a man. She started to question herself. Could she have wounded him instead, made him give up his gun? Did she have to kill him? "Oh, Adam," she gasped, "I killed him! I didn't want to. I had to fire; Henry was reloading and he was just about to shoot him."

Devon could see her agony, but there was nothing he could do but give her reassurance. "You did the right thing, my love. You had no choice – in fact, Fitzjohn should be eternally grateful that you did what you did. You never know, you might get a medal." Devon's efforts to lighten the mood only partially worked.

Hannah closed her eyes and sat back, relaxing in her seat.

***

After a couple of minutes, Devon realised that she had fallen asleep. At last he was able to relax. He knew he had been under huge stress, emotionally and physically, since departing Hatfield four days earlier. The sudden quiet in the room helped his clarity of mind, and he decided the time was right: he had debated the question in his mind for months.

He loved Hannah deeply and knew she felt the same. His reluctance to set a wedding date came from his uncertainty over how he saw his future. He had finally accepted that what he really wanted to be was not a schoolboy comic book all-action adventurer, but a man with a steady job – flying, preferably – a lovely wife, and a home to be proud of.

Devon had already looked at the diary for 1953, soon after the coronation, and found a date to suggest to Hannah. After making enquiries the previous month, he had reserved a time at the Caxton Hall register office in Westminster for the wedding. He could find no sensible reason why he had not discussed his thoughts with Hannah, but as he looked at her sleeping soundly, he resolved not to delay any longer. As soon as she woke, he would ask her to marry him on 1 July 1953.

FORTY-TWO

L ate that evening, long after the group had eaten their evening meal, the adjutant's assistant called Val to the telephone. It was her senior agent in the Berlin MI6 office, Andrew Murray, who wanted to update her on Franken's arrest. Murray had taken a team to the de Havilland office at Tempelhof but, given the hour, he hadn't expected anyone to be there. They broke in to find Franken's note saying that he would be away for two days. The team searched through some filing cabinets and found his home address, then immediately drove to the West Berlin suburb where he lived. Franken's flat was on the first floor of a three-storey post-war block. There was no security on the entrance to the lobby; the team easily picked the lock on the flat's lightweight door and entered.

It was clear that Franken hadn't returned home. There was no food in the small pantry, no dishes to be washed, no recent newspapers, the towels were completely dry, and there was no sign of his wife. Murray sent a car and two men back to the airport to lie in wait for Franken, should he return there, and to search for evidence of accomplices or secret papers hidden away. Murray and Iain Bremner, another experienced agent, stayed at the flat to carry out a more detailed search and capture Franken if he showed up.

Murray instructed Bremner to search the rubbish bins, every cupboard, suitcases, in and under furniture; he was sure that Franken would have left something that gave him away; people always did. Bremner soon found a pair of pliers, some wire cuttings and three battery packs in a small toolbox under the kitchen sink. Not absolute evidence of bomb making but a strong indicator, nonetheless.

Franken's note in the office was dated Monday, and it was now Wednesday evening, Murray was confident that Franken would be back home this evening before returning to work the next morning. He instructed Bremner to turn off all lights, and they sat in the dark, waiting, motionless, their PPKs ready in their hands.

They had a short wait. Just before midnight, the men heard a car stop outside the block of flats. Carefully glancing down into the street from the living-room window, they saw a young man take two bags from the back of the car, gently close the door and enter the lobby. The agents moved silently to stand on each side of the door to the flat, guns in hand.

Franken inserted his key and turned it, kicking the door to encourage it to open. As he stumbled in, burdened with his bags, Murray wrestled him to the floor and pulled his arms behind his back. Bremner wrapped his hand across Franken's face to stop him shouting. In a moment they had clicked handcuffs on him and stuck tape across his mouth. Franken might be a good servant of the communist cause but he was not a trained field agent; the two MI6 men had one of the easiest arrests they had ever made.

The agents drove quickly across Berlin to the MI6 office and took Franken to an interrogation room where they tried to intimidate him: they tied his arms firmly behind his back, shouted into this face, hit the table. After half an hour of this, Murray put the call through to Val at Wunstorf. After a short wait, she came on the line.

"What do you have for me, Murray?"

"We've picked up Franken, ma'am, and brought him back to the office. We found some tools and kit that could be used as bomb-making equipment at his flat, but no explosives or detonators. I've roughed him up a bit but at the moment he's not saying who he works with or for. But I'm confident that after a few hours under the lamp he will crack."

"Right, go ahead and apply the usual encouragement to get him to talk. I want to know if he has any associates in the UK, and what information he has passed on. And, assuming he knew that Leonid was on board the aircraft, how he found out."

"Understood, ma'am."

"Have you searched the de Havilland office in Tempelhof?" said Val.

"Only quickly. Found nothing but aircraft technical information and sales brochures from de Havilland."

"Are you sure? Were there no papers on the radar developments?"

"Nothing that we could see, ma'am, either at the flat or the office. But I've sent a couple of agents, Oliver and Walker, back over to Tempelhof in case Franken went direct to the office, and also to have a good search for anything incriminating. I haven't heard from them just yet."

"Keep at it, Murray, and ring me as soon as you have anything."

Val immediately called Ballantyne in London, even though it had gone midnight, gave him an update and promised to give him a full briefing as soon as possible after she landed back in the UK the next day. Her boss was disappointed that her team had not pressured Franken into talking, but they both knew that it could be a slow, difficult process; some prisoners were very resourceful at resisting interrogation, and had huge strength of purpose when they were protecting a cause they believed in.

FORTY-THREE

"Come in, Ballantyne. You know Colonel Anderson here, do you not?"

"Yes, sir. Good morning, Colonel."

"These days it's just Mr Anderson, Chief. We like to keep a low profile." He glanced at Ballantyne.

"Anderson is leading the hunt for the mole in the Leonid matter. We are searching for whoever tipped off this German fellow, Franken, and who might be passing secrets on the de Havilland radar project. I want you to work with Anderson's team to apprehend the culprit."

The two men knew each other: they had worked together before, very briefly, in Palestine in 1947. Anderson had been an officer in the military police back then and Ballantyne worked for military intelligence. In those days they both wore a uniform, but Anderson now sat relaxed and assured in the civilian clothes favoured by Special Branch officers involved in counter-espionage: a well-cut suit, a plain white shirt, gold tie pin. His standard-issue tan gabardine raincoat was draped over a chair. It clearly helped to mix in Establishment circles, where spies and double agents had seemed to thrive since the war. Ballantyne's MI6 people were of a rougher cut: they cared little for appearances and didn't mind fighting dirty to silently remove enemies of the state. Anderson had risen to the rank of lieutenant colonel surprisingly quickly, and after his army service was slotted into a high-level role at Special Branch. Ballantyne had nothing against him, but would only work with him on the tacit understanding that they were equals.

C leant forward and tapped his fingertips on his desk. "Anderson here has been working on counter-espionage for some time across the government. His initial review of the betrayal in Leonid's extraction has given us a lead to our prime suspect, but we still lack evidence, and you're here to get that evidence." C sat up straight, hesitated, then said, "Ballantyne, the man we believe has been spying for the Russians is… David Porter."

Ballantyne gave a half gasp, half laugh. "Why the hell – sorry, sir. Why do you think this? Porter had an exemplary military record with the RAF and has a bloody good job at BOAC. And he was significant in the Berlin assignment to get Leonid out. He practically masterminded the whole thing. Somewhat contradicts your theory. And that's all it is, isn't it – a theory?"

Anderson interjected. "Not entirely. He shows all the characteristics of a clever spy: he developed a strong connection with Jocelyn Darley, brought in old colleagues who would trust him explicitly, such as Adam Devon from his RAF squadron. Devon, by the way, is not off our list of suspects. Porter lives a lifestyle well beyond his pay scale. You may have seen the new Jag that he drives, and the quality of his watch – a rather nice Patek Phillipe. He and his wife have an expensive flat off Sloane Square. No mortgage. We have had him under surveillance for the past few months, and he lives very well. Porter has had access to the de Havilland offices and could have stolen information on the new radar or had someone sell it to him. But no, we don't have any firm evidence yet, but with Darley's help we will soon be able to trap him. That's where you come in. We want you to use your friendship to find out how Porter passed messages to the German in the Berlin office of de Havilland, but without him sensing we are on to him, of course. There may be others involved that we haven't yet identified."

"Is that all understood, Ballantyne?" said the chief.

"Yes, sir, but let's be clear on this. Porter has a very comfortable job at BOAC and he was recruited by us, MI6, to assist with our assignments that require pilots and aircraft. Now we are asking ourselves, is he a spy? Sorry, sir, but it's highly implausible. And can I ask, is Darley to be trusted? He has all the secret data at his fingertips."

"Nonsense!" said the chief. "You may feel Porter's credentials are sound, but he was recruited by my predecessor, I'll remind you. And Darley's been with the firm since before the war, and is one of our leading industrialists. Anderson, you agree, don't you?"

Anderson cleared his throat and nodded. "Well, sir, we always keep an open mind. As we have seen with the Cambridge circle, you can never write anyone off. But we have no reason to suspect Darley – in fact, quite the opposite. He has offered us whatever help we need at the de Havilland factory. He was as shocked as anyone when it emerged that Franken was responsible for the bomb on the aircraft."

Ballantyne butted in. "And Franken, sir, we are still holding him at the Berlin MI6 office – we can quickly get to his contacts if he talked. But we need your permission to apply the right pressure…"

The chief grew redder in the face as he searched for the right words. "I'm sorry, Ballantyne, but we are not going to have a culture where we abuse prisoners, using torture, physical and mental punishment to get what we want! We're not Nazi gangsters. We have to work within the law."

Ballantyne saw Anderson cringe. He would turn a blind eye to whatever techniques were needed by Ballantyne's team on such a vital prisoner, but he didn't seem keen to argue with the chief. He had his career to protect.

C went on. "Keep the pressure on him – he might break and talk. Now, gentlemen." He leant forward and, using his right index finger to hook the fingers on his left hand, counted off: "One, I want Porter followed twenty-four hours a day. Two, make a list of his friends and associates. Three, contact BOAC and have his office phone tapped. Four, get a warrant to search his apartment – but we will hold on to that for now. We don't want to alert him at this stage."

"Very well, sir, all understood. I will get Val to assist me – she was central to the Berlin assignment and has a good team in the city."

"No, no, Ballantyne." Anderson spoke quickly and firmly. "Keep this between us and my people. I don't want Hetherington-Brown to know our suspicions at this stage. Not that we have any reason to suspect her of anything underhand, but she has had a long relationship with Porter."

"Mr Anderson, you forget that Hetherington-Brown heads up the Berlin station. She has my full support and confidence. Don't think for a moment that her working relationship with Porter will compromise her. I insist on choosing my own team, and this includes Brown."

This time C was inclined to go along with Ballantyne's wishes. He only had to mutter, "Makes sense," for Anderson to back down.

Ballantyne sensed he could take the initiative in running the exercise. "Anderson, if your people could step up the observation to round the clock, that will cover C's first point. I will get a list of his associates drafted. You can get the phone tap at BOAC arranged, and the warrant. I will go and see Darley after Hetherington-Brown lands at Biggin. If Porter was working with someone at de Havilland, an engineer perhaps, then he might help us track down the mole."

"Time is of the essence, gentlemen. Please provide regular reports." C stood up and walked to his office door. "Coffee please, Miss Samways, and book lunch for me at my club, would you?"

FORTY-FOUR

The DC3 made a perfect landing at Biggin Hill and taxied straight to the long-term parking area for transport aircraft, away from the main buildings. They were greeted by the station commanding officer, his adjutant and two plain-clothes MI5 men who escorted Leonid, Fitzjohn, Devon and Hannah to two military police Humber saloon cars. They quickly departed for the safe house, accompanied by four motorcycle outriders and a Land Rover with three armed guards, leaving Val and Casey to walk across the tarmac to the airport buildings. They had received a message while on the flight that they were required to report to the intelligence office as soon as they arrived.

Ballantyne was there to meet the aircraft, but kept out of sight until the Humbers had departed. He gazed out of the small interview room window and sighed. He wasn't looking forward to discussing Porter with Val. He hoped he would soon be able to release the American, Casey, back to his own people; there seemed little point keeping him at Biggin.

"Good morning, sir. This is Drake Casey. As you know, he's with the CIA."

"Good morning, Val." Ballantyne offered his hand to Casey. "Yes, sterling work on the mission, I gather. Would you mind submitting your report to the intelligence officer next door? I need to have a chat with Val. Come back when your report's completed, would you?"

"Sure, I'll see you in about half an hour."

Ballantyne noticed an exchange of looks between Val and Casey, and Val gave a gentle smile.

"Take a seat. I've got some news for you."

"Yes, sir, what is it?"

"I've just come down from London after meeting C early this morning. A chap called Anderson from Special Branch was there too. Do you know him? He was once a colonel in the military police."

"No, I don't think I know him."

"He's leading the Special Branch task force looking into communist spies. Now assigned to investigate the person who he thinks betrayed us on the Leonid extraction."

"Really, and who's that?" asked Val.

"You're not going to like this, but C's convinced it was David Porter. We've been asked to watch him, look at his associates, and find out how he might have relayed information to Franken."

"This is nuts, sir! There's no way David is a spy!"

"I know that and you know that. But C does not, and I'm not sure what Anderson thinks. But the key issue is, while we have to be seen investigating Porter, we also have to find out who the real traitor is."

"Can't we talk to Porter, have it out with him?"

"You know it's never a good idea to let the target know he's being investigated." Ballantyne was getting exasperated. "I want you to dig deep, find out all you can about Franken. Has he ever met Porter? Did they have any relationship? Family connections, school and university friends – the usual drill."

"I will have to follow orders, sir, but the idea that David Porter is a spy for the Soviets is outrageous, and sending us and Special Branch on a wild goose chase will only delay the hunt for the real culprit." Val didn't hide her dismay.

"Remember, Val, the Cambridge spies were also pillars of society, beyond suspicion and totally trusted – until they turned out to be agents of the Soviet Union. So we have to keep an open mind, just in case. And by the way, the chief also has a question mark over Adam Devon. Probably me and you too, such is his paranoia."

Val couldn't speak; she just shook her head. Ballantyne went through the reasoning for suspecting Porter and the actions agreed with Anderson.

There was a knock at the door, and Casey came in. "All done, sir. I now need to get back to London to brief my boss. Once that's done, I'll be on my way back to Berlin. I'm guessing there will be no shortage of demand from new defectors who want to come over." Casey walked over to Val and shook her hand, then spontaneously embraced her. She returned the hug with a warm smile. They stepped back and held hands.

"Take care, Val. Maybe I'll see you around when you're back in Berlin?"

"I'd like that, Drake. I'll look you up after this Leonid business is settled. And take care of yourself. But do me a favour, will you, as soon as you're back? Get some of your people over to Burg and help the doctor and deputy magistrate escape to the West."

"Certainly will, ma'am. Trust me, I'll make that happen."

As Casey left the room, Ballantyne looked at Val and widened his eyes, but said nothing. The obvious affection the two felt for each other was not something he had to concern himself with – as long as it didn't interfere with Val's job.

***

Ballantyne assigned the compilation of the list of Porter's friends and associates to a junior agent in the office. Reis Jones was an astute thirty-year-old with an inquisitive nature. He was good at detail, and within a few hours had a list of ex-RAF personnel Porter was still in touch with, a full family profile, including his wife's relations and her main friends in her county set, and notes on his membership of the All England Club at Wimbledon and Richmond golf club. Most interesting to Jones was a note on Porter's service file that his father had been a member of the Communist Party of Great Britain for a short period before the war. Then he became a Labour party official. He had once headed up a workers' committee and tried to organise a strike at the bank in the City where he worked. Nothing came of it, and Porter's father retired a year ago. But when Ballantyne shared the list with C, he focused on the socialist tendencies of Porter's family. It was easy for C to make wrong assumptions that reinforced his opinion that Porter was a well-remunerated spy for the Russians.

FORTY-FIVE

Angus Ballantyne arrived at the de Havilland complex in Hatfield just before lunchtime, and was shown straight through to Jocelyn Darley's office. Although he was reluctant to disclose C's suspicions about Porter, he needed to ask Darley questions that would give away the focus of his enquiries. He had to accept that.

"Good morning, Angus, lovely to see you. Do take a seat." Darley was as hospitable as usual. "Let me pour the coffee. What can I do for you?"

"We're looking into the explosion on the Dove en route back from Berlin. You're familiar with the details of the assignment that Devon was asked to carry out, and I'm pleased to say it was ultimately successful."

Ballantyne saw Darley frown, then put on what looked like a fake smile. "Of course. Good show, glad to hear it."

Ballantyne went on, "But you'll also know that somewhere along the line there was a mole: someone who knew about the plan to pick up the defector and bring him to the UK, and they passed on this info to Franken. There's every chance that the mole wanted to transmit details of the radar technology that you are developing, and they got to hear of the flight carrying Leonid, the defector, and the team back. We have a suspect, and my job is to find evidence that will prove that he is guilty."

"You have identified a possible suspect? Might I know who that person is?" Darley cut straight to the point.

"Confidentially, I can tell you it's David Porter. We have had our suspicions for some time that he might be enhancing his income by selling information to the Russians, but we only have circumstantial evidence. And we now know that his father is a socialist. I'm working with Special Branch to find the proof we require and to identify any persons he may have been working with here at de Havilland, such as engineers or scientists working on the project."

Darley sat back and mused silently for a few moments. "I'm sure all of our people are vetted, but no doubt your team will look into their backgrounds again. But Porter? I have to say that we took him on trust, on the understanding that MI6 were happy for him to be involved. And now I come to think of it, he was always very interested in details about the Dove's radar capabilities, very keen to talk to the boys in the hangar. I just put that down to his interest in flying. I had no idea he is a spy."

"Well, we're not one hundred per cent sure that he is, so we will let him continue the work he does for us, finding the right pilots and aircraft for our operational purposes. We will be watching him carefully, tracing his every move and who he associates with. That's where we need your help – with keeping a log of his movements."

"I will do all I can, naturally, Angus. Actually, we have a favour to ask Porter with regard to the recruitment of test pilots. That should give me the chance to keep an eye on him."

"But without arousing any suspicions."

"Understood."

"Right. I'll be on my way then, Jocelyn. Thanks for your help."

***

Darley watched out of his window as Ballantyne drove off in his car. He turned and pressed the button on his phone console and instructed Lucy to call David Porter and ask him to come to the office late afternoon – it was important and urgent. Minutes later, Lucy confirmed that Porter would be there at around 6p.m.

Darley felt relieved that Franken had obviously not talked. He hoped that Franken would die in custody, as many agents do under severe interrogation. Darley might have to arrange to have him killed – a poisoning, perhaps? The question of how this could be done sat uneasily in his mind. He would have to contact the Stasi directly to have it arranged. But in the meantime Darley had everything under control, except for one thing: he needed copies of the latest test results for the new radar. He decided to go down to the hangar and look around.

His luck was in – everyone was at lunch. He went to the chief engineer's office, pulled open an unlocked filing cabinet and found what he was looking for in an instant – a couple of files from the last few flights that Devon had carried out before the Berlin assignment, with the radar performance data listed. He walked through to the flight office and to Devon's desk, where he opened a drawer, pulled out an aircraft handling manual for the Dove, some maps and flight plans. He tucked the radar papers into the bottom of the drawer and replaced the contents. He took the other file back to the office. There he drew from his desk a miniature camera, and took several photographs of the papers. He planned to plant the camera in the bottom of Porter's briefcase – or perhaps his overcoat. That would be the incriminating evidence that Ballantyne needed.

Lucy was still at her desk when Porter arrived just after five-thirty, and showed him into Darley's office.

"You made good time, David."

"Good afternoon, Jocelyn. Yes, the Mark VII's a pretty quick machine. Lovely to drive and solid on the road."

"Better than flying a Spitfire?"

"Ah, not quite. Different kettle of fish altogether," said Porter.

"I'd like to have a look at her before you go." Darley had walked over to his cocktail cabinet. "G&T, Scotch perhaps?"

"Thank you – a small Scotch and water. I can give you a spin around the airfield if you like."

Darley stopped, holding the whisky bottle in mid-air, thought for a moment and smiled. "Yes, that would be excellent."

"What was the important matter you wished to discuss, Jocelyn?" Porter asked.

"Yes, of course, we mustn't forget business over pleasure. At de Havilland we are concentrating our front-line fighter developments on jets, and we need more test pilots. I wanted to ask if you could use your extensive network of contacts from your RAF days to recommend men who would like to consider a test pilot training course with us. Our competitors, Avro, Hawker, Supermarine and others are also in the market for test pilots, so competition is tough. We need to capitalise on our network of friends who will steer the pilots in our direction, rather than the others, on the grounds that we offer the best training programme around. And we have to keep this confidential, naturally."

"I agree there is a huge demand for these chaps. Do you have details of the training scheme you're offering?"

"I do indeed. Here they are." Darley passed a file sitting on his desk to Porter. The two men spent time going through the minimum requirements for flying experience. The training plan listed the flight drills and manoeuvres that pilots must learn. It also noted the pay for trainees and graduates of the programme.

"Looks like an excellent scheme, Jocelyn, and I'm sure your pay scales will be very competitive," said Porter. "I'd be glad to help with your recruitment where I can. May I take these papers with me?"

"Yes, do. And thank you, David, that's most appreciated. There will also be a generous stipend to you for your time. Let me know if you have any potential candidates next week, would you?" Darley had topped up their drinks and now stood by his office window. "Yes, indeed, that's a great-looking car. Now, shall we go and have that ride around the airfield?"

Porter knocked back his drink, picked up his coat and placed the papers in his briefcase. He threw these into the back of the car as Darley climbed into the front passenger seat. Porter didn't hold back in his demonstration of the car's capabilities, taking it up to 75mph around the perimeter track of the airfield. He noticed that Darley was already wearing his classic tan leather driving gloves and so pulled over and offered Darley a go at driving. Porter got out of the car to go around to the passenger side but Darley just slid across into the driving seat.

"I'll use the main runway," said Darley. "Nothing flying at the moment."

Darley turned onto the runway threshold and accelerated straight down the centre line, quickly reaching 100mph then, a few seconds later, 105. Easing back on the accelerator, he allowed the car to slow. Darley turned to Porter and laughed. "Great performance, David. I might buy one of these myself."

FORTY-SIX

De Havilland worked a five-and-a-half-day week. On a Saturday morning many of the staff liked to arrive early, so they could get away by noon. Darley was already in his office when he saw the production staff arriving for work. He went down to the hangar and into the chief engineer's office.

Andrew Wren was sitting at his desk. "Good morning, sir, how can I help you?"

"Good morning, Andrew. I need to review the latest radar performance figures that you have – those from the flights immediately prior to the loss of the Dove."

"I'll get them for you." Wren walked over to the filing cabinet and opened the top drawer. Darley was shocked. This was not the drawer from which he had taken the documents, and he realised that there might be further copies of the data. But Wren rummaged through the files, slid the drawer shut and opened the one below. Again he searched it and quickly turned to Darley. "They're not here, sir. But not all of my chaps are in yet; I will ask them if they have the papers when they arrive."

"Please do that, and let me know as soon as you find them. This is very unsatisfactory, Andrew. You know that classified information should be locked away at night."

"Yes, sir. I shouldn't be long. I daresay one of my analysts is working on the data."

By mid-morning, Wren had been unable to find all the papers, and concluded that a file had been taken from the technical department and had no choice but to tell Darley, who was inwardly delighted that his deception had worked. Wren was visibly relieved when he found the MD was not unduly annoyed about the apparent breach of security.

"But there is something else I should mention, sir, that is very strange. Although one copy of the papers is still missing, we found a copy in Adam Devon's desk."

"I see. That *is* strange. But Devon is on leave at the moment, so we can't ask him why he had the file. Thank you, Andrew. I'll take it from here."

After Wren had left his office, Darley asked Lucy to put a call through to Ballantyne.

"Angus, it's Darley here. We have something of a problem, I'm afraid. If you could come up to Hatfield, I will brief you. It's not something to discuss over the telephone. The factory will be closed, but I'll be here all day."

"I see. Concerning our friend, I presume."

"Indeed."

"I will be there in under two hours."

***

Before leaving his office in central London, Ballantyne called Anderson. Special Branch HQ was just along the river and Ballantyne offered to pick up Anderson and take him to de Havilland. An hour later, Ballantyne pulled into the car park outside Darley's office.

"Gentlemen, I'm afraid we have discovered that some radar performance data files are missing. This information is top secret, and if it falls into the wrong hands it would damage the whole programme. Unfortunately, our chief engineer found a file in Devon's desk, hidden away, and a second file is still missing."

"But Devon is closely involved with this programme – wouldn't it be natural for him to have copies of the files?" said Ballantyne.

"No. As the pilot, he has no right or need to see these papers. In fact, he is forbidden from even reading the test outputs. I can only assume that he has passed the missing copy to Porter."

Anderson spoke up. "We have the warrant to search Porter's flat ready. We could carry out a raid first thing in the morning. If we discover any files, we will arrest him on the spot."

"Agreed," said Ballantyne. "I'll leave you to carry out the operation; house searches are not my forte. I'll wait in my office for the outcome. But tell me, Darley, where is Devon? We will have to bring him in to explain why he had a copy of the data in his desk."

"He's on two weeks' leave at the moment, granted by the company after the Berlin affair. I can call him into the office, if you wish?"

"No, don't do that. He lives at Welham Green. I can go there now – it's only a twenty-minute drive. Are you happy to take the train back to London, Anderson? I can drop you off at the station in Hatfield."

"Very well, but please be careful not to allow Devon to warn Porter."

"Leave it to me. I do have some experience of interrogation," said Ballantyne, and the two men stood and left the office.

In the car, Ballantyne felt he had to reaffirm his views. "You know, Anderson, I'm still not convinced that Porter could be our man, and it's even more ridiculous to think that Devon would be passing secret information to him. The key to finding out who was working with

Franken is through Franken himself. I will be getting my people to work harder on him, look again for evidence in his flat in Berlin."

"We can only speculate on motives, but Porter does live a luxurious lifestyle. If we knew where his money came from, we might have a better feel for what drives him. And as you know, his father was a communist at one time."

"All circumstantial. Arresting Porter may well force the real mole into hiding, and we'll never find him. Or her. If I were a betting man, I would look carefully at the technicians on the project – there could be someone there hiding in plain sight, so to speak."

"Yes, but they're all security-checked and no questions arise for any of them. I'll be in touch tomorrow." Anderson got out of the car and walked quickly into the station.

FORTY-SEVEN

It took Ballantyne just fifteen minutes to get to Devon's house, where he was glad to see his car parked outside. He rang the doorbell, and was surprised when a young woman opened the door.

"Good afternoon. My name's Angus Ballantyne – is Adam at home? It's a work matter." Ballantyne's expression was impassive.

"Yes, he's in the garden. Please come in, I'll go and get him. Would you like some tea?"

"Thanks. Good of you."

"I'm Hannah, by the way."

Ballantyne didn't sit down as Hannah went through the hall and kitchen and out the back door. Instead he looked around the living room, not sure what he was searching for, just anything that seemed out of character for Devon, or unrelated to his job. He noticed some papers with a letterhead from Hawker Siddeley – de Havilland's main competitor. Ballantyne speed-read the letter. It was a job offer for Devon to join them as a test pilot on the development of the Hunter fighter. Clearly Devon was being headhunted.

"Hello, Angus, how are you? You're here on business, I gather." Devon walked into the room and looked quizzically at Ballantyne.

"Yes – you won't be surprised to hear it's about the Franken case. Can I ask you a few questions?"

"Of course," said Devon.

"What I want to know is, who in the radar project is authorised to review the test outputs and data?"

Devon sat back and considered the question. "The boffins who take the readings, of course; the senior engineering staff on the ground; and Andrew Wren, the chief engineer. Probably some of the aeronautics team from the RAF. That's about it, really."

"What about you – do you get to see the data?"

"No, that's not my area. I just do the flying."

"And Jocelyn Darley – is he authorised?"

"Oh yes, I would say so, although he is more interested in aircraft sales rather than radar equipment."

"What about others outside the firm? People from the Air Ministry or other government departments, for instance, or perhaps David Porter?"

"You do see Air Ministry people come to the office occasionally, but I don't expect them to review the technical details. They're only interested in whether the radar actually works as promised. As for David…" Devon gave a half laugh. "No, he wouldn't have access to this type of information. Why would he? His role is to provide you types with pilots to do your bidding, whatever the risks." Devon gave Ballantyne a knowing look.

"Any others?"

"Not that I can think of. All the technical chaps have access to all the data – they use it every day, but they're all decent people. I'm sure none of them would ever consider selling secrets. But no doubt you or your people will be looking closely at them all, to satisfy yourselves that none of them would betray our country. Are you thinking that Franken was involved in stealing secret information about the radar, and heard we were carrying a Soviet scientist so he decided to blow us up?"

"Something like that. The question is, who was feeding him information? Could it have been Porter? And if so, how did Porter get the files?" Ballantyne couldn't beat about the bush. He was perfectly convinced that Devon was not involved in any way, despite the files that had been found in his desk. But Ballantyne needed to find out his views on Porter. "You know David leads a very luxurious lifestyle, somewhat reminiscent of Maclean and Burgess, that's difficult to explain on his salary."

"Those two were established communists, though. David has never been involved in that type of thing, as far as I know. Has he?"

"His father was a member of the Communist Party of Great Britain before the war," said Ballantyne.

"Really? I didn't know that, but it doesn't mean that David was a communist too." Devon clearly understood the implication – like father, like son. "As for money, his wife is very wealthy. You knew that, didn't you?"

"Well, yes, I understand she comes from an old country family. But these people don't have real money; their assets are stately homes and family portraits."

"OK, so David has expensive tastes. That doesn't make him a spy."

"I'm afraid we believe it may well be the case. There are data files missing from de Havilland, and I have to tell you that a file containing confidential information on the radar tests was found in your desk."

"Really? Someone must have put it there, or I might have picked it up by mistake. I have never even read the files, let alone deliberately kept hold of one," said Devon.

Ballantyne was perfectly happy to take him at his word. In his line of business, he gained a sense for when people were lying and when they were telling the truth. "Well, you will understand how important it is that you help us find out who has been working with Porter. We need to find evidence to prove he's the mole who passed information to Franken – information that could have killed you."

"*What?* I don't work for you and your lot, Angus. And I don't believe a word of this. Remember, I flew with David on active service in the RAF. He just isn't the type to sell out his country."

Hannah appeared at the door from the kitchen with three cups of tea on a tray. The tension between the two men dissipated, and Ballantyne raised his hands to placate Devon. "Look, let me put my cards on the table. Porter's lifestyle may or may not come from his wife's wealth. And between you and me, I don't see him as a spy either. But we need to either find evidence that he is guilty, or find evidence that points to someone else. We have to accept that Franken was getting information from someone."

Hannah cut in. "What are you saying, Mr Ballantyne? You think that David Porter is a traitor? Really?"

Devon responded. "That's the way it looks at the moment, darling, but it's all nonsense, we know that. Angus's people will soon work out that David is perfectly innocent."

After an awkward silence, Ballantyne finished his tea and stood up. "I need to get back to London now. Thanks for the tea, Hannah. Adam, I suggest you give some thought to who could be spying for the Soviets within de Havilland, and do it urgently."

FORTY-EIGHT

At 5a.m. on Sunday, very few people were on the streets of west London when the three unmarked Special Branch cars swerved around Sloane Square and into Holbein Place, stopping outside a beautiful red-stoned four-storey house. Porter's apartment was on the second floor. Anderson's plan was to take two men with him to carry out the search. Standard procedure dictated that another two men stay in the street in case the suspects tried to make a run for it. The sudden, early morning raid was designed to prevent Porter or his wife hiding any evidence that might be incriminating, and to stop them phoning any accomplices.

The front door still had the night security lock on, but one of the men carried a two-foot jemmy that he pressed into the door frame. In twenty seconds they were in the vestibule. Taking the stairs quickly but quietly, Anderson and the team stopped outside Porter's door and listened for a moment. He could already be talking on the telephone, and they just might be able to hear the conversation. But all was quiet. Anderson rapped hard on the door, rang the bell and shouted, "Open up – police!"

All designed to instil shock and confusion in the suspects.

David Porter was a hugely experienced fighter pilot who had served in a Spitfire squadron in the Battle of Britain and right through the war. He wasn't easily shaken but he jumped out of bed, startled, pulled on some trousers and went to the door.

"David Porter? My name is Commander Anderson, Special Branch. I am investigating an act of treason and I have a warrant to search your premises."

As Porter stepped back, the men entered the flat. Anderson dropped the warrant on the hall table and walked straight through to the living room. One of his men went into the kitchen and the other made to go into the bedroom.

Porter lunged across and stopped him. "No, you don't, my wife's in there. Give her a few minutes to dress."

The officer looked at Anderson, who nodded. "Five minutes, then get in there, Sharman."

"What do you want, Anderson? What the hell's this all about?" said Porter. "You're not seriously thinking I'm a mole, are you? That's bloody crazy."

"Of course you'd say that, but we'll search anyway. I'll let you know if we find what we're looking for."

But after nearly an hour of searching, pulling drawers open, moving furniture and going through personal papers, the officers had found nothing connected with de Havilland or the radar project. Anderson decided that he had to ask some questions. Porter and Penny sat together on the settee.

"How long have you been at BOAC?"

"Nearly four years. Why?" asked Porter.

"And how long have you been co-opted to MI6 and working with de Havilland?"

"Less than a year." Porter's frustration began to boil over. "Look, Anderson, either tell me what you're after or get out."

"That's enough, Porter. We're doing our job and you will be best advised to cooperate."

"I really think you're wasting your time. And who the hell authorised this nonsense?"

Anderson ignored Porter. He was feeling uncomfortably warm, so he took off his hat and raincoat and dropped them on a chair in the hall. As he did so, he noticed a small sweet dish on the hall table. In it sat a bunch of keys. Anderson picked them up and played the keys through his fingers: several door keys, home and office, a car key and one that might open a safe. He walked back into the living room. "Show me your safe, please."

"It's here. Behind the picture." Porter opened it, and Anderson was disappointed when he only found items of jewellery, two ladies' watches and a man's watch, £200 in cash and various papers. As he was taking the keys back to the hall, the fob caught his eye: a silver image of a roaring Jaguar attached to a black leather square. He had a thought. "Where is your car parked, Porter?"

"In the basement."

"Sharman, you and Wilson get down there and search the car."

"You don't have a warrant for that, do you?" said Porter.

"Ah, no. But you wouldn't object, surely?"

"What the hell. Go ahead."

Anderson returned to the living room, to find Penny standing by the window. "Mrs Porter, a few questions, please. I gather your father is Lord Matlock."

"That's correct. Is that relevant to your visit today?"

"Just being sure of my facts. It's a very nice flat you have here. Must have been expensive."

"That's my and my husband's concern."

"But it's not the usual abode for an airline pilot, even one of Porter's standing."

"It was bought for us through a confidential family legacy, if you must know."

This shook Anderson. He had assumed that Porter had channelled a lucrative income from his spying activities into the purchase of the flat. But he resolved to press on. "Does the family also provide for you in terms of life's luxuries – jewellery, watches, holidays, an expensive car?"

Penny stood up and pointed her fingers at Anderson, pistol-style. Almost spitting her words, she said, "Look here, Inspector, you have no right to question me on personal matters. Any more, and I shall submit a complaint to your superiors. Now, get out if you have nothing else to say."

Anderson was affronted. "It's Commander, Mrs Porter, if you please. And rest assured that our searches and questioning have support from the highest—"

There was a noise from the hall as Sharman pushed open the front door, gasping after running up the stairs from the basement. "Sir, we've found something. Tucked away under the driver's seat." Sharman produced a miniature camera. He had wrapped it in his handkerchief to preserve any fingerprints, although none were subsequently found, Darley had cleaned it and was wearing gloves when he placed it in the car.

"Well, that's interesting. Useful for taking pictures of documents, wouldn't you say, Porter."

"This is ridiculous. That's not mine!"

Anderson stepped forward and faced Porter. "Ridiculous or not, David Porter, I'm arresting you on suspicion of treason and of assisting an enemy. You need not say anything, but anything you do say may be used in evidence. Sharman, handcuffs. Mrs Porter, I am also arresting you on suspicion of assisting in a treasonable act."

FORTY-NINE

When Ballantyne arrived in the chief's office for his regular Monday morning meeting, he was relieved to find that C was unusually relaxed – friendly, even. Reports had come through from the technical people who were debriefing Leonid at the safe house in Surrey: they were absolutely delighted with the information he had given them so far. Russian air-to-ground missiles were clearly more developed than British ones – and, as far as the technicians knew, the American's. Leonid's information would enable the West to catch up rapidly. A message had also been received from No. 10: the Prime Minister sent his congratulations to C for the successful extraction of such a key asset. The chief naturally took all the credit for the assignment, and thanked the PM for his kind words.

After a short discussion of the mission's success, Kate Samways brought in a note confirming that Porter had been arrested after a miniature camera had been found in his car. The film in the camera had been developed, and consisted of pictures of the radar data file. Ballantyne's heart sank, but there was little he could do. The evidence was difficult to refute.

"There you are – even those with the most secure background can succumb to temptation when the price is right." C sat back in his chair and tapped a pencil on his desk in time with the lecture he was giving Ballantyne. "Or, of course, it might be ideological, given his father's record. And we must now look very carefully at Devon – he has the closest and longest working relationship with Porter. I know he was on the extraction flight, but Porter must have decided that he was expendable when he decided to blow up the aircraft. There might be others in the ring – technicians at de Havilland, for instance. I'm sure all these people and others are on your list of Porter's associates, Ballantyne, along with his wife's family and connections."

"Yes, sir, we have a comprehensive list of names, but most of them have been cleared and I'm confident the rest will pass muster today or tomorrow."

"I'm not sure I share your confidence, particularly regarding Porter's family association with communism. Sometimes people cultivate their beliefs for a long time before they act on them. Anyway, they're holding Porter at Special Branch. I suggest you get down there and question him yourself."

"Yes, sir, straight away. Good morning, and congratulations on the message from Winston."

As he left C's office, Ballantyne had every intention of interviewing Porter, but first he stopped off at his desk. He wanted to call Val Hetherington-Brown.

***

"Val, Porter's been arrested. Apparently Special Branch found a miniature camera in his car, but nothing else as far as I know. I'm going over there shortly to question him, and will let you know if anything emerges. Off the record, I want you to keep up the search, and the pressure on Franken."

"Yes, sir, will do. I'll call the chaps in Berlin and get them to up the ante, if you see what I mean."

Ballantyne nodded. "Just make sure nothing goes wrong. We don't want to lose our prime suspect."

"Understood, sir. I'll speak to Murray now. We'll start by arresting Franken's wife, and let Franken know she is in custody. And perhaps a touch more encouragement to Franken – a deep, cold bath, head down – might do the trick. I'll work on what we know about Franken and Porter from this end."

"Excellent, Val. Just make sure that Franken stays alive."

FIFTY

Jocelyn Darley had provided Ballantyne with the scant information on Franken that de Havilland had on their employment files, and Ballantyne had passed this on to Val. Darley had admitted that no references were obtained; Franken was recommended, he said, by a retired colleague in the aviation business, now sadly deceased. That wasn't best practice, of course but good people are hard to find, Darley conceded. Such a shock to find out he was a communist spy.

When the Berlin station agents arrested Franken, they packaged up all the documents in his desk and filing cabinets and sent them to London. They found no technical papers on the new radar developments, and they could not find an exchange of messages with anyone who might be a Stasi agent or informer. Val took the time herself to go through the boxes of papers: they contained notes of meetings with potential clients, copies of receipts for expenses, mainly restaurants in West Berlin, his appointments diary. Franken must have got his instructions from somewhere, and he must have a handler to channel any secret information through to his Soviet masters. But no incriminating evidence was found – the man was a disciplined, efficient spy.

A few days after Franken's arrest, his wife was released and she went to live with her parents. From then on she had been carefully watched; it wouldn't be the first time that the brains behind a spy was the suspect's wife. The Berlin MI6 people spent some time taking their flat apart, but found nothing: Franken was clearly clever and covered his tracks thoroughly. The only reason they could hold him was because he gave Devon the bomb to take on the aircraft, although he denied knowing what was inside the box. He said he thought it contained a bottle of kirsch. And Franken still would not admit that he was a Stasi agent, even under the pressure that the MI6 men were applying.

Val sent word for Devon to be brought in. She wanted to interview him, yet again, to try to glean anything useful that Franken might have said about his background, schooling or political connections while Devon was at the de Havilland office at Tempelhof. Devon was still on leave, so he came down to London for an early morning meeting at the MI6 building. Val hoped he could do something to help David Porter prove his innocence, at least.

The discussion with Val was fruitless. Devon admitted that he didn't like Franken and had made no effort to befriend him. Each time they met, they had only talked about details of the flight, how the Dove handled, and other general information Franken would need for his job as a sales executive. But Devon recalled the niggling irritation he had felt when he was asked to deliver the sales brochures, and his surprise that Darley had involved himself so personally. They had administrative staff at de Havilland for that sort of thing,

"There is something that I found odd, Val. Might not be important, though…"

"Tell me."

"Well, on my flights to Berlin, Mr Darley usually asked me to take a package of sales materials – brochures and the like – to give to Franken. And Franken was always very eager to receive these."

Val walked over to the boxes from Berlin, which were stacked in one corner of the room. Devon followed her.

"These, you mean?"

Devon pulled out a couple of the sales brochures. The first one showed a glistening cockpit, another showed different seating configurations, one showed a mock-up of an air ambulance version of the aircraft, and another was a general brochure showing the Dove in flight on perfect sunny days.

"Yes, these are the ones."

Something caught Val's eye, and she picked up another brochure from the box and pulled out one of the promotional bookmarks. "What's this?"

"Part of the sales material de Havilland hands out at trade shows, conferences, etc. There is usually a bookmark in each new brochure. I think Mr Darley uses them to highlight particular pages. I did look at a couple when I delivered them, but there didn't seem to be anything special about the pages."

Val looked carefully at the bookmark, then started to scratch at the embossed image of the Vampire with her fingernail. Soon the card began to fragment. She tore it in half. It looked perfectly ordinary. She tried another one, carefully picking off the embossed picture. Again, nothing. She turned to the pages that had been highlighted. A Dove parked somewhere cold – Norway, perhaps? – with a snowy mountain scene in the background, and a heading in bold lettering: 'All-weather capability'. In another brochure the bookmark was inserted in a page that listed the aircraft's technical performance, with a picture of the Dove at de Havilland's home base. This time the heading read 'Superior performance'.

Val suddenly slapped her hand on the open page of another brochure. "Bloody hell, look!" She almost shouted it, then showed Devon the page. She ran her finger over the heading 'Fuel efficiency', then paused at the capital F. "Look, the page is slightly torn or scraped." Val went back to the Norway picture. Yes, the capital A also looked scratched. She dashed to the door of her office and called over her senior technician, Ian Morrison. "Get these down to the lab straightaway, Ian. I want an immediate analysis of the scratched parts of the pages – here, and here."

"What is it, Val?" said Devon.

"I'm pretty sure that lettering contained a microdot. We have a lab in the basement and the chaps will be able to confirm in a few minutes." Val could see a puzzled look on Devon's face.

"Using microdots is a way of reducing photographs to a tiny scale," she explained. "You need specialist equipment to do it, but it's not inherently difficult. Take the pictures, shrink them down to a pinhead size, and smuggle them to your contact. He then magnifies them and hey presto."

Val went through more boxes. "Not all the documents have bookmarks. Were they there when you delivered them to Franken?"

"No, not all the brochures had them," said Devon.

Val flicked through some technical papers. "No signs of damage there."

Morrison returned a few minutes later. "The boys have examined the pages under the microscope, ma'am, and they definitely think they contained a microdot underneath the lettering. Traces of the adhesive used are still there."

"Excellent! Now find out where Ballantyne is, will you? Ask him to come to my office as soon as possible."

When Morrison left, Val turned to Devon. "It's Darley. He's our traitor."

FIFTY-ONE

Val ensured that C gave authorisation to bring Darley in, even if he was reluctant to do so, as he still hung on to the belief that the culprit was Porter, or someone else at de Havilland. This time it was MI6 who were making the arrest, with Val as leading agent, Ballantyne at her right hand, and backed up by four armed agents. A pang of sadness hit Val as she realised Raleigh was not with her, but she quickly shook it off. They expected Darley to stick to his usual routine, and were confident that he would still be at his desk at six o'clock that evening.

At the office, Val and Ballantyne went straight upstairs and into Darley's secretary's office.

"Is Darley in?" said Val.

"Yes, but he's busy at the—"

They ignored her and burst into Darley's office, where they found him sitting in his chair behind his huge, expensive desk. A bottle of malt whisky and a cut-glass tumbler were on the desk, and he held his gold-nibbed Parker Duofold frozen in mid-air. The element of surprise had worked perfectly, but after two seconds Darley came to life, gasped "*what the hell*", threw the pen down and pulled open the top drawer on the right-hand side of his desk.

Val levelled her PPK at him. "Forget it, Darley! Get your hands away from the desk."

But Darley ignored her command. He pulled out a Colt .38 pistol and clicked off the safety catch. Val immediately fired, aiming two feet to his left, at the huge picture window behind him, which came down in an enormous shower of fragments. The gunshots and crashing of the falling glass had the desired effect. Darley dropped the pistol on his desk and held his hands in the air. "OK, OK, take it easy!"

One of the supporting agents dashed into the office, head held low, responding to the shots, gun in a two-handed grip. Val was pleased to see it was young Mark Taylor – she expected him to develop into an excellent agent. "Everything's fine, Taylor. Get the handcuffs on him."

"You fool, Darley, did you really think you could shoot your way out of here?" said Val.

As Taylor came forward, Darley held his hands out to the front, his wrists pressed together. "Not behind me, please. I would like to be able to take one last glass of malt, if you don't mind."

Ballantyne glanced at Val then silently poured the drink.

"You don't mind, do you?" said Darley.

She laughed. "No, go ahead. I'll have a drink tonight to honour Raleigh. I'll have some consolation in knowing that you will spend the rest of your life in prison, Darley."

"I doubt it, madam. There will be an exchange and I expect to live a very comfortable life in one of Moscow's most exclusive districts. Perhaps even Berlin, after the West has been annexed by Soviet forces. Please don't doubt it: the Soviet invasion will be happening very soon, and the Communist Party here will rise up and take control."

Ballantyne frowned at Darley's bravado. "Enough of that rubbish, Darley. Where are the radar files?"

"In the lower desk drawer." Darley drank the Scotch in one.

"And the microdot equipment?" asked Val.

"Ah, I see. So that's how you discovered my work. Well. It's at my house in Cambridge. I'm sure your agents will find everything they need when they carry out their search."

Val had had enough. "You bloody Cambridge types – tied up in a nice circle of nouveau-communists, ready to change the world. Well, forget it. The red tide is washed up. It's over. And you can be confident that you will spend a long time in prison, Darley. You might not be aware that we lost one of our agents in East Germany, and for that I will make sure you are right at the bottom of the list for exchanges. Forget the good life as a feted communist; the Soviets don't like failure and they won't lift a finger to help you. Take him away."

Val gestured with her pistol to the door, and Taylor led Darley down to the car.

FIFTY-TWO

A couple of weeks later, Hannah made excuses to her friends from the bank for why she wouldn't join them for their usual Friday evening drinks, and walked to Liverpool Street station. She had told Devon that she would come up to Welham Green on Saturday morning, that she had things to do at home. An hour later, she stepped off the train at Cambridge and walked out to the taxi rank. She wore her best grey suit and white blouse: she needed to keep her self-confidence intact and push away the guilt and angst that were almost reducing her to tears. In the taxi she took off her pearl necklace and placed it in her handbag. Only Adam was allowed to admire it on her. Ten minutes later, she arrived at the University Arms Hotel.

Fitzjohn had been precise in his instructions. She was to meet him in the bar at 6.45p.m. – no earlier, no later, the note said. She should bring the cheque for £1,000 and make sure she was free for the rest of the evening. Checking her watch, she saw she was a few minutes early, so she walked across the closely mown grass of Parker's Piece, doing her best to stay calm and manage her disgust at the prospect of what she had to do with Fitzjohn.

Hannah had spent many sleepless nights wrangling with the dilemma she faced. Fitzjohn had only taken on the rescue flight because of the incentives she gave him: money, the promise of secrecy over his diamond smuggling; her willingness, but not desire, to go to bed with him. She knew she had prostituted herself in getting his agreement to fly the mission. She thought she could refuse, renege on the agreement, deny that she had thought he had been serious. But Fitzjohn had done the job, got Adam and the rest of the team out of East Germany. Without his help, who knew what might have happened? If she broke her word now, she felt she would be belittling the value she placed on what he had done for Adam, and for her.

After another glance at her watch, she knew that her time was up. She turned back into Regent Street and climbed the steps to the hotel lobby. But she felt faint and weak. She decided she just couldn't do it; she would be breaching her loyalty to Adam. Although he would never know, she felt it would always hang over her feelings for him. But as she went to turn round to leave the hotel, Fitzjohn came up behind her and gripped her arm. He whisked her to the table he had reserved in the bar.

"Sit here, my dear." He clicked his fingers and a barman hurried over to take their order. "Now, what can I get you? A G&T, I think. And a large Talisker for me."

Hannah couldn't stop her hands from shaking. How could he hold her to what she had promised?

"It's wonderful to see you, my dear, and you are looking lovely tonight. Tell me, have you and Devon set a date for your marriage? You know I believe he is being very slack in this particular area."

"Actually, yes we have. The first of July next year at Caxton Hall. But please don't hold your breath for your invitation."

"Now, now, we must be the very best of friends, tonight of all nights. I can guarantee that this will be very special for you – and, of course, for me. Drink up, then we'll have another one."

Hannah noticed a hotel room key on the edge of the table. "Alright." She wasn't a big drinker, but she suddenly felt that being in an alcoholic stupor would help her get through the evening.

Fitzjohn looked up at the clock in the bar. "I've booked a table in the restaurant for quarter past seven, but before we go through, perhaps you would be so kind as to hand over the cheque."

Hannah opened her handbag and pulled out the cheque. She held it for a moment, realising that she was saying goodbye to the prospect of buying a house with Adam, at least for a few years. Perhaps it would never happen now.

"I don't want to eat, Henry. Let's just get it over with." Her voice cracked as she gasped out the words in fear and anger.

"I'm sure I don't know what you mean."

"Now you want to make a fool of me – as well as a slut."

"Ah, I get your drift. Well, I have some news for you, my dear. You will recall back at Moser airfield our shoot-out with those foul Stasi men? Of course you do, and the problem I had with my gun. Well, thanks to your quick thinking, you shot the bastard who was minded to put an end to me. Handy little toy, that Uzi." Fitzjohn sipped his Scotch, slowly replaced the glass on the table, leant forward and took Hannah's hands in his. "You saved my life, and I owe you a debt of gratitude. So I'm willing to give up my right to the promise you made."

Hannah coughed out a nervous gasp. "*What?* You mean you're letting me off? You don't want me to go to bed with you?"

"That's it exactly, my dear. Debt paid off – no further mention to be made, ever. You know, I am sad about it. You know how I admire you and your... er... attributes."

Hannah sat back, pulled her hands away from Fitzjohn and covered her face. Blood rose warm and pulsing from her neck to her blushing cheeks. She almost laughed, and could say only one thing. "Thank you, Henry, thank you."

"No thanks required, old girl. The promise I extracted from you was a touch outrageous, some might say, so it's only right that I give it up. You did the right thing for me."

"I agree, but thank you."

"Like I say, absolutely no further mention, or thanks. Now, let's go through to the restaurant. I hope your appetite has returned, and I have a surprise for you. But remember, you must never discuss our arrangement or the business activities, legal or otherwise, of Granta, not with anyone. Are we agreed?"

"Yes, of course."

Fitzjohn pocketed the room key, stood and led the way into the restaurant at exactly quarter past seven. They were shown to a table set for four. At twenty past seven, Fitzjohn waved his white linen napkin at a figure standing in the doorway to the restaurant. Hannah turned round to see what the excitement was about, and gasped in shock. It was Adam.

"Over here, old boy!" Fitzjohn half stood to shake hands with Devon, then gestured for him to take a seat. "Lovely to see you, and I hope you like my little surprise."

"Adam, I didn't expect to see you here!" said Hannah.

"And I didn't expect to see you either. What's going on, Fitzjohn?" Hannah saw the distrust in Devon's face.

"I asked you both to join me for dinner to celebrate our success on the Berlin jaunt, and to thank you for your sterling work in seeing off the Stasi thugs in Moser. A very tight situation, expertly handled by Special Agent Shaw here. Forgive my theatricals in inviting you separately to join me, making it a surprise for you both – just a little bit of fun on my part. I will also have the pleasure in a minute or two of introducing you to a very good friend of mine, Miss Amanda Spencer. She and I work very closely on my parliamentary affairs, and she has some further news for us."

A quiet chime from the bar clock indicated that it was half-past seven. Right on cue, Amanda walked into the restaurant and sat down to join them. Fitzjohn made the introductions. He had told Amanda that the dinner was a reunion of old Hong Kong pals; she knew nothing about the arrangements Fitzjohn had agreed to take on the rescue, except that a sizeable fee was involved. Fitzjohn waved the napkin again and with a flourish ordered champagne. As they were toasting each other's health, the waitress took their food order.

"Well now, Henry, this is a jolly party," said Amanda. "Are we here to mark your success in Westminster?"

"Hush, my dear, we will get to that. First I wanted to express my sincere thanks to Hannah for taking out that Stasi agent. And I wanted to make a tangible gesture of my appreciation." Fitzjohn took Hannah's cheque for £1,000 out of his pocket and slowly, deliberately, tore it in half, tore it in half again, and then tore it into small pieces, which he dropped in the ashtray on the table. Hannah and Devon stared at him, speechless. Amanda just sat with a puzzled look on her face.

"You chaps might think I'm a bit of an ogre, but I hope this restores some faith in me. I wish you well in your marriage and building a happy home together."

"That's bloody decent of you, Fitzjohn!" said Devon.

"You're a tricky customer, Devon, but I do believe that you were a terrific Spitfire pilot and officer, a keen sportsman, and you have a great career ahead of you as a test pilot, and—"

"Enough, Henry." Amanda patted Fitzjohn on the back. "You're gushing, and it's embarrassing. I think Adam and Hannah get the message."

Fitzjohn smiled his most agreeable smile. "But I'd like to ask one question, if I may. Devon, a little bird told me that you have been promoted at de Havilland – is that correct?"

"You're not supposed to know about that."

"One of the advantages of having a position in government – you know how it is."

"Yes, I think I do. I'm converting to jets, specialising in testing the latest version of the de Havilland Venom. The new management team have given me the lead role on the programme. As you know from our time in the Far East, the future's all about jet aircraft."

"Oh yes, I recall those discussions vividly. Well, that's super, old boy. I'm sure you will soon be Britain's most eminent test pilot."

"Well thank you, Fitzjohn, and you're not a bad pilot yourself. How's the air taxi business going?" said Devon.

"Splendidly! Plenty of work for both aircraft and all my chaps. We might even be able to acquire one or two more aircraft in the near future. All depends on the bank being willing. We had some teething troubles at first, particularly with a regular client with flights to Amsterdam, but I've ended that contract now." Fitzjohn glanced at Hannah, who tilted her head and nodded in acknowledgement.

Hannah was pleasantly surprised that the meal went so well. There was much talk about the rescue flight and the intrigue surrounding Porter and Darley. Devon mentioned that Porter was back at work, looking at new routes for BOAC flights to North America. They were all shocked when they heard from Fitzjohn that Darley had long been a communist – his father had been laid off in the 1930s from the shipbuilders where he worked in the accounts department, and couldn't find another job. His family's subsequent poverty led Darley to support communism. All this, Fitzjohn said, was confidential; he'd heard the details at a Defence Procurement Committee meeting, and he asked them to keep the news to themselves.

"The MI6 people arrested Porter partly on the grounds that, as his father had once been a communist, there must be a family connection to him being a traitor," said Fitzjohn. "Right idea, wrong person. As I say, it was Darley's background that drove him to follow the communist ideology."

Devon added that he had heard from Val – Franken refused to say a word under interrogation about his relationship with Darley, and no

Stasi contacts had been found, but his fingerprints on the remnants of the bomb and the matching of pieces of wire from his flat were likely to be enough for him to be jailed for life.

When the staff had cleared away their plates and wine glasses, Fitzjohn called for coffee and brandies.

"Henry has much less time for flying these days, Adam, with his new role in government." There was pride in Amanda's voice.

"Really? What exactly are you doing?" said Hannah.

"He has been appointed Under-Secretary of State in the Air Ministry. Conservative headquarters have great hopes for Henry's political future. As have I. We believe that Henry can go all the way." Amanda wrapped her fingers around Fitzjohn's hand and kept them there.

"You mean, to become a minister?" said Hannah.

"Absolutely. And, we hope, to lead the Party – and then, of course, on to number 10."

To become an under-secretary at such a young age was impressive, but Hannah and Devon were rendered almost speechless at the thought of Fitzjohn becoming prime minister. Devon managed to recover enough to say, "Congratulations, Fitzjohn."

With his free hand, Fitzjohn swept back his fringe and smiled. "Oh please, Amanda, I really cannot claim such vainglorious ambitions." He turned to Devon. "With Winston back at the helm there are more opportunities in government for chaps like me – young but with some experience. And the expansion of British industry is firmly at the top of our agenda. After receiving such a glowing report from MI6 on my role in the Leonid job, those in power felt that a reward of some sort was appropriate. Hence my appointment. But it does mean more office work, so it's not all good news. And who knows, Devon, our paths may well cross, with you at de Havilland and me at the Ministry. You can take me up in one of their latest models."

"Now, don't spoil the evening, Henry. I'm sure Adam will be glad to leave the business discussions to de Havilland's office types," said Amanda. "Your career in government won't develop if you spend your time hanging around airfields hoping for a joyride."

"I'm sure you're right, my dear, but the fact remains that I will be working much more closely with defence contractors, aircraft and weapons manufacturers, and so on. It's important that our air force is equipped with the best kit, and I'm sure that Devon and I will form a very worthwhile business relationship."

Hannah looked at her watch. "We really should be getting on now, Adam. I came by train from London – did you drive over?"

"Yes, the car's in the hotel car park. But I guessed I would be having a few drinks tonight, so I booked a room at the hotel. We can both stay, if you like, and I'll drive you home in the morning."

Fitzjohn clapped his hands. "Splendid idea, Devon. Exactly the thought I had, isn't that right, Amanda? We should all meet up for breakfast and you can tell me about your wedding plans, Devon."

ACKNOWLEDGEMENTS

In the 1950s, the Cold War carried a blanket of fear across Europe, and probably the rest of the world. The work of the secret services was carried out by the bravest people and many of them women. Inspiration for the exploits of the character Val Hetherington-Brown came from Kate Vigurs' excellent book, *Mission France, The True Story of the Women of SOE*. Although this history is set in the Second World War, it details the dangers the operatives faced that continued into the Cold War era.

I would like to thank the research team at RAF Museum, Hendon. They provided a comprehensive set of original documents from their archives that assisted with my understanding of the Berlin Airlift and the flight operations that continued for many years after.

Thanks also to Jules Miller, Curator at the Combined Military Services Museum in Maldon, Essex for showing me an actual example of the Marconi Type A Mk III radio and providing advice on secret operations. The collection at CMSM includes an Uzi, and Walther PPK and Webley pistols.

Jane Hammett completed the editing, and provided ideas and thoughts on the text that improved the flow and pace of the story. Thank you for your excellent guidance.

Mike Duval carried out readings of early drafts of the manuscript and provided invaluable comments on the storyline. Thank you, and Lisa, for continuing to provide inspiration for my writing.

As with *The Pearl River*, all the characters are fictitious but have elements of real people I know; family, friends and those I have observed from a distance. Hannah Shaw is based on a good friend of mine and is perhaps my favourite character, with her depth of commitment, bravery and enduring love for Adam Devon.

ABOUT THE AUTHOR

Born in London, but now living in Essex, Mark Butterworth worked in the City of London in financial services for nearly 40 years, including as a Lloyd's underwriter and risk management consultant. Travelling widely on holidays and business, often the two combined, Mark developed his appreciation of the Far East, Australasia, North America, the Caribbean and Europe. Mark held a Private Pilot's Licence for 15 years, including flights from Kai Tak and over the Sydney Harbour Bridge and Niagara Falls. Mark has flown a two-seater Spitfire and made more than 50 parachute jumps. Mark enjoys running, country walking, golf and salsa dancing and has two grown up daughters and a Springer Spaniel called Arthur.